HOME TO STAY

AN ANCHOR ISLAND NOVEL

OTHER TITLES BY TERRI OSBURN

HOME TO STAY

AN ANCHOR ISLAND NOVEL

Terri Osburn

 Montlake
Romance

Published by Montlake Romance, Seattle

www.apub.com

ISBN-13: 9781477818367
ISBN-10: 1477818367

Cover design by Anna Curtis

Library of Congress Control Number: 2013917678

Printed in the United States of America

For Maureen and Marnee.
Without you, this book would not exist.

CHAPTER 1

Willow Parsons had survived. She'd officially run Dempsey's Bar & Grill, the signature restaurant of tiny Anchor Island, North Carolina, for an entire week on her own.

Hallelujah.

Named assistant manager the previous fall, shortly after proprietor Tom Dempsey's heart attack, the owners, which included Tom and his wife, Patty, proved their faith in Will by letting her handle the reopening two weeks before returning from their winter break in the Florida Keys. Will had stressed for a solid month before the big day. Checking inventory, cleaning up the accounting system, and ensuring the staff was as sharp as ever.

And her attention to detail had paid off.

Dempsey's was known for friendly service and the best seafood in the Outer Banks. It was important to reinforce that reputation with a strong opening week. On that front, she would not fail. She liked the Dempseys too much to disappoint them, or let their business take a hit.

The restaurant was already in recovery mode, which was why they'd closed for the winter in the first place. An infusion of cash from their son, Lucas, a lawyer who'd recently returned to Anchor and set up his own practice, had kept them from closing the doors for good, but they'd need a strong tourist season to ensure Lucas's investment wouldn't be for naught.

To that end, Will would do all she could to help the family who had trusted her with their business.

Georgette, the waitress on duty, stepped up to the bar. "The checks are on the tables. As soon as I cash these out, we can start cleanup."

"Sounds good to me," Will said, unloading the empty bottles and glasses from Georgette's tray. "I'll run the register tape while we raise the chairs."

Georgette headed back to the floor with her empty tray as Will dropped the glasses into hot, soapy water. She was tossing the bottles into the recycle bin when the front door swung open and Randy Navarro stepped through.

So much for Will's good mood.

In the year plus that Will had been on Anchor Island, she'd avoided the giant of a man as much as possible. Which had gotten tougher to do in recent months since she'd become good friends with Randy's sister, Sid. Upon arriving on the island, her initial reaction to the man large enough to deserve his own zip code had been fear.

Fear of history repeating itself.

But over the last six months or so, she'd been around Randy often enough to realize his sister's description of him as a gentle giant might be accurate. At times, she even liked the friendly man with a quick smile and whiskey-brown eyes. Which was all the more reason to maintain the charade that he still frightened her.

Will's current predicament made romantic entanglements a luxury she couldn't afford. Getting romantic meant getting intimate, which led to sharing one's secrets.

Will's secret was too dangerous to share.

"Can we talk?" Randy said when he reached the bar.

Until that moment, he'd never attempted direct conversation, and they'd never been alone without Sid or other mutual friends between them. Will wasn't sure how she felt about this new behavior but believed it best not to encourage it.

"Can't. I'm busy." Will dropped clean glasses into hot water and glanced up to see Randy giving the restaurant a once-over.

"Right," he drawled, his deep voice laced with a hint of his Latin heritage. "It's important to have lots of clean glasses for seven customers."

The sarcasm was new.

"There are nine, actually. Two are in the poolroom." Will gave her best smart-ass smile as more clean glasses hit the suds.

"Will," Randy said, impatience in his voice. "I know you don't like me, but—"

"Who said I don't like you?" Not that she *did* like him. At least not *like him like him.*

Great. Now she was thinking like a fourteen-year-old.

He settled his weight onto a bar stool, which creaked in protest. "No one had to tell me. I'm observant like that."

She slung the rag over her left shoulder, shooting for unaffected. "What do we need to talk about?"

"Something that was announced at the Merchants Society meeting tonight." Randy leaned back, draping an arm over the back of the stool beside him. *What did a guy have to lift to get biceps like that,* Will wondered. *A tugboat maybe?* "You have any green tea back there?" he asked.

Will retrieved a bottle from the small fridge under the bar, removed the cap, and tossed it into the can six feet away. "You don't seem like the green tea type."

"You'd have to talk to someone to know what type they are."

Score one for the big guy. "So what happened at the meeting?"

3

After taking a drink, he said, "Thanks to Sam Edwards, *Prime Destinations* magazine is doing a feature article on Anchor Island."

"That's a national publication," Will said, her spine straightening. "They're coming here?"

"Yes, ma'am. A reporter named Rebecca King arrives early next week with a photographer."

"A photographer?" Will's voice climbed an octave higher. She cleared her throat. "So they're going to take pictures?"

Randy narrowed his eyes. "Wouldn't be much of a spread if they didn't include pictures."

So they'd want sand and water and boats. Not people. "Sounds like a good thing for the island. Here's hoping it brings the tourists." Switching glasses from the soapy water into the rinse sink, she asked, "But why do I need to know this?"

"Because they want to feature Dempsey's. With Tom and Patty still in Florida, that leaves you for the interview."

Will stared with what she could only guess was a look of horror. There was no question that she couldn't do this. Her life literally depended upon *not* having her picture in a national magazine.

"That's not going to work," she said, returning to the glasses.

Randy hesitated with the bottle of tea halfway to his lips. "Excuse me?"

"It's not a good idea, that's all." It was the *worst* idea. "They're welcome to feature Dempsey's, but I won't be giving an interview."

"I already talked to Joe about it. He says it's a go."

The other Dempsey offspring, Joe, ran a charter fishing boat business and helped at the restaurant from time to time.

"Then he can do the interview. Problem solved."

Randy crossed his arms, an incredible feat considering the size of his chest. "I realize this island doesn't mean as much to you as it does to the rest of us."

That statement halted the glass washing. "Who said I don't care about this island?"

Ignoring her question, Randy continued. "We have businesses here. Our families are here." That one hit like a blow. No, Will didn't have family on Anchor. Or anywhere else. "If we don't get tourism back up, there are people on this island who will lose everything. That might not mean much to you—you can serve drinks anywhere you want—but it means something to us. It means something to your bosses, and the least you can do is answer some questions for a reporter."

Anger flared in Will's blood. This man didn't know her. Didn't know what he was asking. She cared about this island *and* the people on it. More than she could afford to, in fact.

"Are you done?" she asked, employing extreme patience to keep her voice steady.

By the look of him, puffed up like some bullfrog calling his mate, he was just getting started.

"I may not own a business on this island," Will said, leaning forward. "And no, I don't have family here. But I do have friends, and I do care about this island. Not that I have to explain any of that to you." She pulled the rag from her shoulder and dried her hands. "Feel free to take your tea and go."

Randy remained silent. It wasn't in Will's nature to be outright rude to people, but she was not going to be chewed up one side and down the other by this pissy giant who didn't know a damn thing about her.

And to think, she'd begun to like him.

He broke his silence with a statement she should have seen coming. "Whatever big guy screwed you over in the past must have been a real asshole."

The statement was more accurate than he'd ever know.

"My past is none of your business," she said through gritted teeth. "And it's the asshole in my present that's giving me a headache tonight." A muscle twitched along his jaw, but he kept his mouth shut. "This conversation is over," Will added.

The two parties that had been seated in the dining room were leaving. Will called to Georgette, "Go back and let Mohler know we're closing. I'll start on the chairs."

As Will rounded the end of the bar, Randy cut her off. "Do you need help setting up for the party tomorrow?"

The abrupt change of subject, together with the lack of distance between them, jerked Will to a halt.

"Joe and Beth will be here around five to hang the decorations in the poolroom. You'll have to ask them if they want help. I think you know my answer."

Beth, who was engaged to Joe, and Will had a surprise birthday party planned for Sid for the next night. Will had known Randy would be there but hadn't counted on him wanting to help.

Georgette returned from the poolroom and joined them at the end of the bar. "Milo says we're gonna be in a magazine." Milo was Georgette's husband, who worked for Randy at his water adventures business. "Is that true?" she asked Randy.

"Anchor Island is," he answered. "I'm not sure about you and Milo." The man was in full jerk mode this evening.

"Aren't you a comedian tonight," she said, dropping her tray on the bar and untying her apron. "Put this man out of his misery, Will, and go out with him already."

Will's head jerked to Randy, who looked less than happy with Georgette. The waitress stuck her tongue out as she walked away, saying, "Be a smart-ass with me, will ya?"

"What is she—" Will began.

6

"She's just yanking my chain." Randy withdrew his wallet and dropped three ones on the bar. "I'll be here at five to help set up." Will opened her mouth, but he interrupted again. "Relax. This asshole will be sure to stay out of your way."

With that, Randy exited the restaurant, leaving Will staring after him. Georgette's joke might have been funny if it hadn't hit so close to home. Three years ago, Randy would have been exactly the type of guy Will would go out with.

"You mind if I don't stay to help with the chairs?" Georgette asked, dragging Will back to the present. "Milo made me a late supper, and I'm dying to get off my feet. Three months off has made me soft."

"No," Will said, clenching her jaw to hold back the questions. The clenching didn't work. "About Randy—"

The waitress waved a hand in the air. "I was only messing with him," she said, stuffing a small wad of cash into her back pocket. "I mean, I've caught him looking at you a time or two, but Randy has never pursued a woman as long as I've known him." The waitress shrugged. "Theory around the island is that some chick did him bad, but no one knows for sure. If anyone's going to break through his walls, it might as well be you. Give it a shot if you're interested."

"I'm not interested," Will said. Especially not after tonight.

Someone else would have to knock down the big lug's walls. Will had enough to worry about with this magazine coming to town. If her face found its way into those pages, she'd have to find a new place to hide. And that would mean good-bye Anchor Island.

~

For more than a year, Randy had been tiptoeing around the wiry gypsy with the long dark hair and cautious blue eyes, trying not to be offended every time she leapt at the sight of him. He'd watched her talk with ease to all the people he knew, men and women alike, only to recoil like a turtle into her shell whenever he crossed her path.

The only way he differed from other men was in his size, and since he knew he'd never done anything to her, another big guy must have. Or so Randy suspected. Will didn't exactly confirm his suspicions this evening, but she hadn't denied them either.

Randy wasn't the violent type. He believed in the sanctity of life, and had a natural inclination to protect. But every time Will flinched or got that haunted look in her eye, Randy wanted nothing more than to travel back in time and show whatever asshole had touched her what it felt like to mess with someone his own size.

And then he'd gone and been an asshole to her tonight. Not to the same extent, clearly, but an asshole nonetheless. He had to admire her for calling him on it.

"Did someone piss in your protein shake or what?" Sid asked as Randy passed through the fitness center on the way to his office in the back.

Randy owned two businesses on the island: Anchor Adventures, providing water sports for the tourists—which would reopen for the season in a month—and Island Fitness, which was open year round and making enough money to keep the other endeavor afloat. For now.

Ignoring her question, he asked one of his own. "What are you doing here after hours?"

"Um, working out." She pointed to the large ball pressed between her bottom and the wall. "Been spending my workout time at the garage, so thought I'd get in some late-night hours before the tourists load in."

Sid had recently purchased an old, run-down garage on the outskirts of the island. She'd spent the winter putting every bit of time and energy into cleaning out the cobwebs, replacing broken windows, and breathing life into a boat restoration business of her own.

"You gave me a key, remember?" she asked.

"Right." Randy didn't mind his sister using the gym, but he'd come here to be alone. To spend another night doing creative accounting in an effort to solve his current problems.

Sid stood and let the ball hit the floor. "You seem distracted. Are you sure everything is okay?" She closed the distance between them, went up on tiptoe, and felt his forehead. "You aren't sick, are you?"

Randy smiled. "Being a girlfriend is softening you up. Where did this mothering stuff come from?"

Brown eyes the same shade as his own narrowed. "Keep saying shit like that and I'll show you soft." She crossed her arms. "Seriously. What's up?"

A long sigh left his body as Randy rubbed the back of his neck. Sharing his financial troubles was out, so he opted for irritation number two. "How much do you know about Will's past?"

"Not much," Sid said. "She grew up with her mom, and they traveled a lot, but she's never talked about anything else."

Sid and Will had spent a lot of time together in the last six months. It wasn't his place to disclose details of Will's past if she hadn't been willing to share them before now. And in truth, he didn't have any details, only suspicions.

"Do you know anything about where she was before she came to Anchor?"

"She worked along the coast, but I don't know exactly where." Sid tightened her ponytail. "Why the sudden interest in Will? I know she acts weird around you, but if you're interested—"

"No," Randy said. What was it with women trying to get him a date this evening? "I'm just curious. Seems odd she's been here this long and we don't know much about her."

Sid tipped her head to the side in the gesture that always reminded him of their mom. "Kind of a miracle, actually. Nothing is ever a secret on this island. At least not for long. You'd think someone would have pulled some details out of her by now."

"You're her best friend," he said, moving several free weights from the floor back to their stand. "Does all the girl talk not include past history?"

"You know I don't do girl talk." Sid picked up a towel from the floor and wrapped it around her neck. "Besides, if she doesn't volunteer the information, I'm not going to pry." She dropped onto the gray exercise ball she'd abandoned moments before. "She did say something once about why she's so weird around you. How did she put it?"

His sister tapped her temple, her face tight in concentration. "Something about bad run-ins with muscle-bound guys. I didn't think much of it at the time, but maybe she meant more than some guy just being a jerk?"

Randy was positive whoever the guy was, he'd gone well beyond jerk behavior. But again, he wasn't going to tell Sid that.

"Maybe." Lifting a hundred-pound free weight onto the rack with little effort, he added, "Since she and I are thrown together more, what with her always with you and Beth and me usually with Joe—"

"And Lucas," Sid added. Randy wasn't as friendly with Lucas as he was with Joe, which irked his sister. She wasn't the type to be irked in silence.

"And Lucas," he conceded. "Seems like it would be a good idea to try to get to know Will a bit."

Sid's brows went up, then she smiled. "I see. You *like* her."

God bless America. "I don't even know her, Sid. But I'm tired of feeling like a leper when we're in the same room. Don't make more out of this than it is."

Sid continued to smile. "What you do with Will is your business. I've been telling her for months you're a good guy. If you're finally going to take the time to show her, then I'd suggest starting with an offering of Opal's rhubarb pie."

"Rhubarb pie?" he asked. "Why would I give her pie?"

"Because any half-assed effort at wooing requires gifts, and Will loves that rhubarb pie."

Randy shook his head. "Wooing? You need better ventilation in that garage. The fumes are killing off the few brain cells you have left." With that parting shot, he stomped back to his office, but as always, Sid had to have the last word.

"Getting laid would go a long way to curing this bitchy streak of yours. Skip the wooing and fuck the damn pie."

CHAPTER 2

Randy parked in front of Dempsey's at four forty-five the next day with a ladder and two rolls of masking tape per Beth's request. The request had come through Joe Dempsey, Beth's fiancé and Randy's best friend, who'd stopped by Anchor Adventures around lunchtime.

The typically laid-back fisherman had been worried about his bride to be. She'd been acting odd, and her stress levels were sending her moods all over the place.

Having never been a groom, Randy didn't have much to offer in the way of advice. But he believed all women were stressed and moody in the weeks before their wedding. Pointing this out didn't seem to ease Joe's mind.

Contrary to the night before, Dempsey's was hopping. Good thing he'd left the ladder in the truck. No way would he get it through this crowd without clotheslining someone.

"There you are," Beth said, rushing toward Randy with a string of letters in one hand, which he assumed spelled "Happy Birthday." "Tell me you brought the ladder."

He glanced around the room while rubbing his chin. "I'm not sure bringing a ladder through this crowd is a good idea."

"Fine." Beth took his hand and pulled him along behind her. "Then you can put me on your shoulders. I need to get this sign tacked to the beams at the far end."

He could put her where?

Extending his stride to keep up with the tiny tornado whipping through the room, Randy stumbled through the entrance to the poolroom and caught sight of Joe fighting with a mess of Christmas lights near the right side wall.

"Joe," Beth yelled, "come help me get on Randy's shoulders."

"Help you what?" Joe looked up from the tangle of green wires. "You're not getting on anyone's shoulders."

Beth stopped so quickly, Randy almost plowed through her. "I need to get this sign up on that beam. Randy says he can't bring the ladder through the crowd. What do you propose I do?" Her green eyes sparked with impatience, while pink lips pinched into a flat line.

Joe shot Randy a *help me* look. Randy shrugged.

"Think we can bring the ladder in through the kitchen?" Joe asked, abandoning the lights on a cocktail table.

Randy glanced back into the dining room to assess the space between the end of the bar, which was in front of the kitchen, and the poolroom entrance. Meeting Joe's exhausted expression, he said, "We can try."

The men made their way to the parking lot in silence, but once their feet hit gravel, Randy brought up the unspoken subject at hand. "You weren't kidding. How long has she been like this?"

Joe lowered the tailgate on Randy's Ranger. "A couple weeks. The wedding stuff has her so twisted up, she's going to gnaw through her flowers before she makes it down the aisle."

"I've got everything lined up at my place." Randy took the top end of the ladder as Joe pulled from the bottom. Beth and Joe were getting married on the large deck of Anchor Adventures to take advantage of the bay view. "Is anyone helping her with the rest of it?"

Once the ladder cleared the end of the gate, Joe nodded and they lifted their respective ends onto their shoulders. "Lola's trying, but I don't know how much Beth is letting her do. You know how she is, desperate to please everyone." Randy closed the tailgate with his free hand as Joe continued. "I keep telling her this is her day and she's the only person to please, but the words aren't getting through."

"At least it'll all be over in a month."

"I don't know if I can make it that long." Joe took the lead, heading up the stairs to the wraparound porch and down the left side to the kitchen door. "Getting this thing through the kitchen is going to be a bitch."

"Failure is not an option, my friend." Randy laughed. "Beth needs a ladder and we're going to bring her one." Realizing what he'd just said, Randy asked, "You're not going to let her climb this thing, are you?"

"Hell no," Joe said. "But getting that sign exactly how she wants it could take the rest of the night in her current state of mind. Nothing has been good enough." After pulling open the kitchen door, Joe wedged his body against it and turned to face Randy. "This morning she was bitching that Dozer would need a haircut before the wedding or he'd throw off the entire bridal party."

"What does that even mean?" Randy asked.

"Fuck if I know."

Two sharp turns, three knocked-down pans, and one ladder through a serving window later, Randy and Joe reached the end of the bar.

"What the hell are you two doing?" asked Will, holding three longnecks in one hand and two empty beer glasses in the other.

The men looked at each other, then back to Will.

"Taking this ladder to the poolroom," Joe said.

"Do you see I have a dining room full of guests here?" Blue eyes snapped as she set the empties on the end of the bar.

"Will?" Joe said. "Have you talked to Beth tonight?"

"No." The bartender shook her head. "I've been too busy out here. Why?"

"Because if we don't get this into that poolroom, she's going to use Randy as a ladder. Nobody wants that, right?"

Randy knew he didn't want that, but he wouldn't put it past Will to think it a good idea.

Will looked from Joe to Randy, then back to Joe. "He looks sturdy enough."

"Will."

"Alright, alright," she said, waving her hands toward the doorway at the back of the room. "But don't decapitate any of my customers. I'll bring you guys some drinks in a minute."

Afraid Will might change her mind, and concerned about the mental state of women in general on Anchor Island, Randy encouraged Joe to move fast by pushing his end along.

"Don't run my ass over," Joe said, crossing into the empty poolroom and past the tables to set his end on the floor near the far wall. "We can leave this in the corner until the end of the night. No sense in taking it back out through the crowd if we don't have to."

"You want to leave a ladder sitting in the middle of the party?" Beth asked, popping up out of nowhere and making both men jump. "Do you understand I'm trying to make this nice for Sid?"

Joe ran a hand through his hair. "Beth, honey, Sid's idea of nice is brats on the grill and a keg. She's not going to notice a ladder sitting in the corner."

"That's such a man thing to say."

Randy held his breath, reluctant to become Beth's next target. As he was the only other man in the room, the chances were not in his favor. Joe might have understated his fiancée's condition. In the year Randy had known her, Beth had been nothing but sweet and patient, always with a kind word for everyone.

This woman wearing a haggard expression and a line of moisture across her upper lip was not that woman.

"One Bud, one green tea, and a sweet tea for the lady," Will said, setting the drinks on a cocktail table. "What all are you planning for the decorations?"

"What I have planned and what's going to happen won't be the same if these cavemen don't start listening to me." Beth ripped a piece of crepe paper with her teeth. "I'm trying to make this a nice party."

Will's eyes went wide.

"Maybe you could bring Beth something stronger than iced tea," Randy whispered.

Will ignored him. "Beth, are you okay?"

The sweat was now beading on Beth's forehead, and the color was dropping away from her face.

"I don't think she is," Randy said, moving closer in case he needed to catch her. He'd seen people overexert themselves and pass out too many times not to recognize the signs. "Joe, bring Beth a chair."

"I don't need a chair," she said, ripping another strip of crepe, then wiping her forehead on her sleeve. "We need to get these decorations up before Sid gets here."

Joe set a bar stool behind Beth and edged her onto the seat. "You can sit here and tell us what to do. Think of it as being captain of the ship and we're the crew."

Randy had to give Joe credit for the steady voice, because he didn't look steady at all. He looked like a man out of his depth.

As soon as Beth was sitting, the roll of crepe paper hit the floor and she curled over, pressing her arms against her stomach and letting out a loud groan.

"Beth, baby, what's wrong?" Joe dropped to his knees in front of the stool, trying to see his fiancée's face. "Tell me what's wrong!"

"Grab a bar rag and run it under cold water," Randy said to Will, who stood frozen in fear to his left. With a hand on her shoulder, he gentled his voice. "Will, we need a cold rag. Can you get that for Beth?"

Later it would occur to him that this was the first time he'd ever touched Will. She didn't flinch until she looked him in the eye and her brain caught up to the situation. "Yes. Yes, I can. I'll be right back." She hurried from the room.

Rubbing Beth's back, Randy bent close to her ear. "Where's the pain, Beth? Tell me where it hurts."

"I thought it was just my period," she moaned, then began panting. "Cramps maybe, but this feels like I'm being split in two."

Joe returned to his feet. "We need to get her to the clinic. Hold on for me, baby," he said to Beth, a tremor in his voice revealing how scared the man was.

"Here's Will with the rag," Randy said, taking the wet material Will offered and pressing it against Beth's forehead. Her body heat sucked the water from the linen. "We'll take my truck," he said, tossing the rag back to Will. "Can you carry her, or do you want me to do it?"

Joe ignored the question, sliding his arms under Beth and lifting her off the stool. "Clear a way to the door," he barked, jerking Will into motion.

"I'm coming with you," she said, determination in her voice. Beth curled tighter against Joe, escalating from a groan to a scream, which parted the crowd more than anything Will was doing.

"Daisy," Will yelled. "Take over the bar." A purple lanyard with keys on the end flew through the air. "Call Lucas and Sid and tell them to meet us at the clinic."

The blonde waitress caught the keys with wide eyes and an open mouth, then ran behind the bar to do as ordered.

Beth's breathing grew more ragged as Joe slid her onto the backseat of Randy's truck and followed her in. Will climbed into the passenger seat up front, then propped up on her knees to face Beth behind her. "It's going to be alright now. We'll get you to a doctor."

Joe was holding Beth half in his lap, stroking her hair. "Let's go."

Randy drove as quickly as he could while trying not to jostle Beth around. At one point, Will looked his way. "Could it be her appendix?"

He shook his head. "Hard to tell. Do you know if she still has hers?"

Will returned her attention to the backseat. "Beth, do you still have your appendix?"

Randy heard a growl but couldn't make out the answer.

"She says yes," Will translated. "We need to go faster."

"Almost there," he said, unable to ignore the fact that half of Will's body was pressed along his right arm. Warm curves fit tightly against his elbow, hindering his steering and his ability to concentrate on the road. She'd either gotten over her fear of him overnight or had no idea what she was doing.

He figured on scenario number two.

Arriving at the Anchor Island Health and Wellness Clinic, Randy had barely slid the vehicle into park before Joe's door flew open.

"Come on, baby. I've got you," he said as he coaxed Beth from the truck. She didn't seem capable of uncurling, never mind walking on her own. With his fiancée in his arms, Joe barreled around to the entrance where Will was holding the door open. She hit the large square button that would automatically open the inside door for anyone in a wheelchair.

As they stormed into the lobby, Beth let out another scream, which got the attention of the girl sitting on the other side of the sliding window. "Hold on!" she yelled, disappearing from sight, then bursting through the door on their left. "Bring her back here."

Joe carried Beth through the door. Will moved to follow, but Randy grabbed her by the elbow.

"What are you doing?" she demanded, jerking her arm free. "I need to go with her."

So body contact was once again off limits. "The doc will only kick us back out. They'll let us know when they have some answers."

"But—"

"Your intentions are good, Will, but we'll only be in the way." Randy had been involved in enough trauma and accidents to know doctors needed room to work. You didn't climb mountains, scale cliffs, and race anything with a motor without someone getting hurt.

Will clamped her mouth shut, shot him a dirty look, then began pacing the small waiting area. After a thirty-second pout, she said, "Do you think we got her here on time?"

"Beth has been healthy as long as I've known her," he said, which, granted, wasn't that long. "Whatever it is, they'll take care of her."

"But what if we didn't get here fast enough? What if—"

"What if we grab some water and sit down to wait," he suggested.

Will gave a long sigh, crossed her arms, and dropped into a chair two down from Randy. He struggled not to roll his eyes at the mandatory distance. As if one chair length would protect her from whatever she thought he might try.

"I guess water couldn't hurt."

Randy filled two cups from the water cooler and handed one to Will. "You're a good friend," he said, and meant it. Will didn't reveal much of herself, especially not to him, but she'd just dropped everything, including the busy restaurant she was running, to take care of a friend. That meant something.

"I should have helped more with the party," she said. "I could have had the crew decorate this morning so Beth wouldn't have to."

Randy chuckled, leaning his head back against the wall. "I doubt Beth would have given up that much control. Besides, if it *is* her appendix, this would have happened whether she was decorating or not."

"But she's so stressed with the wedding." Will slid one denim-clad leg beneath her. "I could have taken care of the party. It's not as if Sid cares one way or another how fancy the decorations are."

Randy rolled his head to the right to meet Will's eyes. "The same way you want to go in there and take care of Beth, she wants to take care of Sid. That's what friends do."

Will rubbed her upper arms as if trying to warm herself. "I guess you're right. I haven't had friends like this for a while."

He let the silence hold for a few extra seconds, then asked, "Why's that?"

His gypsy, as he'd come to think of her, met his eyes with wide blue ones. The color reminded him of his mother's birthstone, blue topaz.

"I—"

"Where's Curly?" Sid yelled, charging through the front door of the clinic, Lucas close on her heels. "What happened?"

"Take a breath," Randy said, irritated that they'd interrupted whatever Will had been about to say. "Beth bent over in pain while we were at Dempsey's. We rushed her here, and now she and Joe are with the doctor."

"Did she get hit?" Lucas asked. "Fall off of something? Was there any warning?"

"Joe says she's been acting strange for a couple weeks," Randy answered, "but that might not have anything to do with this. She started sweating, then her face went pale. Next thing we knew, she was bent over and moaning."

"We need to go back there and find out what's going on," Sid said, heading for the door to the exam rooms.

"Wait," Randy said, but in that second, Joe walked through the door, his face fish-belly white.

Everyone in the lobby fell silent, frozen in place as if the slightest twitch would shatter the man before them. Without a word, Joe dropped into a chair.

Randy flashed back seventeen years, to the day his world changed forever. His mother, the beacon of the family, happy and healthy only hours before, was gone. She, too, had curled over in pain.

"Joe?" Lucas said, giving Sid's shoulder a squeeze as he slid by her. "What is it? What's wrong with Beth?"

Joe looked up with surprise in his eyes, as if he'd forgotten they were all there. He shook his head. "Nothing. Nothing's wrong with Beth."

Randy let out the breath he hadn't realized he was holding. "Then what is it?" he asked. "Why was she screaming like that?"

Joe leaned back in his chair. "We're going to have a baby."

CHAPTER 3

I can't believe it," Will muttered for the third time in the last hour. Maybe the fourth. "Did you see that coming?" she asked Sid, who was sitting to her left and staring at her beer bottle.

Sid shook her head. "Nope. Not at all."

The party, though it was more subdued than the word implied, had returned to Dempsey's without Joe and Beth. Beth had been given strict orders to put her feet up and get plenty of rest. Her blood pressure had been through the roof, which had stressed the baby, forcing the little bugger to make his irritation known. Or her irritation. Too early to tell on that one.

So strange. A baby.

"Why do you all look like this is the end of the world?" Randy asked. "She's having a baby, not carrying the plague."

"Mom and Dad will be home tomorrow," Lucas said, returning to the table after calling his parents to share the news. "I told Mom that Beth and Joe wouldn't want them to cut their vacation short, but I think she started packing their suitcases the moment I said 'baby.'"

Relief fluttered through Will. The Dempseys' return meant she wouldn't have to handle the reporter in regards to the restaurant. A selfish thought considering why they were coming back, but a relief nonetheless.

"So much for a surprise birthday party," Lucas added, spinning a chair next to Sid, then straddling it. "Beth pulled out a bigger surprise than anyone planned."

Will agreed with that. But she agreed with Randy, too. "It's still Sid's birthday," she said. "And Randy is right. This isn't bad news. We should be happy for them."

Randy raised a brow in her direction, as if surprised she'd agreed with him. She didn't have to want him near her to admit he was right.

"I wonder if Beth is happy about it," Lucas said. "Joe looked scared shitless. Think Beth is doing any better?"

Will knew how she'd feel if she were faced with a surprise pregnancy, but then again she wasn't mere weeks away from marrying the man of her dreams. And even if she was, Will being in the family way would be a modern medical miracle now.

"She told me last summer that they weren't having kids for a while." Sid dropped her head onto Lucas's shoulder. "Goes to show. Never tempt fate by saying shit like that."

Randy chuckled. "Well, I'm happy for them. Once the shock wears off, they'll see things in a better light."

Easy for Randy to say. He wasn't the one whose life was about to change.

"A new Dempsey." Lucas shook his head, a grin teasing one corner of his mouth. "I guess it's about time. Joe isn't getting any younger, after all."

"Watch it, pretty boy," Randy said. "I'm older than Joe."

"That's what you could give me for my birthday," Sid said, smiling for the first time since they'd left the clinic.

"What?" her brother asked.

"A niece or nephew."

Lucas had made the mistake of taking a drink while Sid was talking. Will got a shower of diet soda.

"Hey!"

"Sorry," Lucas muttered, trying to wipe his mouth and hold back the laughter at the same time.

Randy flicked Sid in the forehead. Sid tried to flick him back, but he stiff-armed her with a hand on the top of her head.

"Knock it off before I end up wearing another drink," Will scolded, but couldn't ignore the pang of jealousy. She'd never had a sibling. Hadn't even grown up with cousins. It would be nice to have a family, even if only to have forehead flicking contests.

"Come on, badass," Lucas said, rising from his chair and plucking Sid from her seat. "I'm saving you from an ass kicking, Randy. I hope you appreciate this."

The large man gave a quick smile, and Will's chest tightened. The reaction took her off balance. He was still the man who'd ripped into her the day before. She and her libido needed to have a chat.

"Don't forget the presents and cards," Will said. "Daisy collected them behind the bar." There had been no time to pass the word that the party was cancelled, so Daisy had let people know as they arrived. Will got up to get the gifts, but Lucas stopped her.

"Relax," he said. "We'll get them."

"Speaking of presents," Sid said, turning to Lucas. "What did *you* get me?"

The look that crossed Lucas's face qualified as too much information even before he spoke the words. "I hid your present in the bedroom. It could take us all night to find it."

Sid turned an uncharacteristic shade of pink. "Then we'd better hurry home." Putting words into action, she tugged Lucas hard enough to knock a lesser man off his feet. From then on, the two might as well have been alone for all the attention they paid to anyone else.

"They make a cute couple," Will said, watching the tall, handsome lawyer juggle the presents his tiny fiancée was piling in his arms. "Disgustingly mushy, but cute."

Randy crossed his arms, his eyes watching the same spectacle. "I hate to tell, but he's softening her up. I wasn't sure he had it in him for a while there."

Will took the opportunity to ask something she'd been curious about for months. "Last summer, when Lucas first came back. It was you who told him that Sid liked to run on the beach, wasn't it?"

He looked surprised and a bit guilty. "A little nudge never hurts," was all he said.

Rubbing a fingernail along a rough spot on the table, Will waited for the tension to squeeze her gut. The feeling she always had around Randy, as if she were being suffocated and needed to get away to breathe again.

She wouldn't say she felt comfortable, but she wasn't choking for air either.

Damn it. If she let herself like him . . .

"You were good earlier," he said, jerking Will from her thoughts. "When Beth got sick. I was worried at first, when you froze."

She *had* frozen. Not because she wasn't good in a crisis. That had never been a problem for Will. The reaction had stemmed from the realization of how scared she was for her friend. How much she cared about Beth. Will hadn't let herself care that much about anyone in a long time.

"You were the one who held it together like a pro," she said, opting to deflect the topic away from herself. "Have you done rescue work or something?"

"When you spend your life walking on the edge, you learn how to handle stress and stay calm." Randy lifted one shoulder. "To some it looks like adrenaline junkies are always flying by the seat of our pants, but that's not the case. It's not luck or skill alone that's kept me alive this long. It's brains, presence of mind, and being able to process a situation in seconds."

Will had never thought much about how adrenaline junkies must think, but what Randy described was very close to how she'd been living for the past few years. A life on the edge, always worried someone might recognize her, learn her secret. The remote nature of Anchor had allowed her to relax a bit, but now that security was being threatened by the magazine coverage.

Time to go back on alert, and be prepared to move on if necessary.

"Guess I'd better go." Randy pushed his chair back and rose to his feet, a shadow falling across the table as if something enormous had risen from the sea.

Will rose with him. She needed to get back behind the bar. "Here's hoping we don't get any more surprises like this one for a while."

"Hey," Randy said, pausing until she made eye contact. "Thanks."

"For what?"

"For not making me feel like a leper for once." Will didn't know what to say to that, so she remained silent. "You have a good night," he said, then flashed the smile that did stupid things to her brain.

As Randy walked away, Will's heart beat double time. That was supposed to happen when he walked into a room, not *out* of it. Time to resurrect the roadblocks. Going soft over Randy Navarro was a complication Will could not afford. Her life was already complicated enough.

~

The lunch crowd had dwindled to less than a dozen by mid-afternoon on Monday. With a good ninety minutes of peace before the dinner service started, Will took the opportunity to do a readout on the register.

The totals looked better than she'd expected. A good sign for the season to come. She was jotting down the numbers in the notebook she'd been keeping for end-of-the-week analysis when two strangers stepped up to the bar.

A petite blonde with a clear presence about her climbed onto a bar stool. A man with long brown hair pulled back in a ponytail sat down beside her, his nose in his cell phone.

"I can't get a signal," the man said, holding the phone in the air over his head and squinting at the screen.

"There's no cell service on the island," Will informed him. One of Anchor's best features, in her opinion. "What can I get you?"

Mr. Cell Phone looked stunned, while the blonde turned in her seat to examine the back half of the dining room. "Did you say no cell phone service?" Ice-blue eyes stared in disbelief. "You're kidding, right? Even third world countries have cell service."

Will flashed her tourist-welcoming smile. "Afraid not."

"That's it, Becks," he said in a crisp British accent as he set a small black duffel on the stool beside him. "We've finally reached the end of the world."

Wisps of light brown hair danced around a narrow face that could be described as feminine if it weren't for the scruff along his chin. The man wore a dark green corduroy jacket with a gray scarf wrapped around his neck. Everything about him said "world traveler." Not the typical Anchor tourist by far.

"Sorry," Will apologized, not sure what else to say. "We do have internet. In some places." She didn't want to imply Dempsey's offered free Wi-Fi, but she was certain wherever they were staying would have it.

"Well, bully for you." The comeback would have been rude if it hadn't been said with that lovely lilt and accompanied by a charming smile.

"Relax, Jude," said the Becks person. "You'll survive one week without your phone." Addressing Will, she said, "I'll take a green tea if you have it."

"Coming right up." Will turned to Jude. "And you?"

He perused the area behind the bar, his eyes practically glowing when he spotted the list of imported beers. "I see you becoming my favorite person this week, love. Slide me over a Samuel Smith, if you please."

Will filled the order, setting both bottles before her patrons. "Safe to say you've just arrived?" she asked.

"Fresh off the boat," Becks answered, flashing pearly whites that must have cost her a fortune. Hazel eyes narrowed. "I've seen you somewhere before. Have we met?"

That question always put Will on edge, but she was certain she'd remember a striking blonde with the name Becks. "Don't think so."

"Have you done any modeling?"

Will snorted, then looked up and realized the woman was serious. "No, I've never modeled." What the hell would she model? Restaurant aprons?

"Really?" The woman stood on the step of her stool to see the rest of Will. "You've got the height for it. And lots of agencies are looking for women with hips now."

Somehow that didn't feel like a compliment. Will turned around to grab a glass off the back counter and checked out her hips in the mirror behind the bar. They weren't *that* wide.

"Your hips are lovely, my dear," Jude said. "Don't mind Becks here. She lacks a bit of tact."

"I know I've seen that face before," Becks said, ignoring her friend. "Where are you from?"

Will *never* answered that one. "Here and there." Tossing the cap from Jude's beer, she asked, "You two want to start a tab?"

"Hell yes," Jude said, lifting his bottle in salute. "I'm going to need lots of these to get through a week with no cell phone."

Becks continued to pretend her friend didn't exist. "How long have you been on Anchor?"

Seemed a harmless one. "Little over a year." Switching to sales mode, Will gave her best pitch. "You won't find better food anywhere on the island than right here at Dempsey's. You two want to try an appetizer?"

"I could eat," Jude said, then asked, "Where's the loo, darling?"

"Far right corner," Will answered, nodding her head in that direction. Placing a menu on the bar, she addressed the blonde as Jude took his bag and crossed the dining room. "The steamed mussels are amazing."

"You really do look familiar," Becks said, accepting the menu. "I know I sound crazy at this point, but are you sure there isn't anywhere I could have seen your face before? I spend most of my time in Boston. Have you ever worked there?"

Will always knew this day might come. Was surprised it hadn't happened before now. Three years ago her face had been plastered on flyers, as well as flashed across the evening news, all over New England. But mostly in Boston.

"Nope. Must be someone who looks like me." Using all her energy to tamp down the panic charging through her system, Will grabbed a half-empty bag of bottles from the recycle bin. "I need to take these out."

Charging through the kitchen, she swung open the back door and tossed the bag into the large blue Dumpster. Instead of returning to the kitchen, she ditched into the office to think through her next move. Only she'd forgotten Patty was in there catching up on paperwork. She and Tom had returned the day before, having driven all day Saturday to arrive on Sunday.

"How's it going out there?" Patty asked, peering over her reading glasses.

"Good," Will said, her voice higher than intended. She cleared her throat. "It's fine. The lunch crowd was good for a Monday."

I may have to leave town, she thought.

"Good to hear." Patty laid down the bank statement in her hand and looked back to the computer screen. "You did an amazing job with the accounting system while we were gone. Where did you learn to keep books like this?"

"Just picked it up as I've moved around." The lie tasted bitter on her tongue. "I'd better get back out there."

"Tom will be in around five to relieve you." Patty removed her reading glasses. "Will, we really appreciate all the work you've put in for us. I don't know how we ever got along without you."

Great. That would make cutting out without warning even harder.

"I'm happy to help," she said, exiting the office, then leaning her back against the cold metal door of the walk-in.

Maybe Becks wouldn't remember. Maybe she hadn't seen the ads listing Will as a missing person. Not that those ads identified her by the name Will. After three deep breaths, she forced her heart rate to slow. There was no reason to jump to conclusions. So she looked familiar. That sort of thing happened all the time.

One more deep breath and Will felt in control again. Stepping out of the kitchen, she was greeted by Jude's broad smile.

"Becks here says you recommend the mussels. We'll take an order, and load me up with another beer, would you?"

"I can do that." Keying the order into the system, Will used the bar mirror to survey the pair.

Becks, a hazel-eyed blonde dressed like something straight out of a fashion magazine, looked like one of those women who could get dressed with her eyes closed and still come out looking trendy. Hardly the type to play tourist on their tiny speck of sand. At one mile long and two miles wide, with no chains or franchise businesses of any kind, Anchor drew families, baby boomers looking for hokey fun and good fishing, and the occasional college crowd.

Upper-crust twentysomethings like Becks and Jude seemed more the big city type. Manhattan, Paris, or London. So what had brought them to the bottom of the Outer Banks?

Georgette appeared at the end of the bar, turned in a drink order, then returned to the floor. Will filled the order, lined the drinks on the bar for Georgette, then opted to remain at the far end until the appetizer showed up in the window.

After the order was filled and she'd set the basket of mussels, two plates, and silverware in front of them, Becks asked, "What sights would you recommend to tourists around here?"

The safer topic let Will breathe easier. "One of the biggest draws is the lighthouse. It's out at the end of Lighthouse Road on the southwest corner of the island."

To Will's surprise, Becks was taking notes. "Right. What else?"

"Oh, um." Will scratched her head. "There's wild horses, the preservation museum, and the beaches."

The pen moved furiously across the notepad. "Good. That gives us someplace to start." Becks elbowed Jude. "Why don't you take a picture of our lovely bartender here? She's like the island welcoming committee. We definitely need her picture."

Jude dropped a half-eaten mussel and wiped his hands on a napkin. "Excellent idea." He pulled a very professional-looking camera from his case. "Smile, darling."

The flash blinded Will before she had time to react.

"There," Jude said, setting the camera next to his plate. "Perfect start to this assignment."

"Assignment?" Will asked, her heart beating as if it were pumping tar instead of blood. "You're not from—"

"*Prime Destinations* magazine," Becks said, extending a hand. "Rebecca King, at your service."

A gray haze danced around the edges of Will's vision. "Will Parsons," she muttered, her brain running on autopilot as she took the offered hand. "Nice to meet you."

CHAPTER 4

When Randy answered the phone in his office at the fitness center, the last thing he expected to hear was Will's voice.

"Get over here now," she'd said in a near whisper, then the line went dead.

If his caller ID hadn't revealed that the call came from Dempsey's, he might not have known where *here* was. His first thought was Beth, but Will would have given more details if there was another medical emergency. Whatever it was, her voice carried enough urgency to get him on the road.

He stepped into the restaurant five minutes later to find Will cleaning tables as if some massive contagion had entered the building. As soon as she spotted him, the cleaning was forgotten and she sprinted in his direction. "What took you so long?" she hissed, glancing toward the bar. "They're here."

From her body language, he assumed the *they* in question was either the FBI or an alien army.

"Who's here?" he asked.

She twitched her head to the right three times. "The reporter and photographer. They're at the bar." He opened his mouth to respond but Will wasn't done. "They took my picture," she said, the twitch migrating to her shoulder.

"Will," he said, sliding his hands into his pockets to keep from holding her still. "Are you on a new medication? Is this a reaction to something?"

"Just get them out of here." She returned to the table she'd been cleaning, bared her teeth, and made a shooing gesture with her hands.

The woman had gone certifiably insane overnight.

"Ms. King?" Randy asked, crossing to the bar.

The blonde spun on her stool, offering a perfectly manicured hand and a blindingly white smile. "I'm Rebecca King. I hope you're Mr. Edwards."

"No, sorry." He took the offered hand as catlike eyes perused every muscle on his body. Appreciation clear in their hazel depths.

"That's too bad." Ms. King crossed her legs, allowing the hem of her tan dress to slide up her thigh. The woman wasn't shy about what she liked. He felt like one of the desserts in Ms. Opal's bakery.

"I'm Randy Navarro. My business, Anchor Adventures, provides water sports, such as parasailing and Jet Skis, for the tourists." Releasing her hand and taking a step back, he added, "I also own the fitness center. I'll be showing you around the island while you're here."

"The fitness center?" the man next to Ms. King said in a pure London accent. "I never would have guessed."

A less flattering greeting, but nothing he wasn't accustomed to. "You must be the photographer."

"Jude Sykes. Have camera will travel." Fancy Pants offered a hand. "Nice to meet you."

"I trust Will has been taking good care of you so far?"

"She has," Rebecca said. "She's already given us a list of the island's best sights." A quick lick of her finger and she flipped back several pages in her notepad. "We're staying at the Anchor Inn and Marina. Can you show us the way?"

"Sure can." Randy looked around for Will. She'd migrated to the end of the bar, her face pale and hands visibly shaking. "If you guys could give me a minute, I need to talk to Will about something. There's a great view of the sound off the side deck if you'd like to check it out."

"I can get some nice late-day shots." Jude pulled the strap to a black camera case over his head. "Take all the time you need, big guy."

The reporter followed the lanky Brit through the side door, giving a quick smile over her shoulder and putting an extra swing in her step. He had a feeling the woman was used to getting what she wanted. That streak would end if she set her sights on adding him to her list of conquests.

Randy gave a quick wave as he joined Will down the bar. "Are you okay?" he asked her. "You look ready to crawl out of your skin."

"I don't like having my picture taken," she answered, her eyes darting from him to the saltshakers she was filling. Her unsteady hand sent salt over the side.

"It's only a picture. They probably won't even use it."

More grains missed the opening and she slammed the canister of Morton Salt on the counter. "I'd have to sign a consent form before they could use it, right?"

"I don't know," he said. "I guess so. Did they ask you to sign one?"

"No." She went back to work on the shakers, her hand steadier. "Do you think we could erase it off the camera?"

"What?" This had to be a joke. "You can ask him to erase it, if that'll make you feel better. But I don't understand. What is the big deal about having your picture taken?"

Will opened her mouth to answer, then snapped it shut. She tried again. "People will . . . If someone sees . . ." She closed her eyes, rubbing narrow fingers across her forehead. "I can't tell you."

Another statement that made no sense. She was hiding something bigger than a bitter breakup with some jerk. "Will, are you in trouble?"

Wide blue eyes met his. A muscle in her jaw twitched. "You better get going. You don't want to leave them waiting too long."

The set of her shoulders said she wasn't going to answer his question. Pushing her would only make her close in even more. She could keep her secrets for now, but this conversation was far from over.

⁓

Randy parked his truck in front of the Anchor Inn, then walked over to the SUV rental to help the island's VIP guests carry their bags inside. Jude slung the camera bag over his shoulder, then dragged a computer bag and large green duffel out of the back. Rebecca carried a large purse and smiled at Randy as he removed a bright blue, hard-sided suitcase from the vehicle.

Keeping his face friendly but not encouraging, Randy motioned for her to take the lead. Jude was already holding the door when she stepped up, and Randy grabbed the handle for the photographer to follow his partner inside.

The only sound in the lobby was the flap of Rebecca's sandals as they crossed the sand-shaded tiles to reach the reservation desk. A pretty young woman with skin the color of milk chocolate ice cream raised green-gold eyes as they approached the counter.

"Yvonne, this is Rebecca King and Jude Sykes from *Prime Destinations* magazine. I believe they have reservations." Randy stepped to the side so the pair could handle the details. "Ms. Granville will take care of you." Setting the blue suitcase next to its owner, he addressed the clerk again. "Is Sam in his office?"

"He is," she answered with a nod. "If you're headed that way, could you let him know our guests are here?"

"Can do." To Rebecca and Jude he said, "Excuse me, I'll be right back."

Leaving the visitors in Yvonne's capable hands, Randy strolled down the short hall to the right of the entrance and knocked on the door marked "Manager/Owner."

"Come in," responded a voice from the other side.

"Our reporter has arrived," Randy said, stepping into the simple but elegant office. Sam Edwards was likely the only person on the island who could ever be described as elegant. There was probably a better, more masculine word for it, but Randy couldn't think of one.

After inheriting three hotels from his uncle two years before, Sam relocated to the island to find outdated, fading businesses in need of complete overhaul. No one believed he'd stay and make a go of things. Rumor had it Sam had worked in some of the fanciest hotels in the southeast, racking up quite a reputation for high standards and high quality.

His uncle was the last of the family to live on Anchor, so it was believed Sam had no reason to stick around. But he had stuck. And he turned the Anchor Inn into a modern hotel, by Anchor standards, that could compete with any along the Outer Banks. He'd even acquired the Marina restaurant in recent months, after selling off the smallest and most dilapidated of the three properties.

They weren't exactly drinking buddies, but Randy respected the hotelier, and they'd gotten better acquainted in the last month working on the planning committee that was tasked with bringing tourism back to the island.

"Have we made a good impression so far?" Sam asked, buttoning his suit coat as he rounded his desk.

"They stopped at Dempsey's on the way in. Will took good care of them." Randy left out the part about Will's sudden bout of insanity. "They seem happy enough."

"Good. We need to keep them that way." Sam lifted a folder from the corner of his desk. "They'll have the best view the inn has to offer, and I've given direct orders for them to receive the utmost professional and friendly service while they're here."

Randy had never seen the man this ruffled. For someone who exuded extreme confidence at all times, the display of nerves reflected how important this article would be to the future of the island. They all had a stake in showing Anchor to its best advantage.

"Yvonne has been an excellent addition to the staff," Sam said, tucking the folder beneath one arm and tugging down his shirt-sleeves. "Remind me to thank Lola for sending her my way."

Lola LeBlanc ran the art store on the island. An eclectic older woman originally from New Orleans, she'd reunited the year before with a man from her past. The reunion went well enough that Marcus Granville was now a permanent part of the island, and his daughter Yvonne a recent transplant as well.

As the men traveled down the hall toward the front desk, Yvonne handed two key cards over the counter to the new guests. "Here are your keys. If you ever have any questions or need anything, feel free to call down here to the desk and we'll take care of you."

"Thank you," Jude said, hefting his camera case onto his shoulder. "We'll do that."

"Thank you, Yvonne," Sam said, stepping into the lobby. "Ms. King, Mr. Sykes. Sam Edwards." He extended a hand with complete control. Whatever nerves he was feeling, Sam didn't let it show. "I've put together a packet on Anchor Island so you can get a little history on our home and decide how you'd like to conduct the week."

Rebecca accepted the folder. "Our research department created a full workup, but I'm always happy to have anything extra." After glancing at the folder's contents, she asked, "How well do you know the bartender at Dempsey's?"

Both men hesitated. Why was she asking about Will? Sam looked to Randy as if he were thinking the same thing, then supplied an answer. "Not that well, actually. I know she's worked at a few businesses around the island, but Will has never been on our staff so our paths haven't crossed enough for me to really get to know her."

"Really? I wouldn't expect that on an island this small." Rebecca slid the folder into her bag. "She has one of those familiar faces, you know? So familiar I'd swear I've seen her somewhere before."

"You know what they say," Randy offered. "We all have a twin in the world somewhere."

An awkward silence settled over the little group, until Yvonne spoke up. "I'm sure our guests would like to get settled in their rooms. Do you want me to ring for Owen to show them upstairs?"

"No," Sam said. "I'll take them myself."

"Then it looks like my work here is done," Randy said, feeling more relieved than he'd be willing to admit. "We can get started on the rest of the island tomorrow. How does nine o'clock sound?"

"Perfect," Rebecca said. "We'll meet you here in the lobby."

"I don't suppose I can get a good cup of coffee around here?" Jude asked. "I'm not really awake until I've had my coffee."

"You're in the suites, which have full kitchens, including coffeemakers," Sam replied. "But we also have the Hava Java coffee shop not far from here if you're looking for something only a barista could make."

"Mr. Randy, we'll be starting at Hava Java." Jude picked up his bags. "That's fun to say."

"Great. I'll leave you with Sam and see you in the morning then."

Randy gave Yvonne a wink, who rolled her eyes and visibly exhaled, then bid a hasty retreat to his truck. He considered mentioning Rebecca's line of questioning about her to Will, but decided against it. She was already spooked enough.

It had always been obvious that Will was hiding something, but until now he'd assumed she was intensely private. Based on her reaction to one casual snapshot, there was definitely more to her story.

CHAPTER 5

By the time Will arrived at Opal's for their regular Tuesday girls' night, Sid and Beth were seated with their desserts, including Will's rhubarb pie. Beth looked tired, but well enough to be out getting treats.

"I heard she's pushy, but I guess you have to be in that line of work," Beth was saying as Will took her seat. "Word is the photographer's a real charmer."

"He is," Will said, dropping a napkin across her lap. "British. Long hair. Pretty eyes."

"You met him already?" Sid asked around her bite of chocolate cupcake. Sid did love her chocolate. "How did that happen?"

"They stopped in at Dempsey's on the way into town. I didn't know who they were at first." If only she'd known. "I thought they were tourists."

"That explains it." Beth wiped her mouth. "Yvonne says the first thing the woman asked Sam Edwards was if he knew you."

"What?" Will nearly choked on her pie. "Why would she do that? Sam doesn't even know me."

"That's what *he* said, according to Yvonne. This King woman commented that you had one of those familiar faces, then dropped the subject."

What could a travel reporter possibly gain from asking about Will? It wasn't as if anyone on Anchor Island knew her secret. No one knew her face had been front page news once upon a time. And she certainly wasn't an important enough part of the island to garner this kind of attention.

"I don't know what she expects people to tell her," Will said, trying to play the whole thing off. "I'm not that interesting."

"Maybe she likes you." Sid raised a brow.

Will remembered how Rebecca King had looked at Randy as if he belonged in Opal's display case. "Trust me. That's not it."

"I'm just saying. You're kind of hot, in that lesbian sort of way."

Will looked at Beth, who had spit a piece of carrot cake into her hand. "Where does she get this shit?"

Beth shook her head, coughing and waving a hand in front of her face. "I don't know, but that one nearly killed me."

Sid smacked Beth on the back. "Take a breath, Curly. If you die, Joe will kill me."

"Why do we hang out with her?" Will asked, trying to keep a straight face.

"Don't look at me," Beth said. "She's your people."

"No way in hell I'm claiming her." Will noticed a day planner under Beth's plate. "What are you hiding under there?"

"Oh." Beth set down her fork and slid the notebook from under her plate. "This is my life at the moment. Everything for the wedding is in here."

"I'm trying to get her to hand it over," Sid said, slicing what was left of her cupcake into three large pieces. "The doc says no stress, and that means no more handling every single wedding detail on her own."

"Lola tried to sneak this out of my bag, but I caught her." Beth held the book with a death grip.

"You have to let us help you." Will held out her hand. "I swear to you, on Sid's life, that we'll set everything up exactly how you want. If the slightest thing goes wrong, you can bury her at sea."

"Who needs enemies when I have you two shits in my life?" Sid shook her head and returned her attention to her dessert. "She won't give it to you."

Beth handed Will the planner. "All the numbers and details are in the back."

"What the fuck?" Sid said.

Ignoring her, Beth continued. "You'll have to stay on the tent company to make sure they're prepared to be here and set up at the slightest chance of rain. Opal is taking care of the cake, but make sure she knows the delivery time. The florist is over in Hatteras, so you need to make sure they schedule plenty of time in case there are ferry delays."

Will felt the heavy weight of stress travel from Beth to herself. She'd figured everything would be done by now and she'd maybe have to arrive early to answer questions. This sounded like a full-time job, with more responsibility than she had running Dempsey's.

And Sid's life was on the line. Which was still a funny joke, but in all seriousness, Will had to make sure this was perfect for Beth.

"My dress arrives this Friday, so I'll need you two to come with me for the fitting and try on your dresses." Beth pointed a finger at Sid's nose. "And do not argue with me. You're wearing a dress. And heels. No boots."

Her finger floated to Will. "That goes for both of you. I know you like the skirts-with-combat-boots look, but that's not going to happen on my day."

A moody, pregnant bridezilla had infiltrated Beth's body. Will hoped the old Beth would return when the event of her life had gone off without a hitch.

43

Now, to make sure there were no hitches.

"We'll be there and we'll wear whatever you want."

Sid opened her mouth, but Will silenced her. "We'll wear whatever Beth wants us to wear, and we'll like it. Right?"

"This is why I want to elope," Sid muttered.

"If you rob me of the chance to put you in a real wedding dress," Beth said, "I will hunt you down and beat you until you can't get up."

Sid blinked several times, then looked at Will. "Who is this woman?"

"I don't know," Will said, loading pie onto her fork. "But if this beatdown occurs, I'm selling tickets. We could make a killing."

Beth finished her carrot cake, sat back, and yawned. "That was good. I think I might have another." It was as if the temper she'd just displayed had dissipated into thin air. "I *am* eating for two, so the doctor said I could eat anything I want. Maybe I'll try the cherry pie."

Going from carrot cake to cherry pie sounded disgusting to Will, but then some people hated rhubarb pie and she loved it. There was simply no accounting for taste.

"Oh, one more thing," Beth said, the cherry pie momentarily forgotten. "The tuxedos have been ordered, but Randy's has to be specially altered. They don't carry them in his size on the rack."

"Why does that not surprise me?" Will asked, not expecting an answer.

"You'll have to go with him up to Kill Devil Hills to get fitted. That's the closest place I could find."

Wait. What? "Why do I have to go with him? He's a grown man. He can go by himself."

Beth held out her hand. "Fine. Give me the planner back."

"You can't be serious."

"The only way to make sure he gets the right vest in the right color and the right fit is to make sure a woman goes with him. I planned to go." Beth pointed at the little tan book in Will's hands. "Now you're taking over, so you have to go."

What a load of . . .

"Sid can go with him."

Green eyes narrowed as Beth leaned forward. Will leaned back.

"I'll go with him. Geez. You're scary when you're like this."

Beth sat back and smiled. "Time to get my pie."

As their friend moved to the counter, Sid whispered to Will, "Are all pregnant women that schizo?"

"Think of it this way," Will said. "At least we're not Joe."

"Amen to that."

~

By the time Randy had returned home Tuesday evening, his face hurt from smiling and his entire body felt as if it had been hooked to a live wire for the last nine hours. Playing tour guide was bad enough, but Rebecca King asked more questions than any woman he'd ever met. He understood that went with the territory, considering she was writing an article about the place, but the woman never took a breath.

One day had tested his endurance. He might have to cry uncle by the end of the week.

First on the itinerary for Wednesday was Lola's Island Arts & Crafts, where at least there would be other people to answer the questions. Rebecca had been silent on the short drive as she reviewed the information Sam had provided for the businesses they would visit that day. Jude had alternated between sipping his coffee and napping.

"Here we are," Randy said as he pulled into the gravel lot in front of the art store. "Stop one for the day."

"Wow," Rebecca said. "It really is that blue."

Randy glanced toward the small building. The color was a bit bright. Maybe he'd seen it so often, the boldness didn't register. "The color matches the owner's personality. Lola is a force of nature."

"I'll take some pics out here and meet you two inside," Jude said, removing the camera from his bag. "This place has great character."

Randy took his enthusiasm as a good sign. The more they found to appreciate about the village, the better the article would be.

A bell jingled overhead as Randy pulled the door open for Rebecca to pass through. She stopped inches inside the entrance, making it difficult for him to step in and shut the door without being pressed up against her.

Randy opted to remain in the doorway.

"It's like an optical illusion," Rebecca said, her eyes taking in the wide expanse of space. "You'd never know any of this was possible from outside."

"We get that a lot." Lola LeBlanc joined them at the entrance with a genuine smile. Her colorful dress floated around her as the breeze from the open door caught the material. "You must be Ms. King."

"I am," Rebecca said, clutching her notebook under one arm and extending a hand. "And you must be Ms. LeBlanc."

"Please, call me Lola." With a conspiratorial wink, she added, "We don't go for much formality around here."

"And so far that's one of my favorite aspects of Anchor." Finally stepping farther into the store, the reporter lifted a shimmering silver vase from a display. "This is beautiful. I can see I won't be leaving empty-handed today."

Lola laid a finger beside her nose. "I'd be disappointed if you did. Let me show you the rest of the place." The two women moved farther into the gallery of eclectic art and pottery. "We don't have many visitors this early in the season, but then that's why you're here. Oh, before we go too far, I want to introduce you to the woman I could not live without."

Randy lingered in the front display area, letting the women pull ahead. From the corner of his eye, he noticed a statue of a woman a few feet to his right. From a distance it looked like black marble, but moving closer he picked up the dark purple hues. She was slender and elongated, her arms holding up long swirling tendrils of hair that looked more like black fire.

The body twisted and leaned back slightly as if standing against a strong wind. Around her feet danced dark flames, and her face looked graceful but strong. The figure exuded confidence and sensuality, while the body language made it clear no man deserved her. This woman knew who she was and the power she held. One name came to Randy's mind.

Willow.

She could have been the model for this sculpture, if the artist hadn't conjured this figure strictly from imagination. Either way, whoever created this piece had a great understanding and respect for the female gender. Which led him to assume the artist was likely also a woman.

After checking the price, he made a note to come back for the large piece. He even had the perfect place to display it. Randy shuffled on to find the women he'd abandoned when the bells over the door sounded again. Jude stepped in and repeated Rebecca's frozen amazement.

"Bloody hell. It's a freaking magic trick." Catching Randy's eye, he asked, "Is this place run by Mary Poppins, by chance?"

"Not exactly. But the owner does have a similar way about her."

"This I've got to see." Jude ambled through the front of the store, glancing right and left as he went. Stepping into the main gallery, he lifted his camera without hesitation and took some shots. "Who'd ever expect to find all this here?"

Assuming the question was rhetorical, Randy remained silent and followed behind. They found the women in the jewelry section and stepped into an ongoing conversation.

"Beth teaches jewelry-making classes for the tourists and does some craft classes for us islanders during the off-season." Lola stood behind Beth's right shoulder, beaming. "She also runs the place most of the time, allowing me to enjoy time off with my sweetie."

"What does your sweetie do on the island?" Rebecca asked.

"Oh, Marcus does as little as possible if he can help it. Says he's retired and plans to enjoy his golden years." The blush was barely visible on Lola's ashen cheeks. "But he does handle the island newsletter and enjoys some amateur photography."

"Then I definitely want to meet this man," Jude said, making his presence known. "Jude Sykes. I'm the picture taker of this crew."

"And a right pretty picture taker at that," Lola said, drawing a blush from the woman in the chair beside her. "Lola LeBlanc, owner of this establishment, and Beth Chandler, my right-hand woman."

"I like you right off." Jude winked at Lola. "This place oozes charm, Ms. LeBlanc. We'll definitely want to use it in the spread. The colors are phenomenal."

"The place is a direct reflection of its owner," Beth said, speaking for the first time since Randy and Jude had joined them. "When I came to the island last year, this is the first place I visited thanks to her colorful flyer."

"You arrived on Anchor Island a year ago?" Rebecca asked, taking the chair Lola offered. The men remained standing, with Jude wandering off to snap more pictures.

"Yes, ma'am. It'll be exactly a year in a few weeks."

"What brought you down here? Do you have family on the island?"

Beth shifted in her chair. "Not exactly. I was coming down to meet my future in-laws."

Rebecca drew out her notepad. "So you were engaged? I'm guessing you're married now?"

More shifting. Randy wanted to rescue his friend's fiancée, but they'd known explaining their story would be complicated.

"No, I decided not to marry that man."

"But you're still here." Rebecca crossed her legs and balanced the notebook on her knee. "Why did you stay?"

Beth chewed the inside of her cheek and glanced to Lola, who squeezed her hand. "I met a man while I was here, and we're getting married next month."

"That's a great story." Rebecca looked as if someone had set a delicious meal before her. "We have to include this. So you showed up on the island engaged to one man and ended up leaving him for another who you met here? That sounds like something out of the movies."

"Right." Beth gave a nervous laugh. "Just like the movies."

"So who is the lucky man? I hope I get to talk with him, too."

"You will," Randy said, taking advantage of the opening. "We'll be out on his boat tomorrow."

Rebecca scanned her notes. "Dempsey Charters?"

"That's right," Randy said. "Joe Dempsey is the owner and operator of the fishing and charter boat service."

"Great." Rebecca looked back to Beth, who had started to sweat. "Whatever happened to the first fiancé? I guess he's back wherever you left him?"

Beth proceeded to do a stellar impression of a dying fish.

"I can't believe I haven't brought out the tea," Lola said, bursting from her chair. "I make a mean sweet tea. Let me get the pitcher from the back."

"Thank you," Rebecca said with a smile. Then she went right back to what was feeling more and more like an interrogation. "So what happened to the fiancé? I'm dying to know."

"He's here," Randy said, worried about the color dropping from Beth's face. "Lucas Dempsey is the island lawyer, as of last fall. He doesn't really cater to tourists, so he's not on our list of villagers to meet."

"Wait." Rebecca looked down at her notes, then back to Beth, then back to her notes again. "Did you say Dempsey? Good Lord, this is better than I thought."

"Randy, could you help me outside?" Beth grasped for his hand, her face pale and damp. "I need some fresh air."

"Is something wrong?" Rebecca asked, all innocent curiosity.

"Beth hasn't been feeling well lately." Randy took her weight as she slowly rose from her chair. "You go ahead and finish with Lola. We'll be right outside."

As soon as they passed through the front door, Beth dropped to the top step and put her head between her knees. Randy filled the space next to her.

"Keep breathing, darling. You're going to be alright." He rubbed in a circular motion in the center of her back.

"That was horrible," Beth mumbled through a face full of curls. "How am I going to survive having to tell that story for the rest of my life?"

And he thought Rebecca asked tough questions. "Forget about how you got here," he said, watching three seagulls dive-bomb a trash can. "All that matters is that you and Joe are happy. You're going to start a family and it's all good."

"But she made it sound like some tabloid story." Beth flipped her head up, then locked her hand on Randy's knee to steady herself. "Whoa. Shouldn't have done that."

"Beth," Randy said, speaking as gently as he knew how. "Lucas and Sid are as happy as you and Joe are. If you hadn't made the choices you did, you'd be four miserable people right now."

Beth sighed. "That's true."

"It all worked out." He leaned his elbows on his knees. "Everyone is with the person they were meant to be with. Focus on that."

"You're right."

Randy was happy to see color returning to her cheeks. They sat in silence for several seconds, when Beth asked, "What about you?" He looked her way and met green eyes filled with concern. "You haven't found the one you're supposed to be with. Or have you, and I don't know about it?"

Randy wanted a wife and family as much as the next guy. Probably more. But he'd never found the woman he'd be willing to risk his heart to be with.

The pain of losing someone you love, with no warning, and no ability to save them, wasn't something Randy ever wanted to endure again. If no one had his heart, then no one could rip it in two. Then there was the chance he would be the one to leave loved ones much too soon, thanks to the history of men in his family dying at much too young an age.

No, his life was better this way.

"I'm happy the way things are, but it's nice of you to think of me."

"I don't doubt you're happy." Beth bumped his knee with her own. "But you could be happier."

Randy chuckled. "You think so?"

"I know so."

He had to give the woman points for optimism. "How about if I agree to never say never?"

Beth nodded. "I can live with that."

CHAPTER 6

Everyone must have decided to stay in Wednesday night, because the dinner shift at Dempsey's was nonexistent. Will relieved Tom at four-thirty and by six was bored out of her mind, so she took the opportunity to flip through Beth's planner. She didn't have to get past the first couple pages to see that the bride-to-be had a thing for Post-it notes.

Perched on a stool at the bar, she tried to decipher Beth's planning process. There was a to-do section, which held the most Post-its. If she'd written on the pages there would have been no need for the sticky notes, but Will tried not to judge.

Then she found the receipts, and her accountant mind instantly flipped to divide-and-conquer mode. The receipt for the catering deposit was stuck to the one for the DJ, but by *what* Will wasn't sure. It looked like a smudge left from a chocolate chip. As these were the top two receipts, she assumed they were the most recent ones. The dates proved her right.

Baby brain really was an evil thing. Beth was what one might call über-efficient. She'd done research for a law firm before quitting her job and moving to Anchor to live with Joe. Which happened after she'd been engaged to Lucas. Which made life a bit complicated for everyone for a while. But since Lucas eventually fell in love with Sid, who had been in love with *him* since they were in high school, the whole thing worked out in the end. Everyone found the person they were supposed to find.

"Hello there, darling. Can a chap buy the bartender a drink?"

Will looked up from the planner to see Jude had taken the stool next to her. He gave a wink, flashed the smile she was certain worked better than any pickup line he tossed around, and tucked a wayward lock of brown hair behind his ear. She was relieved not to see a camera anywhere in sight.

"Sorry, photo boy, but I'm on the clock." She glanced at the mostly empty room behind her. "Though there isn't much need for me to hover behind the bar tonight."

"Ah," he said, "but that's why Becks and I are here, isn't it?" He spun on his stool until his elbows rested on the bar. "I'll have this place looking like heaven on Earth, and Becks will make sure it reads that way."

Speaking of the overly curious blonde. "Where is Becks tonight?"

"She's back at the hotel, presumably working on her notes. When I left, she was planted in front of the laptop, notebook at her side and pencil clasped in her teeth."

"Do you two do many of these kinds of trips together?" Will asked, stepping around the bar and pulling a Samuel Smith from the lower cooler. "Kind of a travel reporting team?"

Jude faced the bar again and accepted the offered beer. "Thank you, my love. Not often, no. This is our . . ." He glanced up in thought. ". . . third assignment together. Becks is a little high maintenance. Best absorbed in short doses, with good long breaks in between."

Will's brows shot up. "You don't like her?"

"Now, I didn't say that." He sipped his beer. "Rebecca is a bit . . . what's the word?"

"If it starts with a *b*, I'll have to switch into my *we are women, hear us roar* lecture, so choose your word wisely."

"No worries," Jude said, tapping the side of his nose. "Wasn't going there. No, Rebecca King is driven. That's what she is. Determined to be a *real* reporter, as she puts it."

Will leaned a hip against the bar and crossed her arms. "What is she now? A fake reporter?"

"Right now she's a travel reporter. A female Rick Steves of sorts. But she wants to be a Christiane Amanpour."

"Oh, one of *those* reporters." Now that she thought about it, Will could see the drive. Not that Rebecca hadn't seemed happy enough to cover their island, but the way she asked questions, more like an interrogation than an interview, screamed hard-core news reporter. "And do you want to be one of *those* photographers?"

Jude waved a hand in the air. "I'm seeing the world on someone else's dime, and not getting shot at for my efforts. I'm happy being *this* kind of photographer, thank you very much."

Since they had a nice, easy chemistry going, Will took advantage of the moment to ask Jude for a favor. "You know that picture you snapped of me the day you arrived?"

His brow furrowed. "We took a picture? Oh, yes. I remember, sure. Beautiful woman behind bar. Those are always my favorites."

The man could flirt with a turnip. Too bad he was on the small side for Will's taste.

"If you say so," she said, dismissing the compliment. "Could you make sure that doesn't make it into the magazine?"

"Shy type, huh?" He shook his head, as if truly disappointed. "If you don't sign a consent form, then we can't use it no matter what. I'm guessing you're unwilling to sign consent?"

"Quite unwilling."

"Does that go for the rest of the night as well?" the Brit asked, turning the smolder up a notch.

"Does *what* go for the rest of the night?" Randy asked, smacking

Jude between the shoulder blades hard enough to knock the wind out of him. As the flirting foreigner coughed and struggled to catch his breath, Randy smiled at Will. "What did I miss?"

If she didn't know better, Will would think Randy didn't miss a thing. His timing was impeccable, and his handling of Jude not the least bit subtle.

"Jude let me know they won't be using my picture in the magazine article," she said. Since she'd let Randy see how panicked she was over the photo, Will wanted him to see how calmly and rationally she'd handled the situation.

Without having to lay a hand on anyone.

"That's right," Jude said, then he cleared his throat. "We were talking about the article. I thought you were waylaid by that brunette near the door?"

"Nah," Randy said, planting his large frame on the stool Will had vacated. "Georgette's husband works for me. She had a question about the reopen date." He gave Jude's shoulder a squeeze, making the smaller man wince.

Looking to his left, Jude said, "I see that lovely woman from the registration desk at our hotel. Think I'll go see how she's doing this evening."

Using the tip of his beer bottle to send Will a silent salute, Jude headed across the room.

Will pinched her lips as tight as she could to keep from telling Randy exactly what she thought about what he'd done to Jude.

"Could I get one of those green teas, please?" he asked, as if he hadn't just physically intimidated a man into ending a harmless flirtation.

So she wasn't going to take Jude up on what he'd clearly been offering. That didn't mean Will appreciated Randy taking matters into his own hands.

Literally.

"Who do you think you are?" she asked, slamming her rag onto the bar. "You could have hurt him."

Randy's head jerked back. With lowered brows, he asked, "Could have hurt who? Pretty boy over there?"

"His name is Jude," Will ground through a clenched jaw. "He was being nice, and you practically knocked his head off."

He rested his elbows on the bar, his hands clenched into fists. Will took a step back.

"From what I heard, he asked if you were *willing*, as if instead of offering drinks you were offering happy endings. Last I checked, this wasn't *that* kind of establishment, and you weren't *that* type of woman."

"What do you mean *that* kind of establishment?" she asked, anger moving her forward again. "You mean a bar where people try to pick other people up? That's exactly what this is." She felt her temper rising. "And you have no idea what type of woman I am. You don't know a damn thing about me."

"Well not because I don't want to," he said, cutting off anything Will was about to say.

"What?" she asked.

Randy put his head down and rubbed a line across his forehead. When he looked back up, the brown eyes were softer. "The only reason no one on this island knows much about you is because you won't let us. You've been here a year and we don't even know where you're from."

Will snatched the rag and wiped up the wet spot Jude's beer bottle had left behind. "I grew up all over. There isn't one place I'm from."

Randy laid his hands flat on the bar. "You had to graduate from high school somewhere. Where was that?"

Gnawing her lip, Will shuffled through all the lies and made-up history she'd created over the last three years. Then she told the truth. "Maine. I graduated from high school in Maine."

She hadn't shared a true fact about her past with anyone since the night she left her old life behind. Doing so felt scary and liberating at the same time.

Randy smiled, awakening the butterflies that had been flitting around her gut a lot in the last week. "I hear it's beautiful up there."

"It is," she nodded. "You've never been?"

He shook his head. "Not yet. Maybe someday."

This was a different kind of flirting. She could laugh off Jude's charmer attempts. He only wanted to have some fun, not get to know her or learn about her past. The photographer had been harmless, even if he was the person in possession of a single image that could ruin her life.

No, that picture wasn't nearly the threat Randy Navarro could be. If she let him.

"I'll get you that green tea," she said.

"That would be nice, thanks."

She stepped toward the mini-cooler near the register, but Randy stopped her, saying, "I really didn't hurt him. I surprised him is all. I'm not that kind of a guy."

Will nodded. "That's what I keep hearing."

"Do you believe it?" he asked, genuine curiosity and a hint of hope in his eyes.

She opted not to answer and opened the small fridge. "We're out of the teas up here. I'll have to get one from the back."

∼

Randy had no idea why it mattered so much what Will thought of him. Maybe because he didn't like how it felt to be feared. The fear brought with it a lack of trust, a belief he was a kind of person that he wasn't.

But again, why did it matter? He'd had his share of people who didn't think much of him. That was part of life. So, why did those people's opinions not matter, but Will's did?

A small voice in the back of his brain whispered *it's because you like her.* But that was crazy. The woman had a hair-trigger temper, then swung back to soft and sweet before Randy knew what hit him. She called bullshit anytime she saw it, was more secretive than a CIA agent, and had the bluest eyes he'd ever wanted to fall into.

He almost laughed at the last thought. Fall into her eyes. What kind of sappy, girly-movie shit was that?

"Hey there, big guy." Beth plopped onto the stool beside him. "Drinking alone?"

"Will went to get me a bottle of green tea."

Her nose scrunched up as her lips twisted. "You like that stuff?"

Randy laughed, feeling his shoulders relax. "It's good for you."

"So is spinach, but I'm not adding it to my diet." She pointed to her nose. "Couldn't even be around it right now. Turns out being pregnant intensifies your sense of smell by about a billion percent. And the strangest scents make your stomach roll."

"That would suck." Randy loved a heaping bowl of spinach but kept the fact to himself. "Where's Joe?"

Beth sighed. "Parking the car. He insisted I not walk any farther than from the Jeep door to the entrance. I'm surprised he didn't carry me up the steps."

"He's worried about you." Randy would likely feel the same way. After watching what the reporter had done to her today, he considered volunteering to help Joe carry the petite woman anywhere she wanted to go. "Does he know what happened today?"

"What happened today?" Will asked, sliding an open bottle of green tea Randy's way. "Did you have another episode?"

Beth shot Randy a dirty look as she answered. "Joe does *not* know, and I'd appreciate it if you two would keep it to yourselves."

"How could I tell him?" Will asked. "I don't even know what it is yet."

Green eyes darted to the door, then Beth leaned in. Will leaned in too, and the scent of lilacs swirled around Randy's head.

"That reporter was at Lola's today. She asked me how I got here. Instead of giving the smart answer, that I'd come here for a vacation"—she poked the bar with one finger—"which would not be a lie, I said I'd come to meet my future in-laws. I don't even know how it went from there. Her questions were like bullet fire, and I kept taking direct hits until she figured out I'd left one brother for the other."

Will jerked upright. "Yikes. It does sound bad when you say it that way." When Beth shot her a pleading look, she added, "I mean, that's so annoying of her."

"I had to cut off the interview and take Beth outside to get some fresh air." Randy bumped Beth with his shoulder. "That's when I told her everything worked out the way it was supposed to, and she shouldn't be worried about what anyone else thinks."

"Easy for you to say," Will said. "Reporter Rebecca hasn't started asking about you yet."

She was right. Randy had yet to face the firing squad that was Rebecca King's interview style. At least not on a personal level. She'd asked questions about the island with rapid-fire succession, but not one had been about him personally.

Maybe she was waiting, looking for a weak spot to attack before she pounced. Or maybe she didn't find him all that interesting.

"It's in a reporter's nature to ask questions, right?" He lifted the tea to take a drink. "We only have to make it through a few more days, then she'll be gone."

"Who will be gone?" Joe asked.

This was beginning to feel like a bad skit.

"The reporter. Though the photographer is nice," Beth said. "And kind of cute." She grinned at Will, as if they were sharing some inside joke. Randy snorted before he could stop himself.

"I hope that's not a snort of agreement," Joe said. "I'll take a beer, please, Will." He planted a kiss on Beth's forehead, then took the stool to her left. "They'll be out with us tomorrow. My biggest hassle will probably be keeping Sid from throwing her overboard if this reporter lady pisses her off."

"She's going out on the boat? That's going to make things worse." Beth said.

"Why?" Joe took the beer Will slid across the bar.

Beth dropped her forehead onto the edge of the bar, turning it from side to side. "No no no no no."

Randy caught Joe's questioning look and tried once again to rescue Beth. "Ms. King visited Lola's today. The subject of Beth originally coming here to meet her future in-laws came up, and the reporter followed the string through to the switch from Lucas to you."

"Crime in Italy." Beth's head jerked back up. "There is never going to be a good way to tell that story."

"Is that what this is about?" Joe said, turning toward Beth as he pulled her chin in his direction. "Are we happy?"

Beth nodded.

"Is Lucas happy?"

"Yes," she said, sounding like a chastised four-year-old.

"Is Sid happy?"

"Disgustingly so," Will answered for her.

Joe's eyes never left Beth's face. "Nothing else matters then, right?"

Randy knew agreeing to that one was going to be difficult for a woman used to worrying what people, friend or foe, thought about her. An endearing quality, but a tough burden to carry all the same. Made tougher by marrying a man who didn't give two shits what anyone thought about him.

Except the woman he loved.

Randy looked up to see Will watching the couple intently. If he didn't know better, he'd think she was wishing for something similar. Not what he expected from a woman who worked so hard to be alone.

Joe dropped a kiss on Beth's nose, then planted a longer one on her lips. Randy looked down at his tea, feeling like an intruder on an intimate moment. From the corner of his eye, he could see Will had found something else to focus on as well.

Him.

When he caught her eye, an attractive blush covered her cheeks.

If she was thinking what that blush said she was thinking, maybe it was time he put a little more effort into getting to know Willow Parsons.

CHAPTER 7

"If Joe and Randy weren't there, I'd have beat that bitch to a pulp and thrown her over the side."

Sid had apparently *not* enjoyed her day on the water with Ms. Rebecca King. Will took a sip of her beer as she watched her friend charge around the pool table to take her next shot. Venting about her afternoon on the water with the not-so-popular reporter didn't seem to be hindering her concentration, as she sank two more balls in rapid succession.

"I'm surprised Joe wasn't willing to help you," Will said. "Did she really insinuate that you and Beth swapped brothers?"

"The bimbo did everything but ask if we continued to swap every other weekend." Sid pointed with her cue stick. "She better hope I don't catch her without someone around to save her skinny ass."

As badass as Sid could be, something told Will that Rebecca King could hold her own in a brawl, and maybe even come out on top. The women were of a similar size, so neither held a weight advantage. Sid would fight dirty, of course, but the reporter didn't look like the type to stick with the rules either.

"What do you think of the photographer?" Will asked. "He seems nice enough."

"I don't know." Sid sank another ball. "He's almost too happy.

Don't get me wrong. I can admire the pretty Orlando Bloom thing he's got going on."

"I'm with you on that."

"But I can't help but think of them as a pair, which makes me dislike him by association."

Will chuckled. "From what he said the other night, I don't think he likes her very much."

Sid stood, dropping the cue by her foot. "Really?"

"Said she's best in small doses with long breaks in between."

"Hah," Sid said. "Score points for picture boy."

"There you two are," Beth said, barreling into the poolroom as if seeking a place to hide. "I need one of you to go order me a burger and onion rings."

Will and Sid exchanged a look, then Will asked, "Why can't you order the burger yourself?"

"I did."

"What?" Sid said.

"I ordered a burger, but I want two," Beth said, rubbing her stomach. "Tom and Patty are out there and I don't want to look like a giant pig."

Will did the math on how much fat and calories were in one Dempsey Burger, let alone two. The numbers left her a little numb, but to be fair, the woman *was* eating for two. Or maybe three if her appetite was any indication.

"Go order for her, Sid."

"Why me?" she asked, bent over the table in position to take a shot.

"Because they know I don't eat burgers, so they'd never believe I was ordering for myself." Will wasn't a vegetarian, but she did avoid red meat.

Sid leaned her stick against the wall behind Will. "Then when she gets busted eating two burgers, it's my ass on the line for aiding and abetting."

"Hooking up with a lawyer has made you paranoid," Beth said, slapping a twenty onto the table. "Get me that burger and you can keep the change."

Burger bribery. Amazing what a desperate pregnant woman would do, but it proved how well Beth knew their little boat mechanic.

"You got it, Curly."

As Sid left the room, Beth climbed onto the high-set chair across from Will, closed her eyes, and laid her head against the wall. "I'm going to be as big as Joe's boat, but right now all I care about is eating those burgers."

"Cravings, huh?"

Will hadn't gotten far enough along to experience those, but she wondered if her little one would have sent up the red meat flag.

"I think they've officially begun." She hung her purse on the back of the chair. "Last night I was dying for pickles. I had to slide out of bed without waking Joe, bribe Dozer with a hot dog to get him to stay quiet, then hold my nose as I ate the things because the smell was nauseating."

"You were craving something that you couldn't even smell without getting sick?"

"I know," Beth said. "Of all the things I've heard about being pregnant, the fact that it would make me completely insane was not included."

"Really?" Will laughed. "Pretty sure that's the first thing anyone told me."

Beth's head jerked away from the wall and wide green eyes stared at Will. "You were pregnant?"

She hadn't meant to let that slip out. Will shrugged and stared at the silver label on her beer. "It was a few years ago. I lost it."

Though not without someone's help.

Beth laid a hand over Will's. "Oh, honey. I'm so sorry. I had no idea."

"No need to apologize." Will accepted the affection for a few seconds, then pulled her hand away.

"And here I am complaining about it." Beth set her forehead in her hand. "God, I'm such a jerk."

"None of that now." Randy's words came back to Will. No one knew her because she wouldn't let them. But there was more to her life than one tragic episode three years ago. "I'm so happy for you and Joe, and I love hearing about the baby. Don't ever think you can't talk about it around me. In fact," she said, "if you could talk about it as much as possible when Sid is around, as I'm sure it'll freak her out, I'll buy you a six-month supply of diapers."

They laughed together, the moment of tension sliding away.

"Were you married?" Beth asked. "Wait. I'm sorry. That's incredibly nosy."

Will shook her head. "No, it's alright. I was engaged, actually." Not that she'd accepted the proposal without hesitation. "So we have that in common."

"What happened to the guy?"

A tougher question to answer. Will used all her energy to stay in the present. "Let's say he turned out *not* to be the guy I thought he was."

"Oh," was all Beth said.

In that moment, Sid returned. "Order is in. Why do you two look like that?"

"Like what?" Beth asked, a bit too chipper.

"Like you're hiding something."

Will wasn't sure when Sid had gotten so astute, but she didn't see any reason not to repeat the little bit she'd shared. These women had become like sisters to her. She owed them something of herself.

"I was telling Beth that a few years ago, *I* was pregnant."

"No shit?"

"No shit," Will answered, the simple response lightening the mood. "I lost it, and things didn't work out with the guy. Now how about those fittings tomorrow."

The other two women sat in dazed silence for several seconds. Beth recovered first. "Right. The fittings." She shook her head as if to clear it. "You have my planner, but I think the appointment is for one-thirty."

"It is," Will said. "I checked. And I called to make sure the dresses were in. They arrived today."

"Damn," Sid said. "I'll be out on the boat."

"Nice try," Beth said. "I've already told Joe you need the afternoon off. He's lined up someone else to cover for you."

The curse Sid said under her breath was a bit stronger than *damn*.

"I've had several versions shipped in. Whatever ones you don't like we can return," Beth said. "And you two don't have to match. So long as the dresses complement each other, I'm good with whatever you pick. Since the ones I've ordered all go nicely together, it should be fine."

Sid looked as if she'd been told a root canal was in her immediate future, but Will was kind of excited. She'd never been a bridesmaid. With the added bonus of watching Beth stick their friend into a fancy dress, this fitting might turn out to be the best day she'd had in a while.

$\sim$

Bartender Willow Parsons was definitely hiding something, and Rebecca King was determined to figure out what. She was certain she'd seen the woman's face before. Gut instinct, which a reporter always trusted, told her there was a story here.

If Will was indeed a person of interest, then Rebecca scooping the story would be the break she'd been hoping for. No more fluff pieces. No more coconut drinks and tiki bars. And no more traveling with mindless photographers only interested in the pretty sunset and bikini-clad tourists.

No one Rebecca had talked to that week knew anything about Willow Parsons beyond the moment she showed up on Anchor Island a year ago. A cursory background check revealed various jobs up and down the coast, but none that dated back more than three years. That provided a starting point.

She'd spent two nights combing most-wanted lists for crimes committed three to five years ago in the New England area, but with no hits. Then she switched to the missing persons cases. Strikingly, there were many more people missing than wanted, and the search was taking longer. If she hadn't had to cater to the local yokels all day, Rebecca might have found something by now.

"Knock knock," Jude said, stepping through the balcony door to her room. Though they'd each been given their own suite, they shared the balcony overlooking the harbor. Rebecca had to admit, the view was stunning. "Heading over to Dempsey's for dinner. You want to come?"

Jude almost never invited Rebecca anywhere when they were on assignment together. They weren't exactly friends, and she didn't have a problem with that. The Brit had his charms, but his only goal in life was to snap some photos and have a good time. The perpetual Peter Pan syndrome incarnate. When she thought of what he could be accomplishing with his talent, Rebecca couldn't help but lose respect for the man.

"I'm good, thanks."

In spite of her clear dismissal, Jude remained. "You haven't left this room one evening since we got here. I realize the tourists aren't here yet, but there is a nightlife on this speck of sand. Don't you think you'd better check it out if you're going to write about it?"

Rebecca looked up from her laptop. "Are you telling me how to do my job? Last I checked, I didn't tell you how to work that contraption around your neck."

"I was simply suggesting that the article should include something that happens after sundown," Jude said through clenched teeth. "Hard to do when you won't leave the room."

"Stick with taking pictures. I'll handle the rest."

With a glare that more than communicated where he'd like to tell her to go, Jude retreated back to the balcony, allowing Rebecca to return to her computer.

"If you do have a secret, Ms. Parsons, I'm going to find it. Then maybe we'll both be famous."

~

Knowing Sam was anxious for an update, Randy arrived at the Anchor Inn bright and early Friday morning. Yvonne let him know Sam was in his office, pointing him in that direction. The hotelier was sipping his coffee while reading something on his tablet when Randy knocked on the door.

"Hey there. Can I get you some coffee?"

"Never drink the stuff," Randy said, shaking Sam's hand before taking a seat. "Anything interesting in the news?"

Sam lifted one brow. "Same old, same old. The rich are getting richer, and the rest of us are stuck shoveling the shit."

Randy guessed Sam to be the wealthiest islander in the village, but compared to the ultrarich decorating the news these days, that still left him at the bottom of the net worth totem pole.

"And that's why I don't read the news." With little time before his tour duties resumed, Randy cut to the point of the meeting. "The visits have gone well so far. We hit every major sight, and a few of the minor ones. The tour has run from the ferry landing to the preservation museum at the other end. We've done nose to tip, with a trip out on the water with Dempsey Charters."

"And how have the islanders responded?" Sam asked, sitting back with his coffee mug.

"Well, I think. Some have taken to the attention better than others."

Sam tensed. "That doesn't sound good."

Randy shook his head. "My sister didn't like the direction of Rebecca's questioning, and to be honest, neither did I." For an article on their island as a tourist destination, Ms. King was entirely too interested in the private lives of the Anchor citizens. "She pushed Beth Chandler into a corner on Wednesday to the point that I had to cut off the interview and take Beth outside."

"Randy, this article is important to—"

"I know how important this article is to all of us. But I'm not going to allow anyone to harass my friends and family." They could find another way to increase tourism, if necessary.

Sam exhaled as he rubbed the back of his neck. "This wasn't the easiest article to line up. I don't want anyone harassed either, but surely we can handle a few probing questions if it means getting a positive article out of this reporter."

"Has she probed you with questions yet?" Randy asked, not sure how much contact Sam had with the pair after he dropped them at the hotel.

"I've barely seen Ms. King. Yvonne says she rarely leaves her room after you drop them off." He grabbed a manila folder on his right and flipped it open. "According to their bill so far, she's ordered room service every night this week. That doesn't bode well for a well-rounded article. I was hoping they'd do some exploring on their own."

"The photographer has gotten around," Randy said, remembering Jude's insulting innuendo to Will on Wednesday evening. "Maybe he's filling her in on the island nightlife. What there is of it."

"Maybe." Sam closed the folder again. "Maybe you could convince Rebecca to make a stop at Dempsey's this evening."

"Not sure she'd agree, but I can try."

"Good. Maybe a couple drinks with the locals will help round out her view of the island." Sam's phone rang. "That's the front desk." Picking up the receiver, he said, "Yes, Yvonne."

After a moment of silence, he added, "We'll be right out." He replaced the receiver, saying, "Our guests are ready to go." Sam rose from his chair. "Two days and this will be over. Let's hope those two days go well."

"I think we're making a good impression overall." Randy followed Sam into the hall. "She seemed genuinely interested during the interviews, and we've caught a few tourists who had nothing but good things to say."

"Is the photographer taking plenty of pictures?"

"Enough to fill several articles worth, I would think."

"Good." When they reached the lobby, Jude was leaning over the reservation desk, flashing a smile Yvonne's way, as Rebecca stood near the door tapping a foot. "Are we ready for another day of exploring our fine island?" Sam asked.

Rebecca smiled, but the sentiment didn't reach her eyes. "Ready as we'll ever be."

Jude stood at the sound of Sam's voice, then lifted his camera case from the floor beside his feet. "Looks like some clouds are moving in. If we want good shots, we'll need to get going right away."

That was the most professional thing Randy had heard the man say. "Then by all means, let's hit the road."

Sam shot him a worried look as the pair filed out in front of him. Randy had no idea what had happened overnight, but there was a definite tension between the two that didn't exist before. Two more days. They just had to play nice for two more days.

CHAPTER 8

Will lost her breath the moment Beth walked out of the dressing room. The spaghetti-strapped confection stopped slightly below her knees. The chiffon handkerchief hem floated around her legs, giving off an ethereal look. It was simple and elegant, with a hint of crystal beading at the top.

It was Beth, and it was perfect.

When she reached the platform in front of the large mirror, stepped onto the pedestal, and turned to face them, even Sid gasped.

"What do you think?" the blushing bride asked, as if she couldn't see the truth for herself.

"Perfect," Will and Sid said at the same time.

Beth swept around. "Do you really think so?"

As if there could be any doubt.

"I don't think so, I know so." Will left her chair to get a closer look. "The beadwork is amazing. The length is perfect for getting married by the water." Will looked up. "Joe is going to fall to his knees when he sees you coming down that aisle."

Beth's smile broadened. "It is the right one, isn't it!" She danced in place, then froze, the excitement falling from her face.

"What?" Will asked. "What is it?"

Green eyes turned misty. "Should I really be wearing white? I mean . . ." She laid a hand over her belly. "With the baby and all."

"Stop right there," Sid said, joining them near the mirror. "I'm no expert on this girly shit, but my grandmother always said every woman deserved to wear white on her big day. No matter what. It says she's special. The most beautiful and happiest woman in the room."

Beth and Will stared at their friend as if she'd been body snatched.

"Don't look at me like that. I have a pair of ovaries, too, you know."

"We know," Will said. "We weren't sure if you knew."

Sid rolled her eyes as Beth and Will laughed together.

"Now it's your turn," Beth declared, clapping from her perch. "I've put one dress in each of your dressing rooms. Try them on and then come out and let me see."

"We don't get to pick them ourselves?" Sid asked. "What if we don't like them?"

"It's her day, remember?" Will said, pushing Sid toward the dressing rooms. "Do what she says."

They reached the dressing rooms, but neither seemed to know which room to enter.

"Will is on the left," Beth yelled across the room. "Sid, you're on the right."

With a deep breath and a drop of the shoulders, Will stepped behind the curtain. She'd not gotten this far in her own wedding planning, and hadn't been in a fancy dress in years. Hanging from a hook to her left was a dress bag. She unzipped it, holding her breath in anticipation of what Beth had selected.

"Please let me like it," she said to her own reflection. Will really wanted to make Beth happy. Having to fake a positive reaction would be tough, but she'd do it if necessary. It was only a dress, after all. She could muddle through for one day to make one of her best friends happy.

Will paused at the thought. Beth and Sid truly were two of the best friends she'd ever had. Maybe *the* best. A childhood of constant movement dictated by her mother's wishes and whims had made it difficult to have friends. Finding a *best* friend had been impossible.

Which made her wish all the more that she could stay on Anchor forever. Since the night she'd left Boston with little more than the cash in her pocket and a driving fear of what she'd left behind, Will had been living apart. Distant from everyone around her.

But today, she belonged. She had friends.

Today, the past didn't matter.

Reaching into the dress bag, Will slid the hanger forward to reveal a simple, navy-blue sleeveless dress. The delicate material was gathered to one side, with a sash that would hang over her right hip, and a draped neckline.

It was exactly what she would pick for herself.

Slipping out of her jeans and T-shirt, Will shimmied the dress over her head, sighing as the soft crepe caressed her body. If Beth had done this well for Will, she couldn't wait to see what Sid was wearing.

Will didn't have long to wait.

"This makes my boobs look huge!" Sid yelled as Will exited her dressing room.

"Your boobs *are* huge," Will informed her through the black curtain. "Now get out here and let us see."

Sid yanked the curtain aside. "What the hell is this thing made of?" She swayed from side to side. "Every time I move, it flaps around. One stiff wind and I'll be flashing the entire crowd my underwear."

Beth put Sid in chiffon? Will never would have thought of it, but damn if the bride wasn't right on this one as well. The dress was strapless, with draped material making what looked to be a large bow across the bodice. Not in an obnoxious or little girl way, but as accent on the otherwise simple dress. The bow even offered more coverage and played down the breasts behind them, which was not an easy task.

"The woman knows us better than we know ourselves," Will said, twirling one finger in the air, directing Sid to spin. "She even got the colors to match." Sid's dress was also navy, slightly darker than Will's, but close enough to look good together.

"You're killing me!" Beth hollered from across the store. "Get over here already."

Sid yanked at the top of the dress. "I guess it is kind of pretty." She swirled her hips, sending the dress into motion.

"It's gorgeous. You'll be lucky if we get to the 'I dos' before Lucas carries you off somewhere."

A naughty smile lit her friend's face. "That's a nice thought," Sid said, turning to lead the way to Beth. She even walked like a girl. That dress was a miracle worker.

∿

Randy walked through the front door of Dempsey's with a sigh of relief. His official duties as island tour guide for *Prime Destinations* magazine were almost over. They could have been over fifteen minutes ago, but instead of dropping Rebecca back at the hotel, he'd insisted they stop at Dempsey's so she could experience the island nightlife on a weekend.

The crowd wouldn't come close to what they'd see in July and August, but it would be lively enough to show the place didn't close up at night. They'd barely made it two feet inside the restaurant when

Jude veered off to the bar. Will smiled as she popped the top on a bottle of beer, then slid it his way. Her hair was pulled into two low ponytails behind her ears, the gold bangles chiming at her wrist as she did her job with grace and confidence—two qualities Randy admired, but wished she'd display a bit more around him.

"I see some of your friends in the corner," Rebecca said. "Who's the one sitting beside your sister?"

Randy followed her gaze to the table at the back of the room. "That's Lucas Dempsey. Joe's brother and Sid's fiancé."

"Really?" Rebecca's cat eyes lit up. "Maybe this little stop wasn't such a bad idea after all."

Well shit. He hadn't brought the woman here to drill his friends and cause a scene. "Let's stop at the bar for a drink first." He steered the reporter to where Jude was flashing his pearly whites at Will. "I'll take the usual," Randy said, nodding a greeting as he did so. "What will you have, Rebecca?"

To his surprise, Rebecca took the stool next to Jude. The two had mixed as well as oil and water all day. When they weren't avoiding each other, they were making snide, passive-aggressive comments that did little to hide whatever rift had simmered between them.

"Since we're experiencing the nightlife, I'll have a gin and tonic." As Will moved to mix the drink, Rebecca asked, "Do you have any siblings?"

The question was aimed at Will and seemed to come out of nowhere. Without missing a beat, the bartender answered, "Nope." She filled a glass with ice, then measured out the gin into a tall, skinny shot glass. "You have preference for lemon or lime?"

"Lemon," Rebecca said, leaning her elbows on the bar. "Where did you learn to mix drinks?"

Will picked up the soda dispenser and pushed the tonic button to fill the glass to the brim. "Where did you learn to be a reporter?"

Randy felt as if he were watching a tennis match and Will had just scored a point.

Rebecca actually laughed, enjoying the verbal volley. "Emerson. Is that your way of saying you learned to make drinks in college?"

"Didn't everyone?" Will squeezed the slice of lemon over the glass, then gave it a gentle stir before placing it on a small square napkin in front of Rebecca. "You guys up for an appetizer?"

If Rebecca's questions were bothering Will tonight, she wasn't letting on. Randy took the opportunity to admire how the gypsy moved so comfortably behind the bar. Since she wasn't paying him much attention, the apprehension he'd become accustomed to seeing in her eyes wasn't there. Even when she slid his bottle of tea across the bar, she didn't pull back instantly as if he might snatch her over the surface and carry her away.

Instead, she surprised him by saying, "Can I talk to you at the end of the bar for a second?"

"Sure." He stepped around the bar stools to join Will at the end closest to the poolroom. "What can I do for you?"

"Why did you bring her here?" she asked, the casual air gone. "Beth is back in the corner with Joe, Sid, and Lucas, and I don't want Rebecca harassing them."

"First off, nice to see you, too," Randy said. "Secondly, I brought her here so whatever article she writes doesn't make it sound as if we roll up the sidewalks at dinnertime."

"Anchor doesn't have sidewalks," Will snarled.

"You know what I mean." Her confidence was more attractive when she wasn't using it to take a bite out of his ass. "Besides, I didn't know everyone was here when I made the suggestion."

Will glanced back to where they'd left the pair. "Shit. Where'd she go?"

Jude was missing too. Randy leaned around the half wall that separated the dining room to see Rebecca headed straight for the corner table. Jude had joined Yvonne, Lola, and Marcus at another table.

"She's headed their way. I'm sure Joe and Lucas can handle her."

He looked back to Will, who looked skeptical. "Think about how Sid feels about Beth, then remember what she thinks of our resident reporter."

Will had a point.

"And the former fiancé thing," he added. "I'd better get over there." Randy took two steps, then turned back. "Send them all another round of drinks on me. I have a feeling I'm going to owe them at least that much."

He arrived at the table to hear Lucas extend a greeting. "So you're the reporter I've heard so much about."

"And you're the jilted fiancé," Rebecca said, beaming that serpent smile of hers.

Beth studied her glass of water and leaned closer to Joe. Sid looked ready to bolt out of the booth, but Lucas must have been holding her down under the table.

"Not exactly," the lawyer said, his face never faltering. "I think she'd have had to leave me at the alter to earn that designation. Would you like to join us, Ms. King?"

The rest of the table looked ready to smack him, but the surprise on Rebecca's face was enough to make Randy want to pat Lucas on the back. This was the first time he'd seen the reporter speechless since he'd met her.

"Let me pull up some chairs," Randy said, grabbing two from the empty table behind them. He couldn't exactly insist they leave after going through so much trouble to get the woman in the bar. "Here you go," he said, offering one to Rebecca.

"So there's really no drama here? No tension?" she asked. The reporter looked as if a puzzle piece weren't fitting into the picture. "I find that hard to believe."

"Sorry to disappoint you," Lucas replied. "There was some tension in the beginning, but everything worked out in the end." He slid an arm around Sid's shoulders and dropped a kiss on her hair. "We're all happy, and that's what matters."

Rebecca looked as if he'd lit a stink bomb on the table. Guess there wasn't much of a story here after all.

"So you all seem to be the first family of Anchor Island. Everywhere I go, I hear or see the Dempsey name."

"It's a small island," Joe said. "With three businesses between us, that's bound to happen."

Will arrived with a tray full of drinks.

"Yes," Rebecca said, watching Will load the drinks onto the table. "It is a small world, isn't it?"

"These ones are on Randy," Will said, setting the last glass on the table, then charging back to the bar.

"The one thing I've noticed about this island is that everyone seems to know everyone else." Rebecca glanced back to Will, her eyes narrowed. "Except one."

"Except who?" Sid asked.

"Your bartender there," Rebecca said. "She seems to be the only mystery around here."

"Will isn't a mystery," Sid argued. "She's private. Not everything is everybody else's business."

Randy shot Sid a look that said *play nice*.

"What do you think of Anchor Island, Ms. King?" Lucas asked, pulling Sid tighter against his side. "Have you seen enough to give us a good review? I know you talked to our parents earlier today, but are there any questions we can answer for you?"

Randy held his breath, waiting for whatever off-the-wall, insulting question Rebecca would lay out next.

"I was wondering when someone was going to ask me that." Rebecca gave Randy a sideways look. "I like it a lot, actually. It's small but not boring. Plenty of history. The pirate lore is popular these days. The food is good, people are nice, and there's something for everyone." She leaned back in her chair. "Add in the beach and the fishing and you've got the perfect island getaway."

The entire table seemed to exhale at the same time. Randy felt a weight lift off his chest. Sam would be relieved as well. They all had a lot to lose, but if this article didn't turn out well, the blame would fall to Sam for bringing Rebecca to town in the first place.

The conversation went well from there, with Rebecca asking about the two pirate festivals, one held in early summer, the other toward the end of the season. The Dempsey brothers and Sid talked about what it was like to grow up on the island, and a truce seemed to have been reached. Leave it to the lawyer of the bunch to pave the way for peace. Score a point for his future brother-in-law.

CHAPTER 9

An hour later, Randy and the reporter were gone. Sid and Beth now sat at the bar, filling Will in on the unforeseen changes in the reporter's demeanor.

"The woman is actually nice. Who knew?" Beth said, sounding more relaxed than she had in days. "We should have put Lucas on the case before now. He can bring anyone around."

"She's lucky she didn't try to flirt with him," Sid said, unwilling to pay the woman a compliment.

Beth turned on her stool, laying an arm across the back. "He had his arm around you the whole time. There might as well have been a sign over your heads that said 'This Man Is Taken.'" A light laughter accompanied the words. It was nice to have the old Beth back for a while.

"She's leaving on Sunday, right?" Will asked.

"Yes, ma'am," Beth answered. "And tomorrow you're heading up to Kill Devil Hills with Randy, so you probably won't see her again."

Will had managed not to dwell on her impending day with Randy. Between the fittings and working a full service, she'd had plenty of distractions. Beth's reminder set the butterflies loose again. She'd wanted to believe they were from fear, but Will recognized anticipation when she felt it.

And she was feeling it all right. Against her better judgment, the man's patient prodding was working. Will didn't tense when Randy was around anymore. Not from fear or distrust, anyway. That was at least going to make spending the day with him easier. Which was the problem.

She didn't want things to be easy with Randy. Will needed to keep him at a distance. Letting her guard down would jeopardize too much. Reveal too much. So she was lonely. That was no reason to give into the temptation that was Randy Navarro.

"Did I hear my name?" said the giant of a man as he joined them at the bar. Will hadn't realized he'd planned to return.

"You did," Beth said. "I was reminding Will that you two are headed up to the tux place tomorrow. Thanks for doing this, by the way."

"My pleasure." Randy took the stool next to Sid, sending Will a smile that revealed he was looking forward to the trip more than she was. "That conversation with the reporter went pretty well."

"Thank Lucas," Sid said. "He's the one who brought out the woman's decent side."

"Speaking of," Randy said, looking around the room. "Where are Lucas and Joe?"

"Back in the poolroom." Sid grabbed her beer and hopped off the stool. "We're headed that way. You coming?"

Will pretended not to be listening, but with the rest of the bar empty, it was tough to look busy. Then Randy said the last thing she wanted to hear.

"I'm going to stay here with Will for now. You two go ahead."

As her friends walked away, Will wanted to yell for them to come back. She didn't know what Randy thought they had to talk about. Maybe he wanted to set up the details for their trip the next day. That shouldn't take long.

Before he had a chance to ask, she set a green tea on the bar.

"Thanks," he said, the smile still in place, though now he was looking at her more intently. As if trying to read her mind. "What did Beth have to do to get you on this trip with me tomorrow?"

The man lacked any ounce of pretense. Something she found unnervingly sexy.

"What makes you think she had to do anything?"

He raised one brow, the smile shifting to a sexy grin.

"Fine," she said. "There might have been a threat involved. I can't tell if it's wedding stress or wacky hormones, but that woman can be scary when she wants to be."

"Maybe she's been spending too much time with Sid." Randy leaned his elbows on the bar, revealing a small tuft of hair through the collar of his polo shirt. Will's hand itched to see if it was as soft as it looked, which would be ironic when he was so hard everywhere else.

The thought spiked her temperature up several degrees. What was wrong with her? She'd been chewing this man out earlier in the evening; now she wanted to chew on him. Maybe *her* hormones were the ones out of whack. The plan was to be a bitch to keep him at a comfortable distance. Going doe-eyed was completely counterproductive.

Desperate to focus on something other than the man before her, Will checked the tape running on the register. "Yeah, maybe that's it."

"By the way," he said from behind her. "You look really good tonight."

Surprise made Will jerk the register tape, resulting in a nasty paper cut along the side of her finger. "Shit," she said, before sticking the injured digit in her mouth. How the hell could such a tiny cut hurt so damn bad?

"What happened?" Randy asked. "Let me see."

"I'm fine," she said around her knuckle. "It's nothing." Will pulled her hand away and watched the puckered slice fill with a line of blood. To stop the bleeding, she pressed her bar rag against the wound.

"Don't use the rag. It's probably filthy from whatever's been on this counter." Randy walked from in front of the bar to behind it and gently took hold of her wrist while prying the rag out of her fingers. "Let me see what we have here."

The man had missed his calling as a paramedic. Though she'd never met a paramedic that smelled this good. Will closed her eyes and breathed in. When she opened them, Randy's face lingered only inches away, one corner of his mouth hitched up in a grin.

Good Lord, what was she doing? And what was he doing? His warm fingers were gentle on her skin. A thumb massaged her palm, making her want to melt into him. Some part of her brain was sounding the alarm—*Danger, Will Parsons! Danger, Will Parsons!*—but her body ignored the message.

"Where's the first aid kit?" he asked, his mouth close enough for her to feel his breath on her lips. "This is going to need a Band-Aid."

Will tried to answer. Tried to break the spell he was weaving in her brain. But her body didn't care about Band-Aids and paper cuts. About secrets or self-preservation. Her body wanted one thing, and that was the man standing beside her.

"Will," Randy said, his eyes dropping to her mouth.

"Yeah?"

"If you don't stop looking at me like that, we're going to give the diners quite a show."

Someone whistled from a booth near the windows, jerking Will back to her senses. With a shake of her head, she pulled away from Randy's warm touch, putting enough space between them for her to think more clearly. Though his scent seemed to have permeated her brain, making it impossible to clear the fog completely.

"I'm sorry," she said. "I don't know what happened."

Randy cleared his throat. Maybe he'd been as affected as she was. "No need to apologize. I hope it happens again in a more private setting."

Again? Private setting? That sounded like an excellent idea.

No it does not, screamed the one sane brain cell she had left. This was not supposed to happen. Will wasn't sure when she'd dropped her guard, but now that it was down, she didn't know how to put it back up. She wasn't even sure she *wanted* to put it back up.

Which was absolutely ridiculous. She'd definitely been alone too long, considering where her mind was going. But who could blame her? Will was a woman after all, with all the needs that any other woman experienced. Needs Randy looked ready to fulfill.

Damn him.

"You need to get back around the bar," she pleaded. Randy didn't move. "Please," she added, keeping her eyes on the tiny paper cut. The bleeding had stopped, but a slight burning pain still pulsed in her finger.

Randy stepped back, but only turned his back to the dining room. "I'm going to need a minute."

Will glanced up to his face, then down, spotting the problem right away. That was quite a problem. Wow. He had definitely been affected.

"Right. Take all the time you need. I'm going to get a Band-Aid from the first aid kit in the kitchen."

Will leaned against the wall inside the kitchen, taking several deep breaths as she waited for her pulse to return to normal. With shaking hands, she managed to apply the Band-Aid, but gave up on a normal heartbeat and aimed for anything better than beating out of her chest. She hadn't been aroused like that in longer than she could remember. The sensation felt foreign and familiar all at once.

This was bad. So, so bad. Even now, she wanted to walk into that bar and jump his bones. All rationale seemed to have left her body. How in the world was she going to spend an entire day with him? What if she snapped and jumped him right there in the truck? Or maybe in the tuxedo store fitting room?

That sounded kind of fun.

So much for slowing her heartbeat. Will lifted the lid on the ice machine, extracting one large cube and running it along her warm neck. She closed her eyes and let her head fall back, the cold, dripping water bringing her temperature back down.

When she opened her eyes, Vinnie, the head cook, and Chip, his sous-chef, were watching her with mouths agape. Great. Now she was putting on a show for the staff. This was not her night.

"Hey, guys," she said, tossing what was left of the ice cube in the sink. "Good shift tonight. Food was great." With that lame remark, she headed back to the bar, hoping Randy had returned to half-mast, so to speak, and joined their other friends back by the pool tables.

～

Randy had managed to return to his bar stool, but only seconds before Will returned. When she stepped out of the kitchen, he watched a drop of water travel down the length of her slender throat and disappear behind the V-neck collar of her Dempsey's T-shirt.

His entire body clenched at the thought of licking that drop off her skin. Son of a bitch, this had not been his intention when he'd returned to the bar. Yes, he'd wanted to talk to Will. To break more ground on getting to know her, making her more comfortable around him. Randy hadn't expected her to melt in his hands, then look at him with that kind of desire in her blue eyes.

As if she'd take him right there behind the bar.

All that from one compliment. One touch. If he ever got more of her, she might burn him alive. There was something exciting about playing with this kind of fire. The adrenaline rush was better than jumping out of a perfectly good airplane.

"Band-Aid on," she said, holding up the injured finger but not making eye contact.

He let her shuffle some papers beside the register, then tear off the tape and fold it neatly before sliding it into a ledger book. Letting her take the lead, he kept quiet, watching her stilted movements. Once she'd run out of busy work, her shoulders rose and fell, as if she'd taken a steadying breath.

Will turned to face him, stepped up to the bar, and said, "About what just happened . . ."

Randy considered apologizing but waited to see what she would say next. He didn't expect the words that followed.

"I'm not sure what that was, but it can't happen again."

At least she hadn't apologized, which meant she wasn't sorry it happened either. He could work with that. "Why not?"

Will's pretty mouth opened, then closed. Opened, then closed again.

"I can't think of a reason either," he said.

"It would not be good." Will was shaking her head, still not meeting his eyes. "Definitely not good."

On that she was wrong. "It would be better than good. But you're probably right."

What the hell was he saying?

"There's too much you don't know about me." Blue eyes faded to a deep gray as she held his gaze. "Too much I can't tell you."

"I'm not asking for your secrets, Will." And he wasn't. Randy could guess at enough to know he wanted to help her forget whatever kept her so on edge. Take her out of the past, if even for a little while. "It's been a while for me, that's all. Maybe too long, judging from how hard it is to sit on this stool right now."

He'd planned on complimenting her. Getting to know her a bit. Jumping into bed with her hadn't been on his immediate list of things to do. Though he *was* a guy. Sex was *always* on the list.

Will looked around as if to make sure no one could hear them. "It's been a while for me, too." The blush that colored her cheeks made him want to touch her even more.

"So we have something in common. Couldn't hurt to help each other out. Right now, not following where that brief encounter was leading was the painful part.

"You make it sound too easy," she said, doubt and need warring in her eyes. "It can't be that easy. Not for me."

"You're right," he said. Of course she was right. She'd only recently begun to relax around him. What the hell was he doing bringing up sex?

"This won't make tomorrow awkward at all, will it?" The smile she flashed was unexpected, but encouraging.

She seemed to be considering the offer, and he enjoyed watching every thought travel across her face. The arguments for and against. What she wanted versus what she feared. When she shook her head while a tiny smiled crept across her lips, he knew which way she was leaning.

Meeting his eyes, she asked one question. "Why did you stay out here with me instead of going back to the poolroom with your friends?"

"Because I like you," he said, going for the truth. "I like the way you look, the way you move. Your confidence and capability. But honestly, because I can't resist the challenge of trying to wipe that hurt and fear out of your eyes."

She didn't run or flinch or show a hint of anger. All emotions he expected. That was another thing. She was always surprising him with her strength.

"I'm not a charity case. I don't need some man to rescue me."

Of that he was sure. "Maybe we can rescue each other."

As her face relaxed, the corners of Will's mouth curved up. "Maybe." She grabbed the bar rag from where he'd dropped it and twisted it in her hands. "I'll think about it."

"You'll think about what?" Beth asked, dropping three empty beer bottles on the end of the bar. "The guys need another round. I could use a refill on my water and Sid is switching to soda."

Randy watched Will, who held his gaze under lowered eyelashes. Neither answered Beth.

"Hello?" she said, waving an arm in the air. "Are you two okay?" Beth crossed the distance between them, stepping up to the stool beside Randy. "What's going on out here? You look like you're planning a bank robbery or something."

Will laughed, and the sound shot straight to Randy's groin. "Or something," she said, throwing the rag over her shoulder. "Two beers, a water, and one soda coming right up."

CHAPTER 10

Sleeping was virtually impossible. Will tossed and turned all night. The last time she'd seen the clock it read 4:00 a.m., but she must have drifted off shortly after that, since she'd definitely had a dream. A rather vivid and less than virtuous dream featuring a very naked, hot, and ready Randy Navarro.

When she'd awakened in a pool of sweat exactly three minutes before the alarm was set to go off, parts of her body that had been too long neglected still tingled. Will dragged herself into the bathroom and stepped under a full stream of lukewarm water, but even that wasn't enough to keep the erotic thoughts at bay.

So she did what any red-blooded woman would do—upped the water temperature and spent five extra minutes on, well, herself. She was only human, after all.

At least the tux fitting wasn't first thing in the morning. Due to the two-and-a-half-hour drive, Beth had scheduled the appointment for after lunch. Randy had something he needed to do with Jude first thing, so Will agreed to meet him at Anchor Adventures around nine-thirty.

Groggy-eyed and exhausted, she pulled up in front of the large triangular building at nine-fifteen. A quick glance inside revealed the place to be empty. When she stepped back outside, the sound of a motor from the right drew her attention. Will followed the decking around to the side of the building that faced the water and spotted a Jet Ski flying across the harbor, spinning and then shooting over its own wake.

Whoever was on that machine knew what he was doing.

"Bloody brilliant!" came a voice from the pier to the left of the deck. Will hadn't noticed him before, but Jude danced around the edge, following every movement of the man on the watercraft. Then revelation dawned.

"That's Randy." How she'd missed the fact was a mystery, since the size of the man on the machine should have been her first clue. Will moved closer. The smile that split his face revealed how much he was enjoying himself. Water shot straight up as he banked hard right and raced toward the pier.

Dark curls hung wet over Randy's ears as he pulled up mere feet from the sand and cut the engine.

"That was perfect," Jude yelled, enjoying himself as much as the man on the water. "Exactly what I needed."

Randy beached the Jet Ski, stepped off to one side, and threw his hair back. Water flew out behind him, forcing Jude to tuck his camera under his jacket. Which reminded Will it wasn't exactly summer temperatures today. She pulled her denim jacket tighter as she reached the bottom level of the deck.

Had Randy hopped on a Jet Ski in ice-cold water for the sake of this article? Talk about dedicated. Sleeveless black neoprene clung to every curve and bulging muscle on his body. Every. Bulging. Muscle. The suit cut off above his knees, revealing calves the size of her thighs that were covered in a light dusting of dark, wet hair. Water slicked down his body.

Will's mouth went dry as the world around her disappeared. Even the squawking of the seagulls faded away. Randy climbed the short ladder that brought him onto the pier, where he reached behind him and pulled something down his back. Before she could process what was happening, he began to peel the suit down over his broad chest.

Will couldn't look away. One rational, prudish brain cell told her to turn around and wait in the van. The other brain cells beat that one into submission and kept her feet planted firmly on the dock. Good God, the man was beautiful. Better than Michelangelo's *David*. Better than anything she'd ever seen in any magazine. Better than even her dream brain had conjured.

She could have this man if she wanted him. He'd said as much the night before. Would it be so bad to give her body what it wanted and to hell with the rest?

That one brain cell tried to talk again, but the others sat on it and cheered for her to go for it.

"Will!" Jude yelled, gaining her attention. He stood beside her, but she had no idea when he'd gotten there. "Close your mouth, darling. I'm afraid one of these horrid birds will go in looking for food."

She stuttered, trying to come up with a plausible excuse for what must have been the very carnal and hungry look on her face. But then she looked back to Randy, who had peeled the wet suit down until it hung off his hips, his pelvic bones forming a V that dipped behind the material.

Nope. She didn't care one bit what Jude thought. If he'd witnessed Heidi Klum climb out of that water dripping and peeling clothing, he'd have looked the same way.

"I suppose, if you go for that type," her British friend said, watching the man walk toward them. "No wonder I didn't stand a chance."

"Morning, Will," Randy said, running his hands through his hair as he joined them. "Guess I stayed in the water longer than I should have."

Will tapped her wrist, which sported bangles instead of a watch. "No problem. I'm early." If she'd have missed this show, she never would have forgiven herself.

"You ever been out on a Jet Ski?" He tapped water out of his left ear. "I could take you sometime if you want."

"Not if you drive like that." How she managed to keep her voice casual, Will didn't know. "Looked dangerous from here."

Randy shook his head, sending more drops into the air. "You'd need to hold on tight, but you'd be fine. I wouldn't let anything happen to you."

Will felt the heat crawl up her body at the thought of wrapping herself around the man before her and holding on tight. She bit her bottom lip, smiling into Randy's darkening brown eyes.

"Well," Jude said. "Now that I'm invisible, I guess I'll go." He slid the camera from around his neck and popped on a lens cap he pulled from his pocket. "Thanks for doing this. We needed some action shots and these will work beautifully."

"Happy to help out," Randy said, keeping his eyes on Will.

She wasn't sure how long they remained there, staring at each other, or when Jude wandered off, but Will finally came to her senses and remembered they were supposed to be going somewhere.

"You must be freezing," she said, pulling her own jacket tight around her neck.

"Not at all. The water feels great."

Will gaped. "That water has to be below sixty degrees. What are you, a human heater?"

He took a step forward, reaching for her hand. "You could say that." Randy pressed her hand to his chest, directly over his heart. Heat seared her skin as his pulse beat against her palm.

"Oh," she said, staring at the broadest shoulders she'd ever seen. Her own heart rate kicked up a notch. "Yes. You're very warm." And solid. And gorgeous. But it wasn't the feel of his skin or the bare chest that turned her to a pile of mush.

It was his eyes. Brown, with tiny flecks of gold she'd never noticed before. The kindness in those eyes is what did her in. That one brain cell found its voice again, saying what all the others were too stupefied to utter.

Oh boy.

~

Randy stayed as still as possible as Will held her hand against his skin. He'd let go of her wrist several seconds before and doubted she realized what she was doing. The topaz eyes darkened as she stared first at his bare chest, then up into his eyes.

Don't flinch, he thought. The slightest movement would startle her, and that was the last thing he wanted to do. Keeping his breathing steady took everything he had. Not pulling her closer took even more.

"I should probably go change," he said, hating to break the spell but knowing they needed to get on the road. "I've got clothes up in my office. Hot coffee, too, if you want to grab a cup while I towel off."

Will's eyes darkened even more, pushing sapphire now. A hint of distrust still danced in their depths, but so did desire.

"Yes, we'd better get going." Will stepped back, sliding her hands into her pockets as she moved. "It's a long drive." She finally broke eye contact, shifting focus to the deck on which they stood. "Speaking of, are you driving or am I?"

There was no question. "I'll drive." He was old-fashioned that way. Motioning toward the building, he said, "After you."

Nodding, Will climbed the three narrow levels to the larger area at the top. "This is where the wedding will be?" she asked, turning to look out over the water once they reached the top. "I hope they get a sunny day like this one."

"The ceremony will be here," he said, indicating the end to their left. "Beth and Joe will stand there, by the railing, so the guests will be looking toward the water. Then we'll have the tent set up over here, with plenty of tables around the sides and space for dancing in the middle."

"Beth is a genius for thinking of this. It's a perfect location."

"It was my idea, actually." He smiled at Will's look of surprise. "I've pictured a wedding out here for a while now. An option I could sell in the off-season. When Beth and Joe started talking about a wedding, I knew I had to offer."

Crossing her arms, Will glanced around the deck again, as if seeing what he'd imagined in his mind. She shook her head. "Just when I think I have you figured out, you go and say something like that."

Randy tilted his head. "Is that a good thing?"

"I haven't decided yet," she said, an honest answer he took as a good sign. If the jury was still out, he had time to win the case. What he was looking to win exactly was still up for debate.

Not that his body didn't already have an answer, but this was tenuous ground requiring his upstairs brain to be in charge. Difficult when she looked at him like an expensive delicacy she'd like to devour.

"I'll get you that coffee while you think on it, then." Randy opened the side door to Anchor Adventures, holding it for her to pass through first. "Third door on the left is the break room."

They passed the employee locker room, from which Randy grabbed a towel, and then a restroom on the left. A broom closet and his office were on the right. Will turned left at the door he'd indicated. "You call this a break room?"

"It's the room we use to take our lunch breaks, so yeah."

She crossed to the counter, running her hand along the surface. "What is this?"

Now that he'd stepped into air-conditioning, his body registered the cold water covering it. Randy toweled off his arms and chest as he answered. "Recycled glass mixed with concrete. We go for eco-friendly around her."

"Eco-friendly or not, it's beautiful." Will pointed to the cupboards. "Mugs?"

"Far right, above the coffeemaker."

As Will filled her cup, Randy took the opportunity to watch her. She was graceful, as always. Found the creamer in the fridge without having to ask. Pulled a clean spoon from the drawer—getting it right on the second try—to stir the drink, rinsed it in the sink, then dried and put it away.

When she turned with the cup to her lips, she leaned her bottom against the counter and blew softly. He'd never seen anything so sexy.

"What?" she asked, catching him staring. "Weren't you going to change?"

He wrapped the towel around his neck. "Yeah, I'm going. Give me five."

As Randy crossed into his office, he whistled a tune, feeling pretty good about the day ahead.

∾

Two-and-a-half hours of pretending she was unaffected by the man in the driver's seat tested Will's nerves to the breaking point. She knew something had changed between them. And so did he. But neither seemed willing to bring this newfound . . . thing into the light of day and acknowledge it.

They were either chickenshit or both waiting for the other to bring it up first. No way in hell was she lifting the lid on this one. Denial was the way to go. Deny, deny, deny.

"Is that it, up ahead on the right?" Randy asked, leaning closer to the windshield.

Will followed his gaze and spotted the sign reading "OBX Tuxedo Shop."

"That's it." *Thank you, Lord.* "We're a little early, but that's better than being late."

The store was in the end unit of a U-shaped shopping center. Two dapper mannequins decorated the window, looking all dressed up with no place to go. When they reached the entrance, Randy opened the door, holding it for her to go through first. A bell jingled overhead, bringing a small Asian man from the back room.

"How can I help you today?" he asked, smile wide and hands clasped.

"We have an appointment," Will said, gesturing toward Randy. "Well, he does. Randy Navarro. One o'clock for a tux fitting."

The small man assessed Randy from head to toe, then back again. "The big guy. She was not kidding."

Randy sighed behind her but stepped forward. "Yes, sir. I'm the big guy. I hope you can help us. This wedding is pretty important."

The tailor looked to Will. "We'll have him looking perfect for your big day. No worries." Before she could correct his assumption, the man shuffled toward the back of the store, saying, "Follow me, please," over his shoulder.

She looked at Randy, not sure whether he meant both of them, but then remembered the reason she was there—to make sure everything was right. Will couldn't exactly do that by hanging out up front with the fancy mannequins.

"You heard him," she said. "Let's go get you a tux, big guy."

"Yes, ma'am," Randy replied, flashing his pearly whites, made brighter by the olive tone of his skin. The simple black T-shirt that stretched tight across his billboard-sized back hugged his biceps like sausage casings. The dark denim of his jeans rode low on his hips, showing off to full effect the perfect ass behind them.

Not that she was looking at his ass or anything.

Following the tailor through a doorway in the back corner of the store, Will felt as if she'd stepped into a private club. Every detail, from the burgundy drapes to the countless tie racks and stacks upon stacks of starched white shirts, said *manly domain*. To the left stood a wood-framed three-way mirror with a short, round wooden pedestal in front.

Their host snagged a long cloth tape measure that hung over the right third of the mirror. "I am Mr. Lee, and I will be handling your fitting today." With a keen eye, he assessed Randy. "The pants will not be a problem, but we will have to bring in the waist quite a bit on any pair that will fit those thighs."

Yes, Will thought, those were some formidable thighs.

"The shirt will be a different matter." Mr. Lee pursed his lips. "We will make it work. Step into the dressing room on the right, please. I will hand in two pieces to start."

Randy raised a brow in Will's direction, then disappeared behind the curtain. She realized why Mr. Lee had picked this particular dressing room right away: it was taller than the others. A reminder Randy was well beyond average height. From what Will could surmise, Randy was well beyond average in every category.

Damn him.

Minutes after Mr. Lee had handed in the black pants and white shirt, Randy emerged, looking like a fancified Incredible Hulk. The shirt gaped open over his broad chest, clearly not able to close. The sleeves were too short, and Randy held the pants up with one hand.

Will covered her mouth to keep from laughing at his expense, but then those brown eyes turned her way, full of self-deprecating humor, and she let the mirth come through.

"You look like someone zapped you at a party and turned you into a giant. Only the zap didn't work on your clothes."

"The pants aren't bad," he said, looking down at his toes poking out from under the material. They were attractive toes. "But if this is the biggest shirt they offer, I'm in trouble."

"Ah," Mr. Lee exclaimed, appearing from behind another curtain at the end of the stalls. "As I thought. We have much work to do, but this is a good start."

Twenty minutes later, Randy had been measured, poked, pinned, and, from Will's vantage point, possibly felt up, but Mr. Lee looked pleased with his notes. He'd hemmed and hawed through the proceedings, the more stressed sounds accompanying the neck and chest measurements.

They'd probably have to build a new shirt out of a ship's sail.

"We have you all set," Mr. Lee said, gracing them with a confident smile. "Will take ten days, then you come back and we see how things fit."

"The wedding is three weeks from today," Will said. "Ten days should be no problem."

Mr. Lee gave a thumbs-up. "We will have your man looking all dapper for your day. Leave it to us."

"It's not my day," Will said, finally able to correct the presumption. "We're both in the wedding, but it's not our day."

"Ah," he said, placing a finger beside his nose. "Day will come for the two of you. I can tell these things." She opened her mouth to argue, but he raised a hand to stop her. "You believe what you want, but I know. I am in the business."

Will was so startled by the vehemence in Mr. Lee's voice, she could do little more than stare in wild-eyed amazement. She didn't know what business he thought he was in, but right now he needed to get out of hers.

CHAPTER 11

W e are not having a day," Will said as Randy turned the key in the ignition. "I want to make that clear right now."

He buckled his seat belt. "No offense, Will, but I don't remember proposing."

"You didn't have to. Your little tailor dude did it for you."

This woman had serious issues to get this worked up at the mere mention of marriage. He hoped the topic alone was the problem, not the topic with him included.

"He's an old guy trying to lock in more business. He's harmless." Randy put the truck in gear. "You really need to relax. No one will be twisting your arm to make you get married."

Glancing over to his passenger, he saw the color drain from her face and kept his foot on the brake. "Will?"

She stared ahead, eyes unblinking, but her hands were gripped tight enough in her lap to turn her knuckles as white as her face. Randy slid the gearshift back into park and held silent. Will might be sitting beside him, but she was miles away in her mind. Whatever memory was washing over her was definitely not a happy one.

He could wait. See if she'd tell him where she went. After nearly a minute, she came back. "What are you doing?"

"Nothing," he said, softening his voice as much as he could. "Waiting."

"For what?" She tossed her hair over her shoulder, her movements jerky and tense.

He laid both arms on top of the wheel. "For you to come back from wherever you'd gone." Randy looked down, debating his next move. Pretending had never been his strong suit. "I don't know what happened in your past, but considering what sent your mind racing back there, I have some guesses. Whoever hurt you is never going to do it again. Not as long as I'm around, okay?"

"I don't need a protector," she said, eyes focused on something in the distance.

"How about a friend?" he asked. That one seemed to get her attention because she finally turned to look at him. "I want to be your friend."

Will snorted. "With benefits?"

He felt the sting of the accusation but held her gaze. "With or without. I'm here."

As her shoulders dropped, she ran a hand through dark hair, shoving the mass of thick waves off her forehead. "I appreciate that, but there are ghosts from my past that would take more than muscle to defeat."

"Are you sure?" he asked, trying to lighten the mood. "I have a lot of muscle."

Her laughter filled the truck cab, hitting him in the chest like a blow. "Yes, you do." Crossing her arms over the purse in her lap, she turned his way again. "We never had lunch, and I'm starving. You want to eat?"

Feeling as if they'd made some kind of progress, he put the truck back in gear. "I could eat. How do you feel about Thai food?"

"I feel like it's been way too long since I've had it." Will gave him a weak smile, the ghost from her past still hovering in her eyes. "You know a Thai place around here?"

"I do. It's back up the Banks a little, but worth the drive."

"Then Thai it is," she said with a nod.

The restaurant was mostly empty. Randy and Will opted for an outdoor table, as the temp had warmed up nicely and the patio was in the sun.

"What do you have in mind?" Randy asked, once the young waitress had taken their drink order and left them to peruse the menu.

Will kept her eyes on the list of offerings. "I'm thinking pork. These specials look good. Pepper ginger maybe. What about you?"

"I'll stick with my usual," Randy said. "Start with the Tao Hu Tod, then the vegetable Pad Thai."

Her eyes tracked across the menu to find the descriptions of what he would order. She blinked, looked up to meet his eyes, then blinked again.

"What?" he asked.

"Tofu? You're starting with tofu?"

Randy laughed. "I'm a vegetarian, Will. And tofu is good, especially the way they make it here."

She dropped the menu to the table. "You're a what?"

"You serve me green tea. Why would the fact I'm a vegetarian be a surprise?"

Will shook her head, started to speak, then closed her mouth. She finally pointed a finger his way. "Look at you. Doesn't that take a lot of protein?"

Randy crossed his arms on the table, leaning forward. "There are lots of ways to get protein in your diet. Besides, I'm not some freak show exhibit. I work out. I'm healthy. That wasn't always the case for the men in my family, and most of them died relatively young." He shrugged. "I don't intend to follow in their footsteps, so I go my own way."

"How young is relatively young?" Will asked, eyes narrowed.

Not a topic he liked to discuss, Randy focused on the large vacation homes across the way, and the water beyond them. "Around forty. Some a little older, some a little younger."

Will reached across the table, laying a hand across his forearm. "I'm sorry. I was aware that both your parents had died when Sid was pretty young, but didn't know about the rest. Or think about the fact that you weren't exactly an adult when they passed either." She gave his arm a squeeze, and with a smile added, "That won't happen to you. You're too healthy. And stubborn."

She sat back, sliding her hands below the table. "Besides, Sid would kick your ass for dying on her."

That was probably true. The comment reminded him how close Will and Sid had become. "Speaking of my sister, how did it go getting her in a dress yesterday?"

"Oh, she fell in line real quick once she caught a glimpse of herself in the mirror. The dress Beth picked out is gorgeous, but then Sid could make a burlap sack look sexy."

"How about you?" he asked, curious to know what Will would be wearing when he had the pleasure of walking down the aisle with her on his arm. "Do you like the one for you?"

Will's face went soft, as if he'd flashed her a picture of cute kittens or something. "It's beautiful. Exactly what I'd have picked for myself." Her eyes brightened. "And wait until you see Beth. As if she's not glowing enough whenever Joe is in the room, she beams in that dress. I have to make sure this wedding is perfect. I'll never forgive myself if something goes wrong."

"Nothing will go wrong. We've got this." Randy winked at her.

"Since when is this a *we*?" Will lifted the menu off the table. "I'm the one stuck with the bride's planner. It's *my* ass on the line."

He pushed her menu down with one finger. "Have you always been this stubborn?"

"Excuse me?"

"The venue is *my* place, and was *my* idea. The groom is my best friend, and I've come to care about his bride as well. I'm offering to help make sure this wedding comes together the way it should, and you act like I'm asking for a kidney. Why is it so hard for you to accept some help?"

"I can accept help. When I need it and when I ask for it." Blue eyes narrowed again, this time lacking their previous sympathy. "Maybe you're the one who can't stand to be told you're not needed."

Right. He was the problem here. This little meal was going downhill fast, but he wasn't backing down on this one. She needed him, and he would make her realize exactly how much.

"Do you know the dimensions of the deck on Anchor Adventures?"

"No," she said, the word clipped with impatience.

"Do you know what's available on the deck, in regards to electricity, space, and lighting?"

"No," she all but growled.

"But you're prepared to finalize plans with the tent company, the disc jockey, and the caterer without that information?"

Will closed her menu and slammed it onto the appetizer plate in front of her. "You've made your point. I need information that *you* have to make this wedding happen."

Information that he had. She couldn't even say the words. "You'll have to do better than that," he pushed. "Try again."

She looked ready to swallow her tongue, a rising temper evident through the flush of her cheeks. "Fine," she growled. "I need you. Happy now?"

"Yep." Randy sat back in his chair and motioned for the waitress. "Now, let's eat."

∾

Such a pompous ass. What was his problem? Why did he have to push so much, work his way in like that? Will didn't like being off balance, and that's all Randy seemed to make her feel. Off line. Unsure. And worst of all, there were moments when he made her laugh.

Gorgeous and built and kind and pushy and funny and . . . Damn if she didn't like him. Even when he poked to make her admit things she didn't want to admit. So she couldn't do everything on her own. That didn't mean she couldn't try. Having to admit, out loud, that she needed him to pull off this wedding left a bitter taste on her tongue.

Will didn't make it the last three years by depending on people for help. Depending on the wrong person is what had screwed up her life to begin with. If she hadn't leaned on Jeffrey in the wake of her mother's death, Will would be back in Boston sitting in a corner office dealing with spreadsheets and profit-loss statements, not tending bar on a remote island, looking over her shoulder, prepared to cut and run without warning.

It was the cutting and running that freaked her out more than anything these days. Will had made the idiotic mistake of falling for Anchor Island. It felt like home. Her friends felt like family, much more than the people to whom she was blood related. *They* had been raised with money. Raised with the fancy name that wielded power and influence.

Will may have shared the name on paper, but that was the only thing she had in common with her biological family.

"I'll leave the check here for you. No hurry; let me know when you're ready." The waitress dropped a slip of paper on Randy's side of the table. "Can I get you a to-go box for that, ma'am?"

Will's plate was still half full. After their brief spat, her appetite had disappeared. "No, I'm good, thanks."

Randy finished the last bite of his Pad Thai, which he ate with chopsticks, of course, and wiped his mouth. "If this place were closer to home, I'd eat here every day."

Closer to home. The phrase hit a nerve with Will. Would she ever be able to call someplace home again?

"The food was good," Will admitted. "Thanks for suggesting it."

Their argument had ended as quickly as it had begun, with Randy appearing to have some sort of instant amnesia about the whole thing. He didn't have much of a temper and seemed to fizzle back to the happy-go-lucky guy in a matter of seconds.

He noticed her plate for the first time since the waitress had set the meals on the table. "You didn't eat yours. You said you were starving."

She glanced to her watch. "I guess I wasn't as hungry as I thought. We need to get on the road. I told Tom I might be late, but at this rate he'll be stuck with half the dinner shift before I get there."

Will glanced over Randy's shoulder and caught a redhead staring hard at their table. Did she know her? After a week of Rebecca going on and on about how familiar Will looked, she should have known better than to stay off the island for too long. The redhead said something to her friend, a tall man with arms covered in tattoos, then headed their way.

Will's palms began to sweat and her heart rate went through the roof. There was nowhere to run. No way to jump the railing to their right without drawing attention or having Randy think she'd lost her mind. Will put a hand over the side of her face and turned her body as far away from the woman as possible without falling out of her chair.

A quick look over her shoulder revealed the woman had reached the table behind them and continued on. A roar filled Will's ears. The moment of truth was about to find her in a Thai restaurant in the middle of the Outer Banks, and there was nothing she could do to stop it.

Shit shit shit shit shit.

"Randy? Randy Navarro?"

Will spun in her chair as Randy looked behind him. In seconds he was on his feet, wrapping the stranger in a giant bear hug and lifting her off the ground.

"What are you doing here?" he asked, planting the woman gently back on the patio. "I expected you to be on that Cancun trip this month."

"I couldn't go without my Randy."

Her Randy? The roar continued in Will's ears. Adrenaline left from the fear mixed with a flash of jealousy to create an ego-splitting cocktail in her bloodstream.

"I had to take this year off," Randy said, keeping the woman pulled tight against him. Stepping to the side, he said, "Kayla Fontana, this is my friend Will Parsons. She lives on Anchor with me."

That needed an immediate correction. "I don't live with him," Will said, struggling to keep her voice level. "We both live on the island." Her hands were shaking, so she kept them hidden beneath the table.

It was Randy's turn to blush. "Right. No. That's what I meant."

Kayla laid a hand on his cheek. "You're cute when you're making an ass of yourself." She turned to Will, extending a hand. "Nice to meet you. Hope this big lug is treating you right. He's a great catch if you can pin him down. God knows enough of us have tried."

Enough of us? What the hell? Did he have a harem they knew nothing about on Anchor?

"No pinning down going on here," Will said, taking Kayla's hand for a brief shake. "We're in the same wedding. I'm friends with the bride, he's friends with the groom."

Kayla punched Randy in the shoulder. "Going after another bridesmaid? And I thought I was special." Randy performed a great interpretation of a drowning fish as Kayla laughed. "That's how we met." She gave Randy a heated look. "Those were the best ten days I ever spent in Tibet."

Will used her napkin to wipe the sweat from her upper lip as she pondered this odd revelation. It seemed there was much about Randy Navarro that the people around him didn't know. Like that he traveled to exotic places to have ten-day sexcapades with bridesmaids.

"We never did make it to Shishapangma, did we?" Kayla said. "Not that I minded." Her voice dropped a telling octave. Will knew exactly why this woman didn't mind missing out on Shishapangma, whatever the hell that was.

"Well, I'd love to sit here and watch you two catch up, but I really have to get back." Will stood, desperate for a moment alone. "I'll be at the truck."

As she walked away, she caught Kayla's voice on the breeze. "Oh shit. Did I screw that up for you?"

Randy's response was lost in the distance.

CHAPTER 12

Yes, you may have," Randy said, watching Will walk away with her back straight, shoulders tense. She'd been acting odd right before Kayla came up behind him. As if she'd seen something that scared her. "But I think you might have helped me, too."

"Really?" Kayla asked, stepping out of his arms. "And how did I do that?"

He nodded in the direction Will had gone. "Hard to explain." Taking Kayla's hand, he said, "I really do have to go. I'm driving and she needs to get to work. How long are you going to be in the Outer Banks?"

"Arrived today and we're here for a week. I want you to meet Austen." Kayla waved someone over. "And be nice. He's scrawnier than my usual, but I can't resist the tats. And by some miracle, he's actually a stand-up guy."

A lanky man with tattoo sleeves, large gauges stretching his earlobes, and a silver hoop in his left eyebrow joined them. Kayla made the introductions, explained they were there with Austen's family, which Randy planned to tease her about later, and agreed to make time for a visit to Anchor during the week.

After exchanging numbers, Randy took care of the check and headed for the truck, not sure what he'd find waiting for him when he arrived.

Since he had the keys and the truck was locked, Will had taken a seat on the tailgate. As he approached, she kept her eyes locked in the other direction, feet swinging as if she didn't have a care in the world.

Her face belied the body language. Jealous was good. Not in the long run, but a good sign for the moment. But his past wasn't the real problem. Hers was.

"Hey," he said, advancing slowly, hands in his pockets. "You okay?"

"Fine. Why?"

That sounded anything but fine.

"Oh, I don't know." He took a seat beside her, straining the shocks on the truck. "You cut out of there pretty quick. I'd like to think you were jealous, and that's what Kayla assumed, but she didn't see your face seconds before she called my name."

Will kept her face averted but tightened the grip on her purse. A move so subtle he almost missed it.

"There seems to be a lot about you that people on Anchor don't know," she said.

Deflection. A nice try.

"You thought she'd recognized you instead of me." Randy sighed. "Will, why does having someone recognize you send you into a panic? Why can't you have your photo in a magazine?"

She finally turned his way. Tears swam in her blue eyes. "I can't answer your questions."

He brushed a tear away with his thumb. "Why not?"

Using the sleeve of her denim jacket, Will wiped her face. "It's complicated."

"Doesn't have to be." If she'd tell him, maybe they could fix it. Whatever *it* was.

Will half laughed, half hiccuped. "Trust me. If I could make it all go away, I would." She slapped both hands on the tailgate and hopped off. "I really do have to get back. Tom is expecting me."

Randy stood, encouraged by the fact Will didn't step back. "You don't have to do this alone, you know. You have friends. We're here to help whenever you need us."

Will dabbed at the drops clinging to her long eyelashes. "That's a nice idea, but right now I need to get home." Her voice hitched on the word *home,* then she moved around him and hurried to her side of the truck.

The woman took stubborn to a whole new level. Whatever she was dragging around from her past, Randy was certain it couldn't be as bad as she believed. There was no way she'd killed someone. Or been involved in some giant espionage scheme. If she was in the witness protection program, she was the worst witness ever, since he was pretty sure those people were supposed to act natural at all times.

So what was it? What put that fear in her eyes? He carried the thought back around to himself. Randy had assumed Will had been hurt by a large man in the past, as his size was the only reason he would be the one to set her off. She didn't have the same reaction around Joe or Lucas. Or even their dad, Tom Dempsey, who might not be as wide as Randy, but he was just as tall.

Nothing about a rough ex-boyfriend explained why she didn't want to be recognized. And how would total strangers know her face anyway? As he opened his door and climbed into the truck, the truth dawned.

That ex was looking for her.

Didn't explain how strangers would know her face, but the thought of some asshole hurting Will, then hunting her down like an animal, made him see red. A primal and wholly unfamiliar need to cause pain filled Randy's limbs. He bit his tongue to keep from asking the questions.

Who is he?

Where is he?

How do I find him and break both his legs?

A sudden violent streak was the last thing he needed to show Will. Randy steadied his features and leveled his breathing. His grip on the steering wheel was tighter than necessary, so he concentrated on his knuckles, mentally loosening one at a time.

They made the trip home in silence, Will lost in her own thoughts and Randy attuned to every breath she took. There were no scars on her face, so the damage had to be elsewhere. Not that most of the damage wasn't mental. The idea that she believed Randy to be a monster simply because of his size made more sense now.

And intensified his determination to show her differently.

~

An hour into the drive, Will had finally managed to relax enough to notice the tension coursing through Randy. He played it off well, smiling at her on the rare occasions they made eye contact, but she wasn't fooled. If he was wound up over her refusal to answer his questions, then that was his problem.

She'd give anything to lay this burden on someone else's shoulders, but that wouldn't change the facts. Wouldn't alter her reality in any way. Randy couldn't storm up to Boston, kneecap Jeffrey, and release her from the constant fear of being found.

If Will was certain of anything, it was that Randy would never kneecap anyone. Regardless of that muscle twitching in his jaw.

They parted friendly enough. Will thanked him for lunch, realizing she was so off balance by what felt like a near miss that she hadn't offered anything toward the restaurant bill. Randy thanked her for going, looked as if he wanted to say more, but instead nodded and closed the driver's door on her VW Bus once she'd climbed in.

He remained in the parking lot watching her drive away, fading in the distance in her rearview mirror. Such a strange day. The man managed to turn her on, piss her off, make her laugh, *and* dry her tears all in one afternoon. He probably assumed she was bipolar, or at least mildly unstable.

Either way, the impression could not be good. Though why she cared, Will couldn't say. Randy was a good guy. A kind man. Traits that made him a rare creature in her experience.

"Nice of you to join us," Tom said as Will stepped behind the bar. Speaking of kind men, Tom was another one. In fact, Anchor Island seemed to be a haven of good guys. Maybe that's why she loved the place so much. "I take it our island giant will have a tuxedo for the big shindig?" her boss asked.

"We'll see in ten days," Will said. "Considering the numerous ways that tailor invaded his space, I'd say Beth and Joe owe the giant a debt of gratitude for doing all this." She dropped her purse and keys in a drawer under the register. "Sorry I'm so late. We stopped to eat and lost track of time."

"Not a problem." Tom collected a stack of wet rags from the end of the counter. "There's been a change in the schedule for tomorrow."

"You need me to change shifts?" Will didn't usually work Sunday mornings after working late on Saturday, but she could do it if Tom needed her.

"Nope." A broad smile split his face. "You're taking the day off."

Will stuttered. What the . . . "Why? I don't need a day off."

"Yes, you do." The rags dropped into a basket inside the kitchen. "You've been working too much. Lucas is covering your shift, and you're going to take an entire day to do whatever you want."

She followed the older man into the kitchen. "But I want to work." Will didn't like having free time. It gave her too much time to think and only served as a constant reminder that outside of the jobs she did around the island, her life was empty.

"Well, you're not working here. At least not tomorrow." Tom took her by the shoulders. "Will, relax. Breathe. Read a book. Watch a movie. It'll be tough, but you can do it."

After a tap on her cheek, he moved into the office, Will still on his heels. "Have I done something wrong? Messed something up?"

His brows shot up. "Where's all the paranoia coming from? You're a star employee. Think of this as your reward. I learned the hard way what working too much can get you." He held a hand over his heart. "There are worse things to have than a day off. Now, I'm heading home to Patty."

"I'll be here early Monday," Will said, hurtling the words at Tom's retreating form.

"I'm sure you will," he said. "Now get out there. You've got customers."

~

Rebecca King awoke on her last day on Anchor Island with a smile on her face. She'd taken this assignment expecting to find a hole-in-the-wall vacation spot she could make sound like paradise. Instead she was leaving with the key to her future.

"You ready?" Jude asked, knocking on her open balcony door, duffel in hand.

"Yes, I am," she answered, then noticed the dark circles under her colleague's eyes. "If you feel like you look, this is going to be a long day for you."

"I feel worse." Jude dropped onto the ottoman inside the door. "Decided to party it up with some tourists last night. Forgot I'm not as young as I used to be. Why are you so chipper?" he asked. "Was this assignment so awful that you're happy to be leaving?"

Rebecca slid her laptop into its case. "Not awful at all. In fact, this is the assignment that will change my life."

Jude narrowed his eyes. "I must be more hungover than I thought. I didn't hear any sarcasm in that comment."

"Are you going to be sick? I don't want you puking in the car."

"You're up to something." Jude returned to his feet, pausing to hold his head. "Bloody hell, that hurts." Once his color returned to normal, he trailed behind her. "What evil deed are you concocting? You're like a Disney villainess. Destroying someone is the only thing that makes you smile like that."

Rebecca rolled her eyes. She wasn't destroying anyone. Simply reporting the truth about someone who might not want the truth revealed. Wasn't that a reporter's job?

"You have such a high opinion of me, Jude. It's a wonder we don't work every assignment together."

"If that's a threat, it's just mean. Now tell me what blew sunshine up your arse in the last twenty-four hours." Jude pulled the hotel room door closed behind him. "You weren't this cheerful yesterday."

Yesterday she hadn't found the answer yet. Today was a different story. Literally.

"Can't a girl be in a good mood?"

"A girl, yes. A she-cat with a mean streak, no," Jude said. "Spill."

There were only so many insults Rebecca was willing to tolerate, even in her current positive state. "Shove it, Jude. There. You happy? Feel free to sleep all the way back to the airport."

"Now that sounds more like the Rebecca I know and love." The smarmy Brit pushed the button for the elevator. "Sleeping will not be a problem. Standing for very long is another story." Dropping his duffel and camera bag to the floor, Jude took a seat in a chair along the wall.

Rebecca ignored him. Not even Jude Sykes could ruin this for her. Willow Parsons was her ticket to the big time. Or rather, Maria Van Clement was.

~

By noon on Sunday, Will had been to the coffee shop, the real estate office, and Lola's art store, but no one needed her to work. This was why she needed a hobby. In the last three years she'd done nothing but work. That's what she was used to doing. Who she was.

Growing up with a mother who never worked, cleaned house, or boiled water, let alone cooked a meal, had in some reverse-psychology way instilled a strong work ethic in Will's brain. She'd made sure the bills were paid, food was in the house, and clean clothes were in the drawers. It wasn't so much that her mother was lazy; she'd just been raised a certain way. When you've had servants from the day you were born, doing for yourself is as foreign as living on the moon.

Will considered going to Dempsey's but knew Tom would only kick her out. Why they were so damn determined to make her take time off was a mystery. Beth was the pregnant stress ball, not Will. A week with a reporter breathing down her neck had made her a little tense, and whatever sparks were flying between her and Randy didn't help, but they wouldn't blame her for being wound too tight if they knew why these things bothered her.

Not that she could tell any of them.

"An extra pair of hands, willing and able," Will yelled as she stepped through the open garage door of Sid's under-construction business. The mechanic was perched on a tall ladder working on some kind of pulley contraption.

"Those hands are not wanted here," Sid yelled back, keeping her eye on the task at hand. "I'm under direct orders not to let you work today."

Tom had her blackballed? That was low.

"Come on," Will whined. "I have to do something. Let me hold the ladder. Anything!"

Sid finally turned to face her. "What is wrong with you? Most people would love a day off. Hell, some people purposely take days off just to fart around." She began to climb down. "It's a nice day. Go sit in the park, or read on the sand."

Didn't Sid realize that sitting still, even with a book, wasn't an option? Will needed to be doing something. Planning something.

Wait. The wedding. All those details Randy mentioned.

"Do you know if Randy is home?"

Sid's eyes went wide. "Who are you?"

Will shook her head. "What?"

"The Will I know wouldn't spend an entire day with my brother and then purposely go see him again the next day." Sid pulled a large handkerchief from her back pocket and wiped her hands. "Did something happen yesterday? I told him to woo you, but I didn't think he'd do it."

"You what?" Woo her? Didn't wooing lead to marriage? There would be no wooing. "Why would you do that?"

"Don't get your knickers in a twist," Sid said, holding up her hands. "He was asking some questions about you and I thought he might be interested. Since both of you could use some mattress dancing, I encouraged him."

Mattress dancing? Where did she get this shit? "You know how I feel about your brother. Why do you think I'd want to be wooed by him?" Will couldn't believe she'd used that word.

"I have no idea how you feel about my brother. He's never done anything to deserve the cold shoulder you gave him for so long." Sid shoved the handkerchief back in her pocket and advanced on Will. "You've been talking lately, even spent the entire day together, and I didn't hear that anything horrible happened."

"The day wasn't bad," Will admitted, reluctantly. "But that doesn't mean—"

"Randy is a great guy," Sid continued, cutting her off. "I found my happy with Lucas, and I want to see my brother find his happy, too." One pointy finger poked Will's chest. "You'd be lucky to have him."

Blinking, Will rubbed the spot where Sid had poked. "That might be the sweetest, most girly thing I've ever heard you say."

"You've insulted my brother. Don't start insulting me."

Will sighed. "You need to learn how to take a compliment."

Sid tucked a wayward curl behind her ear. "Tell me my truck kicks ass, or my garage is killer. Those are compliments."

Throwing an arm around her friend's shoulders, Will said, "You have the most badass truck on this island. And this garage is going to rock." Giving her a squeeze, she asked, "Better?"

Brown eyes the same color as Randy's narrowed. "Are you hugging me?"

Will tensed. "Maybe." She loosened her grip and put distance between them, not interested in another poke.

"Are you going to see Randy?" Sid asked.

"I have to do something, and he's got the info I need to lock down the final details on Beth and Joe's wedding."

Sid walked behind the counter on the left side of the room and pulled out a large envelope. "Could you give him this?"

"Sure," Will said, tucking the envelope under her arm. "Do I need to give him a message with it?"

"Nah." Sid went back to the ladder. "But do me a favor."

"What's that?" Will asked, tilting her head back to follow Sid's ascent.

The mechanic stopped halfway up and turned. "Make him open it while you're there. I don't want him to be alone when he sees it."

That meant whatever was inside was either bad news or a sad memory. The thought of being Randy's emotional support wasn't something Will relished, but she'd do it for her friend. Both the one before her and the one she was going to see.

"Fine, I'll do it. But I'll need his address."

CHAPTER 13

Randy swept the mess onto the dustpan and emptied it into the garbage. That was the one negative about living on an island. Sand. The stuff was pervasive, and though he swept the wood floors daily, there was always more the next day.

Sunday was his day to clean the house and work on the business financials. He'd been at them all morning, taking a much-needed break to do the floors. When swinging a broom was more attractive than staring at financial reports, things were not looking good.

Someone knocked at his front door as Randy pulled the garbage bag from the can in the kitchen. Odd, since he wasn't expecting anyone. Even more odd when he spotted Will through the glass, waving from the other side.

"Hey there," he said, pushing the screen door open. "Come on in."

Randy hadn't entertained a female in his house in longer than he could remember. At least one to whom he wasn't related. Sid came over often enough, usually to bust his chops and mooch his food. Though that cut back when Lucas moved in with her. From what Randy heard, the lawyer could turn out a gourmet meal with the best of them.

Will stepped into the foyer carrying a large envelope and a day planner. He closed the door and turned to find her standing wide eyed, staring into his living room. She looked great. Dark jeans that tapered into heavy black boots. Long dark waves draped across the shoulders of her denim jacket.

"You can go on in," he said, feeling like a teenage boy staring at the hottest girl in school. A role he was too damned old to play. "Unless you aren't here to stay."

"Well . . . I . . . ." She pointed to the open space beyond them. "Did I step through some kind of portal? Because there's no way a house on Anchor looks like this."

Contrary to most everyone else on the island, Randy didn't go for the beach cottage look. He liked clean lines, limited decor, and solid, neutral colors. Sid often told him the place looked like a cross between a hospital and a museum, but he felt at home in the minimalist setting.

"You're still on Anchor." He felt like an idiot hovering in the entryway and needed something to do with his hands before he reached out to test the softness of her curls. "Can I take your jacket?"

Will sloughed off the denim while keeping her eyes on the living room. "This could be in a magazine. A very chic, modern design magazine." She moved toward the metal-frame coffee table as Randy hung her jacket on a hook near the door. "It's like Zen meets understated simplicity. Masculine without the sports pennants and oversized furniture."

"Do you expect every man's home to look like a frat house?" he asked, following her into the living room, trying to keep his eyes at shoulder height. He considered asking what kind of men she spent time with but remembered that was not a positive subject.

Will moved to the fireplace, running a finger along his newest acquisition—the statue from Lola's that had reminded him of her. He'd actually swung over to buy it after Will had left the day before.

"This is beautiful," she said, in hushed tones. "A touch of feminine curves in a room filled with hard lines."

"It's from Lola's," he explained, leaving out his impetus for buying it. He had yet to learn why she was there. No need to scare her away before they'd even sat down. "Not that I don't appreciate the company, but is there a reason for this unexpected visit?"

"Oh." Will turned, holding up the items she'd tucked beneath one arm. "I came to get those details you mentioned yesterday. The deck dimensions and stuff for the wedding." She extended an envelope his way. "But first, Sid asked me to give you this. Tom insisted I take today off, and I'm not used to sitting still, so I've been all over the island trying to find someone who would let me work, with no takers," she rambled. "Sid said no, too."

"So that makes me your last option?" he asked, taking the envelope and dropping it onto the coffee table. "Flattering." Though he was happy to even be on her list.

"She asked that I have you open that while I'm here," Will said, shuffling her feet and looking everywhere but at Randy. "Said you'd need a friend around when you saw it."

Sid's request piqued his curiosity, but not as much as the implication that Will was willing to be the friend in this scenario. "Have you had lunch?" he asked. "I've got some chili I made last night ready to heat up."

"I'm guessing it's meat-free?"

He padded barefoot into the kitchen. "Yes, ma'am. And you'll never miss it."

Will took a seat at the island. "I'm game." She dropped the planner on the counter, crossing her arms over it. "I didn't even think to ask if I was interrupting something. I'd have called first, but Sid doesn't have a phone in yet at the garage."

Randy pulled a pan from the cupboard beside the stove, then stepped to the fridge to get the chili. "Paperwork. With two businesses, I usually spend my Sundays working the books. Adventures opens the Monday after the wedding, so I'm working on being ready when we open the doors."

"You don't sound very enthused about that."

"I have tea and water. Which would you like?" he asked.

"Water is fine." Will propped her chin on her palm. "You don't like the financial side of running a business?"

"It's not that I don't like it," he answered, sliding the bottle of water across the island. "The numbers haven't been as easy to deal with lately." That was the understatement of the year.

Her response was completely unexpected.

"I could take a look for you." Will spun the cap off the water bottle. "Patty let me clean up the books for Dempsey's while they were gone, and they're looking much better now."

His books were his business, but hadn't he harassed her the day before for being too stubborn to accept help?

"Do you have some kind of background in accounting?" Randy asked, realizing the woman couldn't have been a bartender her whole life. "Is that what you went to college for?"

A look of unease crossed her face. "I had a couple classes. Forget I asked." She took a drink of the water, keeping her eyes averted. "I didn't mean to butt into your business."

Randy knew Dempsey's had been in trouble enough to require an infusion of money from Lucas the fall before. If Will worked some kind of magic on their books, and Patty was pleased with it, then what did he have to lose?

"The program is open on the laptop," he said, pointing toward a doorway on the other side of the living room. "First door on the right. I'll heat this up and bring it in."

Will sat up straight. "Really? I mean—"

"Really." Randy pulled a bamboo spoon from the large utensil holder next to the stove. "Have a look. Maybe a second pair of eyes will see something I'm missing."

If he didn't know better, Randy would swear that was excitement in Will's eyes. Since when did the prospect of financial reports and bank statements elicit excitement in anyone? And how could he get her to look at him with that same kind of enthusiasm?

"Great." She hopped off the stool, snagging her water as she went. "Let's see what we've got."

~

Two hours later, Will was running on an adrenaline high from finding three key areas that would help Randy get control of his numbers. Few people understood why a child who grew up on the edge of society, living like a gypsy, would ever want to venture into accounting, but Will loved the clarity of it. Numbers didn't lie. They weren't ambiguous. And they rarely changed.

With accounting, you knew where you stood, but there was also a flexibility required to be really good. An ability to see things that might not be obvious to anyone else. With a mother who knew nothing about managing money, Will had found the need to be creative with numbers from an early age.

By establishing a career in accounting, she could put the kind of out-of-the-box thinking she'd been doing most of her life to work for other people. And she enjoyed solving intricate financial puzzles like the one she'd worked through with Randy.

"Where did you learn to do that?" he asked as they returned to the kitchen. He put their empty bowls into the dishwasher while Will took a seat and opened Beth's planner on the island. "Your talents are being wasted behind a bar."

Will enjoyed the compliment, but to answer the question would reveal too much about her past. "Let's say I have a head for numbers." Which was true. She always had. "And I like tending bar. There's actually a good bit of math involved. Two ounces of this to one and a half of that, and then a splash of something else. These are serious calculations, and one ounce off can kill a drink."

He closed the dishwasher, then wiped his hands on a towel. "I'd never thought of that, but I guess you're right."

"Okay, I helped you. Now it's time for you to return the favor." She pulled the pen from the leather loop along the side of the planner. "Maybe we should draw the wedding layout for the deck. Too bad we don't have any graph paper."

Randy held up a finger, then disappeared in the direction of the office. Will spun on her seat, staring once again at the open and spacious living room. The furnishings were minimal and screamed modern, but they also gave off a kind of welcoming warmth. Maybe it was the gray of the couch, or the thick black area rug under the contemporary coffee table.

What artwork did cover the walls, which wasn't much, was simple, understated, and carried an Asian influence. A content-looking Buddha hovered on the coffee table. Will had never studied Eastern religions, but the serene and happy-looking fat man had always made her smile.

There was also the envelope Randy had yet to open. They could get to that after the wedding details were down. That way, she could leave as soon as she'd fulfilled her duty and been present when Randy saw whatever it was Sid sent over. As much as she'd enjoyed straightening out his books, she realized that every minute they spent together deepened their budding friendship.

In truth, Will was incredibly attracted to the big guy with the quick smile and gentle ways. Which meant she should be bolting for the door.

"Ask and ye shall receive," Randy said, reaching the kitchen with graph paper in hand. He set it on the island, opened a drawer on the other side, and withdrew two pencils. "Now we're ready. How about I draw up a rough version of what I see, then we can work out the details together?"

"Sounds good to me." And it did.

She and Randy made a good team. He never pushed to be in charge. Never threw his weight around, so to speak. There were moments when he forced her to be open minded, or admit he had a point, but those encounters were over as quickly as they began, with no male ego victory dancing involved.

Randy swung around the island, taking the stool to her right, which worked out well since she was left-handed and he wrote with his right. They even fit together physically.

Time to put the brakes on that line of thinking and concentrate on the task at hand.

And then she got a whiff of Randy's clean scent. It hadn't distracted her nearly as much in the office, because she'd been engrossed in the numbers and he'd not been this close. Their shoulders were practically touching as he leaned over the paper. She could feel the heat from his body along her entire right side.

He'd drawn the seating area for the ceremony, as well as the tent positioning, before Will pulled her brain back to the graph paper.

"We don't want the tent overpowering the ceremony, looming too close, so setting up a longer and slightly narrower one on the first level down will leave the top open for the actual ceremony."

"Right," Will said, watching his fingers as they lightly grasped the pencil and floated across the surface of the paper. The light touch was contradictory to his size and stature.

Would he be gentle in a more . . . intimate setting as well?

Holy cheese and crackers. What was wrong with her? Maybe he'd put something in the chili that sent her libido into overdrive. Could the right combination of vegetables do that? Hell if she knew, but as Randy was keeping this visit completely platonic, Will needed to remember to do the same.

Randy hadn't slid in so much as a single innuendo. No sly looks beneath his lashes, or even a raised brow. Though they were practically thigh-to-thigh, he didn't appear to be the least bit affected by their proximity.

Meaning she was in this state of heightened awareness alone. Lovely.

"The only problem might be the catering," he said, leaning back from the paper. "They'll have to haul everything down a level, so it increases the chance of dropped food."

He looked at Will as if expecting an answer, but her mind was blank. Time to get her shit together. She put all her energy into examining the graph paper and saw an idea.

"What if we switch them?"

"Switch what?"

She pulled a blank piece of paper from the stack and began to draw. "What if we hold the ceremony closer to the water and put the tent on the larger top deck?" Will remembered from the day before that there were two ways down to the pier. "The guests can go from the parking lot, along the left walkway, and down toward the pier."

"That might work," Randy said, pondering her suggestion.

Will flipped open some pages in the planner. "We're looking at fewer than fifty guests, so there's plenty of room down there for the chairs. And this way, Beth and Joe will practically be on the water. It'll look gorgeous from every seat."

"I think you're on to something." Randy slid her drawing his way and placed a large square for the tent along the side of the building. "If we put the food at this far end, then the caterer won't have far to go at all. Less chance of trouble and more room for a dance floor."

He sat back and rubbed a finger along his chin. "Is there anything you can't do?" he asked, flashing Will an admiring grin that sent a blush up her cheeks, and heat to other places.

"Golf," she said, trying to keep things light.

"Golf?"

"Yep. Tried it once. I was awful."

Randy let out a full body laugh, and Will couldn't help but laugh with him. He'd have laughed harder if he'd been there to see her swing that golf club.

Once the laughter faded, Will felt Randy's eyes on her. Like the whiskey they resembled, spending too much time drinking in that look would make for a fun night but leave her with nothing but regrets come morning.

"Okay then," she said, flipping to a blank page in the to-do section of the planner. She took notes as she spoke. "I need to find out how much table space the caterer requires, then see what Opal has in mind to put the cake on. At least the wedding is in the afternoon, so that gives the florist plenty of time to decorate once the tent is up."

"The tent won't take but thirty minutes. Have the guys arrive no later than eight that morning." Randy leaned close enough for their thighs to touch, sending Will's pen slashing across the page. "Sorry," he said, putting a few inches between them.

"No problem," she said. "Eight for the tent people. I'll tell the florist nine and find out what time the caterer will need access to your kitchen."

"Oh," Randy said, putting his pencil to the graph paper again. "Here's the dimensions of the decks, and I'll put an X at the location of each outlet. If we put the DJ at the opposite end from the food, he'll have an outlet here to hook into." He placed an X near the front corner of the building.

Will folded the graph paper and stuck it inside the front cover of the planner. "That does it then." Thank the heavens. She couldn't handle being this close to the man much longer. Her brain cells were starting to fry, and the urge to turn and kiss him was getting harder to suppress.

But there was that damn envelope. Crap.

Randy put the pencils back in the drawer, leaving the few sheets of blank graph paper on the island. "I'll put those away later," he said, looking as if he didn't want their visit to end.

Truth be told, she didn't either. Which was all the more reason to cut and run.

"If you'll open that packet from Sid, then I can head out." She could have ditched him. Claim she'd forgotten, as he didn't seem to be thinking about the envelope either. But she'd promised Sid.

"I'd forgotten about that." Randy motioned for her to precede him to the couch. "Might as well get this over with. Sid doesn't get wound up about much, so I'm curious to see what's in here."

So was Will.

Randy opened the flap, giving Will a quick look as if to say *are we ready?* With a nod, she said, "Let's see it."

He tipped the envelope down at an angle, sending a large photograph sliding onto the coffee table. It looked to be a family of four—a beautiful woman, a very large man, a serious-looking teen boy, and a small, dark-haired girl with a smudge of dirt on her cheek.

Will hovered on the edge of the couch. "Is that your family?" she asked in hushed tones.

Randy nodded but didn't speak. He lifted the picture as if it might disintegrate in his hand. One fingertip touched the face of the beautiful woman, clearly his mother, to whom Sid bore a striking resemblance. His face took on a distant look.

Feeling the need to say something, Will asked, "How old were you there?"

"Eighteen," he answered, never taking his eyes from the photo.

Silence hung like a fog in the air, but Will let it stay this time. Though he did his best to control his emotions, she could see pain and joy warring in his features. He'd clearly not seen this picture for many years, if ever. She had no doubt his mind was somewhere in the past, remembering the day it was taken, the moments before and after.

A full minute later, Randy turned the picture over. Written in Sid's clear hand, it read, "Aunt Belinda found this in an old box." That was it. Nothing sentimental. No dates, names, or locations. But then again, the brother and sister likely didn't need a reminder of those incidental facts.

Unable to help herself, Will scooted closer to him. "Want to talk about it?"

He jerked as if he'd forgotten she was there, which she couldn't hold against him. Being faced with unexpected memories like this wasn't easy. Sid should have given Will a clue so she could have prepared him.

I don't want him to be alone when he sees it.

Maybe Sid had given her a clue.

Randy ran a hand through his hair as the picture dropped onto the table. "I'm going to need something stronger than tea for this. You want some wine?"

Will's plan to leave as soon as her envelope-opening duty was done went out the window.

"I'll pour while you talk," she said.

CHAPTER 14

Randy showed Will where to find the glasses, the wine, and the corkscrew, but his mind was still hovering somewhere in the past. When that picture landed on the coffee table, his heart had stopped, while his brain switched into overdrive. The trip back in time was so fast, and so abrupt, he wondered if his body would ache later.

"Here you go," Will said, handing him a glass where he stood near the sliding glass door at the back of the kitchen. "Do you want to sit?"

"Let's go out here." He slid the door open and waited for Will to step through. "We can sit on the glider at the end there." Randy pointed to the far left end of the porch.

She took a seat, squeezing as close to the arm as she could get. He didn't let it bother him. At least she was still here. Her presence seemed to make the memories easier to deal with.

Randy filled the space beside her, putting the glider into motion and staring out over the lapping waves. His house was only feet from the sand, and he'd left the outside much as it had been when he bought the place. Inside was modern and contemporary. Outside was rustic and weathered.

"Sid looks a lot like your mom," Will said, opening the conversation. As much as she dodged personal questions, in most respects,

Will wasn't the type to dance around an issue. He liked that about her. "You have her eyes, too."

"Angelita Pilar Navarro. A beautiful name for a beautiful woman." Randy took a sip of wine before continuing, letting the weight of his mother's name, something that hadn't crossed his lips in many years, settle into his bones. "That picture was taken shortly before she died."

"So you all knew she was sick? Is that why you look so serious in the picture?"

Randy shook his head, watching a butterfly hover on the edge of the porch railing. "We had no idea she was sick. The photo was taken right after she and I had a big fight." He tilted his head back, closing his eyes and seeing the look on his mother's face when he said he was leaving. "I wanted to see the world. She didn't want me to go."

"But you went anyway."

He nodded in the affirmative, too choked up to say the word.

Will remained quiet beside him. Rolling his head her way, he tried to read her expression. Did she think he was a bad son? Was she pitying him, or would she tell him that was typical teenage behavior and to get over it?

No censure showed on her face when she turned his way. Only a small smile. "Survivor's guilt doesn't change the fact that you did nothing wrong," she said, her voice a whisper. Then she looked down and laced her fingers with his. "You wanted to live, and you had no reason to think anything bad was going to happen to her." Their eyes met again. "And none of those facts change a damn thing, do they?"

She got it. He squeezed her hand.

"Thanks for that. I'm guessing you have a similar experience?"

Will tilted her head to one side. "Kind of. I said hello to the wrong person. Let him in and then leaned on him during a rough time in my life." She paused, biting her bottom lip. "I sometimes think, if I could go back to that moment and take back that hello, then none of the bad stuff that followed would have happened. My life would be so different."

As Randy's porch faced east, the sun was slowly dropping behind them, turning the horizon a deep purple before their eyes. He and Will watched the colors shift and darken as their hands remained entwined. A new thought struck him.

This would be a nice way to end every day.

The sentiment would likely send Will running, so he kept it to himself.

"If you could change the past, then you wouldn't be here on Anchor, would you?" he asked. The question would have been prying the day before, but it felt right in the moment. He felt a fissure of tension in the hand still resting in his own.

With a pinched expression, she answered, "No, I wouldn't."

Randy followed his gut on his next move. Lifting their clenched hands, he dropped a kiss on Will's knuckles. She turned his way, but didn't withdraw her hand.

"Maybe everything does happen for a reason," he said, settling their hands back atop his thigh.

Will relaxed into him, laying her head on his shoulder. "Maybe so."

∼

Will leaned on Randy for several minutes, watching the water pull at the sand, listening to him breathe beside her, his solid shoulder beneath her ear. So much for maintaining any kind of fearful facade. Or keeping her distance.

He'd always seemed so happy, like he didn't have a care in the world. Turned out, he had scars like she did. Maybe not as deep, but they were there.

"Explain something to me," Will said, sitting up and turning her body his way. "Why would a person who's seen so many people you care for die way too young spend his adult life looking death in the eye and daring it to take you?"

He tapped the arm of the glider, completely relaxed. "I don't look death in the eye."

She raised one brow, sending him a *no, really* look.

"Okay, it's not knitting, but I never take unnecessary risks. I never climb without safety ropes and at least one other person along. I don't scuba dive alone, or in caves." Randy shimmied his shoulders. "Too easy to get stuck. I don't ride any machine I'm not positive I can handle, and I never jump out of a plane without packing my own chute and having a backup ready to launch."

Will nearly laughed. Did he hear himself?

"What's the highest mountain you've climbed?"

"About twenty-two thousand feet, but I still want to do Shisha-pangma, which is twenty-six thousand."

The reason he never made it to Shishapangma was something Will didn't feel like discussing at the moment.

"That doesn't sound high to you? Or dangerous?"

"I see where you're going with this." Randy took a sip of his wine, clearly buying time to think of a good defense. "It's really not that dangerous if you know what you're doing. Hell, snowboarding down the side of a mountain is more dangerous than climbing one."

Will crossed her arms. "So you've snowboarded down the side of a mountain? And this isn't a death wish?"

"You're not going to let this go, are you?" Randy swiped a hand through his hair and gave a long, heavy sigh. "Fine. Yes, some of the stuff I do is dangerous, but the rush is worth it. And like I said, I don't do anything half-assed. No 'Hey, watch this' and take a flying leap. There's a difference."

"Well," she said, sliding some humor into her tone, since she didn't want this encounter to end with an argument. They'd come too far for that. "When you put it that way."

He granted her a smile in return, bobbing the side of his knee against hers. "My dad always talked about the places he'd go. The things he was going to do . . . someday. When he had enough money. When his kids were grown." Shifting focus back to the horizon, he added, "I Ic ncvci gor back to Pucito Rico to vlslt hls family. I don't want to live my life *someday*. Then you never end up living at all."

Now he had a point. Will had always been too focused on preparing for tomorrow to make sure she was living in the present. That didn't sound like a very satisfying way to be.

"Do you ever do anything just to do it?" he asked, pulling Will from her life analysis.

"You mean for no reason?"

"No, I mean because you want to. Not because of what it'll get you, or because someone else expects you to do it." He turned, leaning an elbow on the back of the glider. "Do you ever do anything for *you*?"

Everything she'd done in the last three years had been for her own survival, but did that count? Look at how she'd handled a day off. She couldn't even sit still and enjoy some time alone.

Alone. Even when she was working, surrounded by people, Will still felt alone in the world. Though she didn't feel all that alone right now.

"I'll take the hesitation and that confused look on your face as a no," Randy said. "There's a concept in the Eastern religions that suggests one live in the now. Not the past or the future, but strictly in the moment."

Will pulled her legs up until her chin rested on her knees. "How could you not think about the future?" Or in her case, keep one eye over your shoulder watching for the past to creep out of the shadows.

"What good does worrying about a year from now do you today?" Randy absently toyed with her sleeve, making it hard to concentrate on the conversation. Not that she understood what they were talking about.

"The decisions you make today affect where you'll be in a year," she said. "You can't ignore that."

Randy shook his head. "There are a million factors that affect where you'll be in a year, and ninety-nine percent of them are out of your control."

Oh, now he wanted to break out the math. "That's a gross exaggeration."

"That is reality, my friend." A long, narrow finger pointed at her nose. "You need to learn to live in the moment."

What would it be like to pretend the past couldn't affect her? To stop worrying about the wrong tourist stepping up to her bar? Or that an annoying reporter will figure out why Will's face looked familiar?

Which reminded her. "That reporter left today, didn't she?"

"You see," he said, throwing up his hands. "You can't even stay in the now for this conversation."

"That's not true," Will defended herself. "I asked about something that happened today. So that's the now."

Randy finished his wine and rose from the glider, sending Will sliding back and forth. "You asked because you were worried she was going to figure out where she saw you before." Growing serious, he asked, "*Has* she seen you somewhere before?"

Will swished the remnants of her glass, keeping her eyes on the dark liquid. "I don't know."

That was true. She had no way of knowing if Rebecca had seen her face before or not. Will *did* know she'd never seen Rebecca

before, but that didn't mean much when Will's face had been plastered across the New England media once upon a time.

"Well you can stop worrying. She's gone. So what do you say?"
he asked, extending a hand. "Want to do some living in the
moment?"

With the departure of the reporter, Will's current source of
anxiety was gone. There was no reason to believe Rebecca would give
her a second thought once she reached the ferry. Maybe it was time
to put the past where it belonged—behind her.

But she had to be sure of Randy's intentions. Regardless of
attempting to live in the moment, planning any sort of future that
included a relationship was still impossible. If that's what Randy
expected, she'd have to walk away.

"The moment?" she asked, ignoring his hand until she knew
what he was offering.

"No yesterday. No tomorrow." He stepped closer. "Only today."

That sounded good, but her brain wasn't going to cave that eas-
ily. "If I take that hand, where am I going?"

His eyes turned dark, but the grin retained its mischievous
charm. "If I'm finally convincing you to spend real time with me,
inviting you to my bedroom first thing wouldn't be a very smart idea,
now would it?"

A tremor of disappointment trailed down Will's spine. Not that
she'd have had sex with him tonight. As tempting as the thought
may be.

Sliding her hand into the large warm one he offered, Will rose
to her feet. Randy held his ground, which put their bodies less than
an inch apart. Sex may not be on the table this evening, but it would
be soon. If they were going to do this, they would take it all the way.

Eventually.

"One condition," she said, enjoying the feel of his arm as it wrapped around her waist. "It's our little secret."

Deep brown eyes narrowed. "Not sure I like that part."

Will went for logic. "Sid suggested you woo me not long ago, didn't she?"

Randy took a half step back. "Maybe."

"Relax," she said, tapping his chest. His wide, solid chest. "Sid told me. She also told me she wants to see you find a happy ever after like she has. If they think we're an official couple, that's what they'll expect for us. And not only Sid, but Lucas and Beth and Joe. It's as if they've all caught the love disease."

"You make them sound terminal."

"Think of it as contagious."

The rumble of laughter that rolled through Randy's body sent heat to all the right places on Will's. "I see. I don't like the idea of sneaking around, but I suppose what we do is no one else's business."

"Good man." Will drained the rest of her wine. "Now I'd better be getting home." It was dark now. Too dark to see Randy's eyes clearly. But she could almost feel his thoughts dance along her skin.

"I think we should do something to seal the deal," he said, voice dropping an octave and the Latin accent stronger than usual. "Something symbolic. You know what they say. Begin as you mean to go on."

Oh, he was good. Too good. Extending her arms around his neck, Will gripped her wrist with her free hand and pressed her body against the wall of a man holding her tight. "That sounds fair," she whispered, rising up on tiptoe to reach his lips.

Instead of leaning forward, Randy stayed still, letting Will make all the moves. Good thing she was tall herself. When she brushed his full lips with her own, the taste of wine and heat threatened to scorch her brain. *Why weren't they going to have sex tonight?*

"I'm liking this moment," he said, his breaths shorter than before. "I'm interested to see what the next one will bring."

"Uh-uh," Will murmured, brushing her lips back and forth across his as she shook her head. "No thinking about the future."

With a solid tug, she pulled him down far enough to get off her toes and take his mouth the way she wanted. Full on, wet, and hungry. His lips were soft and gentle, as she'd expected, but his arms pulled her tighter, revealing how affected he truly was.

Her breasts were pressed against his massive chest, making it possible for her to feel every breath he took. She wanted to breathe him in, hold tight until they'd lost track of where one ended and the other began. With a nip of his bottom lip, he came alive.

Randy lifted her feet off the ground, turning until she was pressed against the wall of the cottage, one leg over his hip as he ground against her. Will drove her nails into his shoulders.

"I like this moment better," she said, when Randy slid those talented lips down the side of her throat. "A lot better."

But then he was kneading her ass, and she was grinding as hard as he was, and it had been too long. Will hovered on the brink of losing control. When Randy returned to her mouth, sucking on her tongue while grazing a thumb over her nipple, fireworks exploded behind her eyes. Holding on for everything she was worth, Will rode the wave, belatedly realizing that Randy was holding her at least three feet off the ground.

At some point she'd wrapped both legs around his waist, but she had no memory of doing so. Her arms remained clasped around his broad shoulders as she returned to Earth and caught her breath. Randy still panted but didn't make a move to find the pleasure for himself that he'd given to her.

"Are you okay?" she asked, which seemed like a stupid question, but blood flow hadn't fully returned to her brain yet. Of course he wasn't okay. The man was in full erection, which was proportional to the rest of him by all indications, and in dire need of relief. Relief she'd taken for herself.

"Give me a minute," he said, shifting her enough to lower her legs back to the floor. He leaned his elbows against the wall behind her, pinning her in place.

Not that she had any desire to move.

"I owe you an apology," she said, toying with the damp curls at the back of his neck. "That was only supposed to be a kiss."

Randy pulled back, wiping the sweat from his brow on his shoulder. "Trust me, you don't ever have to apologize for something like that."

"But you—"

He lifted one hand. "It's been a while for me, that's all. I'm not a monk, but I've been living like one for about a year now."

"Try three years," Will said, biting her bottom lip. Had she really admitted that? Well, it did explain her . . . response.

His brows shot up as he stared into her eyes, their noses mere inches apart. "Three years?"

Will nodded.

Randy gave her hip an extra squeeze before stepping back. "Then you deserved that." After a quick peck on the lips, he took her hand and pulled her toward the sliding glass doors.

"Where are we going?" Will asked, a sliver of anticipation racing down her spine.

"I'm going to take a cold shower," he said, letting her step through the door first, then sliding it closed behind him. "And you're going home before we take this too far and ruin the progress we've made."

Will tsked. "Who's not living in the moment now?" Not that she didn't agree with him. Having sex today would be a mistake.

They needed to ease into this. Though her body was ready to ease into Randy's bed.

Reaching the entryway, he snagged her jacket from a hook on the wall and threw it around her shoulders. "When your hormone levels return to normal, you'll thank me."

He was right, of course. Though after what had happened on the porch, she owed him big time. When they did take the final step, she'd be sure to repay the debt.

CHAPTER 15

Randy spent his Sunday evening mentally reminding himself why he should not and would not drive over to Will's place and finish what they'd started. Considering how he'd spent the last year, when they eventually made it to bed, he should be able to keep her there for days.

After a restless night, he'd spent a long day Monday pumping iron and dealing with a broken elliptical. The machine was in use when it broke, increasing its speed to the point that he'd had to rescue poor Mrs. Wollinski from the contraption. Thank God the woman didn't break a hip.

He knew Will was working the evening shift at Dempsey's. They hadn't discussed when they'd see each other again, and Randy considered waiting until she sought him out, but in the end he realized he didn't want to wait. Simply put, he wanted to see her.

Dempsey's closed at nine on Mondays, at least until the season kicked into full swing, so he timed his entrance to eight forty-five. This way, he wouldn't disturb her from the job, and they could talk while she closed the place down. Randy was more than willing to lift a few chairs if it meant watching Will's blue eyes dance as they shared some lighthearted flirting.

As he'd hoped, the place was nearly deserted when he stepped inside.

"You're in late," Daisy said, sliding up beside Randy as he settled onto a bar stool. Will was nowhere in sight.

"I'm here on wedding business." He didn't like Will's preference that anything between them remain a secret, but he'd agreed to the term and would honor her wishes. "Figured it would be better to catch her at the end of the night."

Not the best story in the world, but then he had little experience with subterfuge.

"You're helping with the wedding?" Daisy asked, brows up.

"It's at my business so my input is kind of required." Her shock hit him the wrong way. "But what's so strange about me helping with a wedding?"

Daisy shrugged. "Most guys I know wouldn't do it, that's all." She moved the empty bottles from her tray onto the bar. "Mitch would rather have a spike driven through his forehead than help me plan anything. I can't even get him to pick paint colors for my living room."

Mitch also worked at Dempsey's, but bussers weren't really needed until business picked up. The pretty young blonde looked so frustrated, Randy offered a suggestion.

"Threaten to paint it all pink."

"What?" Daisy said, blinking in confusion. "I don't want a pink living room."

Randy turned to face her. "I didn't say paint it pink. I said threaten to. He'll get involved real quick after that."

The waitress scrunched up her face, pondering his suggestion. "You really think that would work?"

He nodded. "I'm sure of it."

Daisy's face lit up. "Thanks, I'll try it," she said, dropping a kiss on Randy's cheek before heading back to her last remaining customers.

When he turned back to the bar, Randy spotted Will leaning in the doorway to the kitchen, one brow higher than the other.

"Are you trying to cut a path through the entire Dempsey staff, or is it only Daisy and me on your radar?"

Surely she was kidding. If he'd ever intended to cut a path through the women on Anchor Island, Randy wouldn't have gone on a voluntary drought for the last year. Nor would he dabble with a waitress fifteen years his junior.

This jealous streak of hers had him worried.

"Are you this distrusting of every male you come across, or am I just lucky?"

The twinkle returned. "Touché," she said, pushing off the door frame. "I do have trust issues, but I was actually kidding on this one."

"That's good and bad," he said, leaning back on the stool.

"What's that supposed to mean?"

"Well, it's good that you aren't really jealous of Daisy, but bad that you're so good at schooling your face, I can't tell when you're kidding."

"Ah," she said, taking a green tea from the fridge and removing the cap. "That means I have the upper hand. I like that." The bottle slid across mahogany in his direction. "To what do I owe the pleasure of this visit?"

Will kept her eyes on the glasses she was dropping into a sink behind the bar. Her features had gone tight, her shoulders tense. Maybe they hadn't made as much progress as he'd thought.

Randy glanced around to make sure Daisy couldn't hear him. "I wanted to see you," he said. No reason not to be honest.

Blue eyes darted toward the clock behind the bar. "At closing time." She continued to avoid eye contact. "Not very smart."

"Why not?" Randy said, not sure what the problem was. "Seemed rude to try to talk to you while you were working. This way, I can help you close up for the night and we can talk."

"And then Daisy can spread the word tomorrow," Will said, almost under her breath.

Before Randy could respond, the waitress returned. "Final ticket is done." She set a tray loaded with two dinner plates, two glasses, and an empty breadbasket on the bar. "I'll load these into the dishwasher, then start sweeping." With a light punch on Randy's arm, she added, "Feel free to help, big guy. These chairs aren't going to lift themselves."

Will's full lips flatlined as she kept her head down, moving glasses from soapy to clear water.

"I'll get on that in a second," Randy said, focusing his energy on trying to read Will.

He couldn't figure out what he'd done to piss her off. The day before they'd parted on more than friendly terms. So why did this visit make her so mad?

Daisy headed for the kitchen, and Will turned to the cash register. She tapped the screen three or four times and what must have been the closing tape starting running from a small box to the right of the keyboard.

Randy waited for her to tell him what was bothering her, but instead, she headed for the front door without so much as a glance in his direction.

Before she'd clicked the lock, he was behind her.

"Do you want to tell me what's going on here?" he asked. "I was under the impression after yesterday afternoon that you'd be happy to see me."

"I'm trying to make Daisy think I'm not happy to see you," Will said, finally meeting his gaze, her face flushed. "When I said our little secret, I meant it."

This was why he didn't like that part of the deal. "I told her I was here about the wedding."

"At nine o'clock at night?" Will hissed. "She's going to wonder why you didn't use the phone."

She had a point. "I'm sorry. I'm not used to keeping secrets. I wanted to see you."

Her body wilted and she leaned against the door with her arms crossed. "Then maybe this is a mistake." Will shook her head. "I'm too much of a mess for this to work."

"You're a beautiful mess," Randy said. Her eyes softened and he wanted to pat himself on the back for saying the right thing. "Breathe, gypsy. We'll figure it out."

≈

Will struggled to keep her heart in her chest, but it was no use. The damn thing lay prostrate at Randy's feet, and she feared getting it back wasn't going to be easy.

"How are you not running the other way?" she asked. Leave it to her to find the one man who didn't run. Or push. Or have a mean bone in his body.

Damn him.

Another step and his clean scent filled her senses. The heat of him threatened to melt her into a puddle right there on the dusty floor next to her heart.

"Maybe I like a challenge." Randy tucked a dark curl behind her ear.

Will's knees threatened to buckle as she found herself lost in his whiskey-brown eyes. At this rate, she wouldn't be a challenge for much longer.

"I can't find the dustpan again," Daisy said, stepping out of the kitchen and sending Will and Randy jumping in opposite directions.

"What the hell is wrong with you two?" she asked, hovering behind the bar with a broom in her hand. "Why are you over there at the door?"

"I was locking up," Will said, racking her brain for some excuse for what they were doing. "I saw a spider and Randy killed it for me."

Great. A bug in a restaurant. Could she not have come up with anything less damaging?

Daisy took the broom in both hands as if ready to defend herself against an attacker. "Is it dead? I don't do spiders."

"All gone," Randy said, rocking on his heels, his eyes on the floor as if making sure their imaginary arachnid was indeed deceased.

"So do you know where the dustpan is?" Daisy asked again.

"Sometimes Chip moves it to the far side of the kitchen after he sweeps his station," Will said. "Try over there."

As the waitress disappeared, Will slumped again. "That was close."

"You're the one who made the rules." Randy slid his hands into his pockets. "You sure we can't be open about this? We're consenting adults. I don't see the problem."

Will could almost feel Sid's poke as she railed about Randy getting his happy ever after. She couldn't be that for him, but without revealing why, Sid would never understand. As badass as the mechanic pretended to be, she had a soft heart and loved her brother more than anything.

"No," Will said. "Nothing has changed. At least not on that front."

"Then maybe we should start on the chairs. I need something to do with my hands or our secret will be out the minute Daisy returns."

Will knew what she wanted to do with *her* hands. "The chairs. Good idea."

Thanks to Randy, the closing routine took half the normal time. Daisy was happy to get out early, and Will was able to relax once the waitress had driven away, since that meant no more pretending there was nothing between her and the big man working by her side.

Will spun the key in the lock, tugged on the restaurant door to make sure it was secure, then turned to find Randy looming in the dark on the top step.

"Thanks for helping," she said, shuffling from foot to foot. "I think you made Daisy's night by getting her out of here quicker."

"My pleasure," Randy replied, his voice carrying softly on the breeze. "Want to sit out here for a while?" He gestured toward a bench on the porch.

"I can do that."

They dropped onto the bench, Randy waiting for Will to sit before lowering onto the seat beside her. He didn't seem as imposing tonight. Maybe she was getting used to the size of him. Used to being with him and not feeling as if something bad was going to happen. Part of her argued that feeling safer with him around was worse than the fear.

But the other part, the part that liked being near him, ignored the warning.

"Sorry about earlier," she said, watching a moth dart around the streetlight at the edge of the parking lot. Will understood how the moth felt, drawn to something that could do it harm. "I really do have a good reason for acting the way I do. It's hard to explain."

"If my guess is right," Randy said, "you've been in survival mode for a while now. Being suspicious is part of that." He laid an arm across the back of the bench, turning his body toward hers. "But you're still here. That's a good sign."

His face was hard to make out in the low light, but she caught a glimpse of white teeth and could imagine the grin that accompanied it.

"Does anything ever bother you?" she asked, truly curious. "I've never met anyone so mild-mannered."

"Well," he said, followed by a long sigh. "When I think about another man hurting you, I want to find him and break both his legs. So that bothers me."

Will held her breath. "How do you know a man hurt me?"

Randy leaned close, the hand behind her toying with a loose lock of her hair. "For months, I watched fear fill your eyes whenever I was around. With Joe or Lucas or even Tom, you're relaxed. But not with me."

With a lump in her throat, Will whispered, "I'm sorry about that."

"No apology needed. It took me a while to realize it wasn't about me." He lifted her chin until her eyes met his. "Then last weekend, when we talked outside the restaurant, I knew."

The truth swirled at the end of Will's tongue, choking her with the need to blurt out everything. The need to share the burden of what had happened to her. Of what could happen again if Jeffrey found her.

But emotion drowned out the words, and tears flooded her vision. For the first time in more than three years, Will felt safe. As the first tear fell, Randy pulled her into his arms, holding her as she sobbed into his neck. Rocking her back and forth, rubbing her back, whispering reassuring words against her hair.

The crying jag lasted several minutes and left Randy's collar a sopping mess. As she slipped into the hiccup phase, Will reached into her purse for a travel package of tissues. It was bad enough that she'd soaked his shirt; using it as a snot rag was out of the question.

He gave her space to clean herself up but didn't completely let go. A mixture of relief and mortification made it hard to meet his gaze. "How could you not think I'm insane at this point?" she asked, followed by a hiccup that jerked her body.

"Fear can do crazy things to a person," Randy said. "That doesn't mean *you're* crazy."

Will sniffed while dabbing at her eyes. "You probably won't believe this, but I'm actually a very even-keeled person."

"You'll get back there again." With a squeeze of her shoulder, he asked, "Which shift are you working tomorrow?"

"I always open on Tuesdays," she said, exhaustion washing over her. "Which means I should probably get home."

Randy rose, pulling her with him. "Then why don't you let me make you dinner tomorrow night? I'll regale you with stories about Sid as a child, and all you have to do is listen."

With a jerky breath, Will was relieved to find the hiccups had subsided. "I'd like that. But Tuesdays are our girls' night meetings at Opal's place."

"That's right. I guess keeping this a secret means bowing out of Opal's to have dinner with me wouldn't work."

She smiled. "That would be hard to explain."

"Then how about Wednesday?" he asked.

His persistence was flattering. "I can do that."

A car drove by but Will hardly noticed. Randy looked so happy in that moment, they could have been the only two people on the island.

"Then it's a date," he said, taking her hand in his as they walked down the stairs.

A date with Randy Navarro. Will waited for the unease to creep in, but it didn't come. When they reached her van, he pulled her into his arms and dropped a warm but chaste kiss on her lips.

"I'll be home tomorrow night," he said. "If you don't want to wait until Wednesday to see me again, you could always drop by."

The words were filled with such boyish charm, Will couldn't help but smile. "Do you have a favorite from Opal's?" she asked.

"Hmm . . . I don't splurge often, but it's been a while since I had some of that chocolate torte she makes." His smile grew wide. "I happen to know she uses a vegan recipe."

"You're so well-behaved, even with desserts?" Will admired his discipline.

"I'm trying to be well-behaved right now, but it's harder when you look at me like that."

Another car went by and Will realized someone they knew might see them, so she stepped back. "I'd better get home. I'll see what I can do about that chocolate torte."

Drifting backward toward his truck, Randy replied, "I'll leave a light on."

CHAPTER 16

Sid and Beth were both seated at Opal's by the time Will arrived and had ordered her pie already. She'd been distracted all day, thinking about Randy and how good she felt whenever he was around. But it was more than a physical thing. His kindness wrapped around her like a warm blanket. His mere presence felt like a protective barrier between her and the rest of the world.

The world that had been one giant threat for way too long.

But then she had to remind herself that Randy didn't know everything, and even if she revealed the rest, the threat was still there. Looming around the next corner.

"I hear Randy helped you close up last night," Sid said in lieu of a hello. "Is there something you want to tell us?"

Will hedged by filling her mouth with rhubarb pie. Sid waited, undeterred.

"He remembered a detail about the deck at Adventures that we missed the day before." She threw in a shrug for good measure and reloaded her fork. "Since he was there, we put him to work."

"He couldn't have called over with the detail?" Sid asked, removing the rest of the liner from her cupcake. "He had to stop by and tell you in person?"

Whether she was guessing right or not, Will couldn't let Sid get her hopes up. She was not going to be Randy's happy ending, and it was best if everyone understood that.

"I have no control over how your brother chose to tell me." Changing the subject, Will turned to Beth. "We've got the layout for the deck all set. The ceremony will be closer to the water, with the tent set up on the top level, closer to the building. That gives us more room inside, cuts down on the travel distance for the food, and gets the DJ closer to the outlets."

"Is that what you and Randy came up with on Sunday?" Sid asked. "*At his house?*"

The woman would not let this go. If Will didn't know Sid's heart was in the right place, she'd be getting royally pissed right now.

"Yes, I went to his house this weekend, which you know since you gave me the address." Will set her fork on the plate and wiped her mouth. "If this is going to turn into an inquisition, I can take my pie and go."

"Let's calm down, ladies," Beth said, joining the conversation for the first time. "We're all on the same team here, and no one is going anywhere. Sid," she said, turning on what Will considered a mom voice. "Will and Randy have been nice enough to help with the wedding. Stop harassing her because you've got the love bug and think everyone else should have it, too."

Sid stabbed her cupcake but remained silent.

"Thank you," Will said, happy to have an end to the questions. "The caterer asked if kaiser rolls were okay, but I told them no seeds, so they're supplying plain dinner rolls."

"That's good." Beth cut her carrot cake into pieces. "The last thing I want is seeds in my teeth as I visit with the guests."

They passed the next several minutes in silence, something new for their little gathering. Sid was pouting, which wouldn't normally bother Will, but there was something more worrisome on her face. A trace of hurt in her eyes.

Guilt weighed heavily on Will's shoulders. What was she doing? Sneaking around. Lying to her best friends. For what? A short break from loneliness? Some sexual release? They hadn't even had sex yet and the complications were mounting.

"Randy and I are becoming friends," she said, breaking the silence. It wasn't the entire truth, but it was something.

Sid stopped with the last bite of cupcake halfway to her lips. "You are?"

"We are."

Her friends looked at each other, Sid seemingly speechless. That was something new.

"That's great," Beth said, her smile beaming as she exchanged an enthusiastic look with Sid.

"Now don't *you* start," Will said, dropping her fork again. "I like Randy. He's a good guy, as Sid has always said. I know the two of you are lovesick and want everyone else to pair off and go all googly-eyed, too, but that's not going to happen with me and Randy. You guys need to face that right now and stop this tag-team Cupid stuff."

"But if you like him—" Sid started.

"Uh-uh," Will said, holding up a hand to halt whatever was coming next. "Believing he's a good guy and going all till-death-do-us-part are two different things. I'm flattered you think I could be the woman for him, but I'm not. Okay?"

Regardless of the fact she wanted to be, some things were impossible.

Sid's shoulders dropped, but she looked less petulant. "It's your loss."

"I won't argue with that," Will said. Whoever ended up as Randy's forever would be a very lucky woman. "Now, can we talk about something else? How's the baby stuff? Any movement yet?"

The rest of the chat centered around Beth's baby bump, which was nonexistent as of yet, and ideas for the nursery. The future parents were also torn over whether to find out the sex when they had the chance. Joe wanted to know, but Beth wanted to be surprised. Will had no doubt when the moment of truth arrived, Beth would cave and demand to know as well.

The women were heading home by eight, each with a dessert for the road. Will set the chocolate torte on her passenger seat, then stared out the windshield, debating whether to drop by Randy's or not. She couldn't help but feel like a hypocrite.

She'd had to make it clear that she and Randy would not be traipsing down the aisle together. Well, other than at Beth's wedding, but not at their own. So why did she still feel guilty?

Pulling into Randy's driveway a few minutes later, Will smiled at the fact he really had left a light on. The porch light beamed bright, casting a yellowish glow across the worn planks.

After three deep breaths and an extra minute to gather her courage, Will walked up and knocked on the door. Torte in hand, she mumbled, "A quick visit. Drop off the food, make a little small talk, then get out."

Then Randy opened the door looking like sex on a stick and all thoughts of a short visit melted away.

∽

Until he saw her standing in the glow of his porch light, Randy hadn't believed she'd come. He'd hoped, but every time Will had a few hours away from him, she seemed to change her mind about them.

"We need to talk about us," she said, once they'd reached his kitchen.

And here they went again.

"Nothing good ever follows a statement like that," he said, sliding the torte into the fridge. "Let's sit down on the couch."

Hesitantly, Will nodded. Then she froze. Pointing into the sink, she asked, "What is that?"

Randy followed her gaze. "That's a wine glass."

"It has lipstick on it."

He looked closer. "Yes, it does. I had company earlier." Knowing what it looked like, and not interested in giving Will a reason to storm out, he explained. "Remember Kayla? My friend we met at the Thai restaurant over the weekend?"

"Yes," Will said, lips tight.

"She and her *boyfriend*," he emphasized the last word, "came down to see me today. Austen, the boyfriend, and I had tea while Kayla had a glass of wine."

Will chewed the edge of her bottom lip. "Oh. That must have been nice."

"We enjoyed catching up," he said, escorting Will toward the couch. "I like Austen, so I'm happy for Kayla. She deserves a good guy."

When they were seated on the L-shaped sofa, with more distance between them than he liked, Will said, "That's nice. Every girl deserves a good guy, actually."

"True," he agreed. "Now you want to tell me why you look ready to crawl out of your skin?"

Will exhaled. "I need to make sure you know the limits here."

"The limits?"

"This can never turn into anything permanent." She said the words so quickly, he wasn't sure he'd heard her right.

"Okay. Anything else?"

She looked disappointed he didn't put up more of a fight. "So you're good with that?" she asked, gnawing on her bottom lip again.

Randy considered his answer and opted to ask a question of his own. "Why exactly can't whatever we start turn into something permanent?"

Will dropped focus to her shoes. "I thought you understood my situation."

Scooting closer, he asked, "How can I understand if you won't tell me exactly what your situation is? If someone is hunting you down, you have to know we'd never let him hurt you." With more force he said, "*I* wouldn't let him hurt you."

Blue eyes locked with his. "That means more to me than you'll ever know, but it's even more reason you have to understand what I can give you, and what I can't. I want you, Randy, but I don't know how to have you and not screw everything up."

Not the answer he was expecting. "What do you think you're going to screw up?"

"You," she said, hopping up to pace along the coffee table. "I can't offer anything more than right now."

"I'm not asking for more than that," Randy said, lurching to his feet. He shouldn't have pushed her so hard. "There are no guarantees in life. I know that better than anyone. But we're staying in the now, remember? We're not talking about a lifetime commitment here."

"But that's what you deserve. Sid is right, you're a great guy, and you deserve someone who isn't a basket case running from her past, unable to promise anything beyond next month or even next week."

"We need to slow this down here." Randy ran a hand through his hair, then stepped around the table to take Will's hands. "I know our friends are planning weddings and having babies, but that doesn't mean every date has to end with a proposal. Or start with one. I sure as hell don't want you to disappear in a week, but I'm not sizing rings and picking out his and hers towels."

"That's good," she said. "Because I did that once and it did not turn out well."

"First of all, I'm not that guy. And second, there's no pressure here." He pulled her around the coffee table and back to the couch. "Tomorrow, you're coming over for dinner. Two adults, sharing a meal. We tell some stories, enjoy a glass of wine, and you go home whenever you're ready. We don't have to think about anything beyond that."

Her hands relaxed in his as her brow settled into less of a scowl. "I suck at this in-the-moment thing, don't I?"

Randy nodded. "You could use some work at it, yeah."

"Okay." Will shook her head, sending dark waves dancing around her shoulders. "No more freaking out. I promise, the woman who shows up at your door tomorrow night will be sane and rational."

"And I will feed her a fettuccine alfredo that will knock her socks off."

"With chocolate torte for dessert?" Will asked.

"I think that can be arranged." Randy grinned.

"Now that's an offer I can't refuse."

Randy brushed a knuckle over her cheek. "Are we okay now?"

Will bobbed her head in the affirmative. "We are. Though I wouldn't blame you for calling this off right now."

Whether she believed him or not, Randy was certain they could overcome her past. Together. All she needed was time to see that she didn't have to handle everything alone. Not anymore.

"Maybe I should let you taste the torte now," he said. "To ensure you come back."

"I *should* probably try it," she said, a teasing light in her eye. "To make sure it's as good as it sounds."

Randy pulled her toward the kitchen. "Prepare for a life-changing experience, Ms. Parsons."

Will laughed as he handed her a spoon. "I bet you say that to all the girls."

"Don't be silly," he said, opening the small plastic container. "I don't share my torte with just anyone. Consider yourself special."

He was rewarded with an attractive blush as they slid their spoons through the layers of chocolate. Will *was* special. And he was determined to make her see it.

~

With May inching over the horizon, warmer winds danced over Anchor as the days grew noticeably longer. Will was a ball of nerves as she showered and dressed for dinner with Randy. After much debate, she slipped on the matching bra and panties long relegated to the back of her underwear drawer.

The lace made her feel pretty, and the extra support for the girls provided a much-needed boost to her confidence. Not that sex with Randy was a definite part of this dinner, but a girl should always be prepared. It wasn't as if there was a question whether they *would* have sex—it was more an issue of when. And if they didn't dive in and do it soon, Will worried her libido might actually suffocate her in her sleep.

Randy wasn't likely to put up a fight or babble once again about waiting and taking things slow. Will had gone without for three damn years. Screw slow.

And now that they were on the same page, understanding they had today but no illusions about tomorrow, she was content to move things along without worrying about guilt or miscommunications.

Since the meal was at Randy's house as opposed to a restaurant, she hadn't expected him to be dressed up, but when he answered the door with wet hair, a half-buttoned shirt hanging over well-worn jeans, and bare feet, Will couldn't help but feel overdressed.

She'd worn silk, for God's sake. And ditched her combat boots for heels.

"Wow," Randy said, staring wide eyed upon opening his front door. "You look incredible."

Will crossed her arms, feeling like an idiot. "I wasn't sure what to wear. Guess I chose wrong."

Randy shook his head. "There is nothing wrong with that." After several more seconds of staring appreciatively, he remembered his manners. "I'm sorry. Come in. Please."

She stepped over the threshold, noticing her high heels made them almost even in height. As he closed the door, a light breeze blew his clean scent her way. The cologne mixed with the damp curls falling over his forehead sent a zing down to her toes.

"I hope I'm not too early," she said, seconds before being spun into his arms with one solid tug. They were suddenly nose-to-nose. "Well, hello."

"Hello to you," he mumbled, lashes lowered over brown eyes staring intently at her lips. "I missed you." Randy followed the breathtakingly honest words with a searing kiss.

Will's brain turned to mush as she held on with all her strength. If he loosened his arms even a fraction, she would land in a heap of silk on the floor.

"Maybe I should wear heels more often," she uttered, once her brain began to function again. "That was some welcome."

"The greeting would have been the same no matter what, but feel free to wear those any time. It's not often I get to look a woman in the eye without having to look down."

"Good to know," Will said as Randy led her through the living room and into the kitchen. The house smelled like an authentic Italian restaurant. "This place smells amazing."

"Tell me about it." After pulling out her stool, he stepped around the island and removed the lid from a skillet. "My mouth has been watering for nearly an hour."

"Then by all means, let's eat." Turning to the dining area behind her, Will said, "I see the table is already set. Should I pour the wine?"

Randy nodded his head to the right. "Chardonnay is on the door."

By the time Randy brought the plates to the table, Will had filled the wine glasses. "The candles are a nice touch," she said, taking the seat he pulled out for her.

"Overkill?" he said, taking his own seat.

Will slid the linen napkin onto her lap. "I'm in silk and heels. I think that makes us even."

"That reminds me." Randy buttoned his shirt the rest of the way. "I ended up at the gym longer than I'd planned. Grabbed a quick shower while the noodles cooked."

Now the wet hair and bare feet made sense. "I feel bad that you had to rush around."

"You shouldn't," he said, lifting his wine glass. "If I'd had any more time, I probably would have put on cheesy music and lowered the lights. Then you'd realize how inept I am at all this."

He hadn't come across as inept so far, but the lack of ego made him more attractive. If that were possible.

They spent the duration of the meal with Randy telling stories about Sid and how she'd tried hard as a little girl to emulate their mother. Will struggled to imagine a tiny version of Sid stumbling around in her mother's high heels, sporting a string of pearls. The image simply did not compute.

As Will finished the last bite of her fettuccine, Randy asked, "Ready for dessert?"

There was no way she could eat another bite. "The torte will have to wait. That was delicious, but filling."

The honest answer was that she was too nervous to eat anything else. Though announcing *I've decided we're going to have sex and it's making me nervous* would drop a giant ball of awkward into the evening.

They cleared the table together, but Will gave up and moved to the other side of the island after bumping into Randy. Twice. This was not a good sign for displaying the slightest level of grace when it came time for the mattress dancing, as Sid called it.

Once the dishwasher was loaded, Randy turned, looking as lost as Will felt. "I feel like a thirteen-year-old about to play his first game of spin the bottle with the hottest girl in school. Tell me I'm not alone here."

Will laughed, relieved by his confession. "I never wanted to kiss the hottest girl in school, but if you flip that scenario to the cutest jock, then yeah, I'm with you."

"How about we sit down on the couch?" Randy rounded the island and led Will to the living room. "You can kick off those shoes, and we'll both stop acting like whatever happens tonight is going to alter the course of the universe."

"I can get behind that." Will dropped to the sofa and slipped her strappy heels off, pushing them under the coffee table so they wouldn't be in the way. "That feels so much better."

"Good." Randy dropped down next to her, draping an arm across the back cushions. "I know you don't like to talk about yourself, but I'm curious what kind of kid you were. I picture a bookworm who kept to herself and loathed any project that forced her to work in a group."

Will pointed at her nose. "Dead on. Looking back, some might say it was a lonely existence." At the time she felt incredibly alone, but keeping her distance from others meant less heartbreak when her mom decided they should move on again. "So long as I had my books and music, I was happy."

"What did you read?"

"Total romance junkie," she said, with no shame whatsoever. She never had understood others' need to hide the covers, as if they would be cursed to hell should anyone know what was inside. "I don't read as much anymore." She'd had to leave her books behind when she fled in the night, and even a small collection was too much to drag around these days.

Randy crossed his ankles on the coffee table as he slouched down into the couch. "You should check out Sid's secret stash."

"You know Sid reads romance novels?" Will asked, remembering that Beth had shared the fact in confidence, since Sid had threatened dire consequences if anyone else found out.

"She's been reading them for years, though I'm sure she thinks I never figured it out."

Will narrowed her eyes. "Not much gets by you, does it?"

"I'm observant, is all." Randy toyed with the hem of her dress, letting his fingers brush the sensitive spot along the side of her knee. "I listen. I pay attention."

Following her instincts, Will toyed with a curl hanging over his ear. "Are you paying attention right now?" If he was, then he could surely sense the erratic beating of her heart.

"I am," he whispered, sliding her dress a little higher. "I hope I'm reading the signals right."

Tension sizzled through her body as the anticipation that had been building for days reached flood-stage levels. "Let me give you a hint. I don't plan on going home for quite some time."

"Good to know," he replied, dragging her onto his lap.

CHAPTER 17

If Will hadn't given him the go-ahead when she did, Randy worried his body might start shutting down. It had been all kinds of hell keeping his hands to himself for days, but then she showed up in that dress, the black accentuating the flawless skin along her shoulders, and the strappy shoes showing off her legs to perfection.

How he hadn't collapsed right there at the door he'd never know.

Her hair was as silky as the material barely covering those incredible legs, and the sounds slipping between her full lips when he ran his tongue down the narrow column of her neck threatened to send him over the edge before they'd even started. He needed to get a grip before he embarrassed himself.

As if lounging across his legs wasn't enough, Will shifted over and laid back on the couch, taking him with her. Thank Buddha his couch was wide enough to hold them both without someone landing on the floor. Then again, in the current circumstances, he didn't mind the need for close personal contact.

"I couldn't stand another night of waiting," Will breathed into his ear.

Randy would have responded but was too busy dropping kisses along her shoulder blade.

Sliding a hand beneath his shirt, Will ran her fingernails up his back, muttering, "We can stop if you think it's too soon."

That got his attention.

"Will," he said, dropping a hand to her thigh and taking a short break from pressing his lips everywhere possible. "Look at me." The nails stopped as eyes the color of a stormy sky met his. "I'm going to make love to you all night long. If that's okay with you."

With a grin that sent his temperature soaring, she nodded. "That is more than okay with me."

And that ended the conversation for several minutes as they tested the stability of the sofa. Will shoved a hand into his hair, pulling him hard against her mouth, then slid the other around to the front of his shirt.

"This needs to come off."

"As you wish," Randy replied, letting her undo the buttons. Even as she concentrated on the task at hand, her hips never stopped driving him crazy, as if they moved of their own volition.

He leaned against the back of the couch so she could reach the last button, then let her pull the shirt off one arm at a time.

"You're so beautiful," she whispered as her fingertips danced lightly over the dark hair along his chest. "I've been dying to touch you since that day I saw you climb off the Jet Ski. Since you laid my hand over your heart."

She laid her palm flat against his skin the same way she had that day.

"You can touch me anytime you want," he said. "I'm all yours."

A look of wonder mixed with desire in her eyes. "You're almost too good to be true." With those powerful words, Will dropped a kiss at the base of his neck, then trailed delicate kisses down his pecs as far as she could reach.

Meeting his eyes again, she said the last thing he expected to hear. "I need to be on top for this."

Happy to accommodate her, Randy twisted as he lifted her from beneath him, planting her firmly along his body once he'd landed on his back. Will looked like a kitten ready to explore her new toy, and he contemplated how much of her playing he could withstand. Not that he wouldn't employ every ounce of patience to let her have her fill, but there was only so much a man in his position could take.

"You're like a dream," he said, pushing her hair out of her face. "I'm afraid I'll wake up and this will all have been my imagination." Black silk gathered high on milky-white thighs as she straddled his hips.

"I'm very real," she said, her hands sliding over his abs and down along his rib cage. Leaning forward until she hovered inches from his mouth, she said, "Let go for me, Randy. Let go."

Her words, or maybe it was her breath along his skin, ignited a level of desire that took them both by surprise. Randy sat up, pulling Will hard against his chest. With a firm hand, he slid the tiny strap of material from her left shoulder, revealing a red slip of strapless lace that lifted her breasts as if they were an offering to the gods.

Denim became the enemy as Will pressed down on his erection. She moaned from deep in her throat before he took her mouth with his. The kiss was searing and sensual and snapped what little control he had left.

In one quick move, Randy was on his feet with Will wrapped around his torso. He licked the sensitive skin along the top of the bra, dipping his tongue low behind the material. Will writhed, dropping her head back as he carried her down the hall to his bedroom. With her arms tight around his neck, she begged in words he was too aroused to comprehend.

"I don't want to let you go," he said, leaning her against the bedpost. "But I want to see the rest of you. I need all of you, gypsy."

With one slender finger beneath his chin, she brought his eyes to hers. "Put my feet on the floor and step away." For a split second he feared she'd changed her mind, but the storm still raged in her eyes, and the smile on her face indicated following orders would be to his benefit.

Once he'd done as ordered, she said, "Maybe you could get out of those jeans while I do this."

Randy didn't know what *this* was going to be, but he knew he didn't want to miss it. His Levis hit the floor in a matter of seconds. The black boxer briefs did little to conceal how hard she had him. Dark blue eyes surveyed his condition and looked very satisfied with what he had to offer.

"Your turn," he said, though his mouth was so dry, the words were barely audible.

With little more than one lift of a brow, Will slid the remaining strap off her right shoulder, then shimmied, sending the whiff of silk into a delicate heap at her ankles. Red lace panties rested several inches below her naval, the sides little more than tiny bits of ribbon. A matched set.

Randy would never look at red lace the same way again.

~

Will tried not to think about how long it had been since she'd been naked in front of a man. The last time she could recall wasn't a pleasant memory, but she would wipe that clean this evening. Tonight would be the beginning of reclaiming herself. Tonight was about her and Randy, and nothing else mattered.

Correction. One other thing mattered.

"I hope you're prepared for this," she said, trying to sound as sultry as possible while asking about condoms.

"As prepared as possible," he said, his eyes roaming her body like a dying man seeing an angel before him.

So much for sultry. "I mean . . . protection?" She didn't want this minor technicality to ruin the mood, but precautions had to be taken. "Please tell me you have some." She might dissolve into a puddle of tears if he didn't have what they needed.

Brown eyes went round. "Oh, right. I've got plenty. Now I need you to come over here before I embarrass myself from looking at you."

Relief tumbled through her as a heat that had dropped to a mild simmer built low in her belly. Joining Randy at the bed, she let him pull her down next to him. The demanding giant that had carried her through the house, which was one of the hottest things a man had ever done for her, had fled, leaving the patient, gentle giant toying with her hair.

"That was a nice little shimmy there," he said, the gruffness of his voice indicating he wasn't as calm as he might appear. "Like a curtain dropping on a beautiful work of art." A warm finger crept along the lacy edge of her bra. "Is this pretty set for my benefit?" he asked, as if inquiring about something that had nothing to do with her being nearly naked on his bed.

"I bought them for me, but thought you might appreciate them, too."

"Oh, I do." He rolled closer, pinning her half under his body. "Let me show you how much I appreciate them."

A shiver trembled through her limbs as his full lips descended to her breast. With one finger, he pressed the left cup down until cool air brushed her nipple. In what seemed like slow motion, he pressed his mouth to the tender bud, suckling until Will's mind went numb, then biting just enough to increase the moisture between her legs.

As if he sensed her reaction, Randy's hand trailed over her ribs, dipped behind the band of her panties, and slid between the folds now wet and ready.

"Oh, God," Will murmured, as her hips rose off the bed.

Ignoring her cry, he shifted to her right breast, pulling the fabric down with his teeth before giving her other nipple the same attention he'd lavished on the first. All the while, his finger was firm and kneading. Then he added another, pressing deeper. Will opened her legs wide as she panted out his name. Every nerve ending in her body was on fire, connected by a live wire to his mouth and fingers.

One finger entered her and suddenly there was no surface beneath her. No walls holding her in. Randy's teeth pinched her now rock-hard nipple as he pressed another finger inside, his knee pressing her legs farther apart.

Before Will could find her bearings again, his hands were on her hips, pushing her higher up the bed. His tongue dipped into her naval, then large hands were sliding the wet red silk down toward her knees. When they cleared her toes, Randy lifted her hips, pressing a kiss into dark curls as she planted her heels on his broad shoulders.

He dropped a kiss lower, where his fingers had worked mere seconds before. Will clutched the sheet, her body jerking with sensations she couldn't even name. With a tight grip on her ass, he sunk deep, his tongue reaching her core, and she panted and begged and whimpered what must have been incoherent gibberish.

Her body was no longer under her own control. She was at Randy's command, responding to every stroke, every nudge, every need he drew from her. Her mind spiraled, her head nodding from side to side. The wave was too strong. Will felt herself going under seconds before a scream filled the air.

Her body clenched, jerked, thrashed, and then settled into a shaking mass atop tussled sheets that felt like a cloud against her skin. Will had never had an orgasm like that. Ever.

There was a ringing in her ears, and her teeth tingled. The world might have spun off its axis, she couldn't be sure.

As the tension seeped away, replaced by a joyful, wilting feeling, she heard the sound of tearing paper. Looking down, she watched Randy slide the condom over his erection. She wasn't sure when his underwear came off, but this first glimpse of what was to come, no pun intended, resulted in an odd and unexpected reaction.

She began to giggle.

～

After giving a woman a mind-blowing orgasm, Randy didn't expect a fit of the giggles.

"I hope this means you're happy with the night so far," he said, sliding his knee between her thighs and dropping wet kisses across her shoulder. His body hovered at the breaking point, but he refused to crawl on top of a woman who was shaking with laughter.

Will coughed, tried to sober, then giggled some more. "I'm sorry," she said through snorts and spurts. "I don't know what's wrong with me. I . . . You're . . ." She seemed to be pointing at a specific part of his body, which was in danger of abandoning the party if she kept up the giggling.

"I'm what?" he asked, not sure he wanted to hear the answer.

"Big," she said, the giggles fading away to be replaced by one of the wickedest smiles he'd ever seen. That brought all parts back to the party.

"Well," he hedged, ignoring the heat crawling up his neck. "I'm a big guy."

Will's smile grew wider. Pushing against his chest, she said, "And I'm a lucky girl." Seconds later, she had him flat on his back, once again straddling his hips, hovering above him like a sexual witch teasing him with what might happen next.

Licking her lips, sapphire eyes locked with his as she slowly lowered onto him, taking him in, inch by inch, until he was sheathed to the hilt inside of her. Palms pressed against his chest, she lifted, moaning as she went, his hips bucking in response.

Placing a finger over his lips, she shook her head, sending waves of black swirling around her shoulders. "My turn," she said, sliding down again.

Randy invoked every ounce of control to give her what she wanted. To let her ride him, setting the pace, rolling her hips in a way that threatened to snap the thin hold he had on his body.

She hadn't said he couldn't touch. Running his hands up her rib cage, he cupped the sides of her breasts, rubbing his thumbs over her nipples. The buds were small and still wet from his earlier attention. The more he rubbed, the quicker Will rode. He dropped a hand to rub the spot he knew would send her over the edge.

Will drove down hard, taking him deeper, driving him closer to his own breaking point. With teeth clenched, she rocked back, driving up then down with sheer determination. Pulling up his knees, Randy lifted into her, dragging a growl from deep inside his chest and sending a surge of raw, throbbing energy tearing through his body.

～

Will toppled onto the bed, curling tight against Randy's side. She'd never felt more sated in her life, but was already thinking about when they could do it again. As his heart beat a mile a minute beneath her ear, Randy tightened his arm around her and dropped a kiss on the top of her head.

"Wow," he said, in a voice that sounded as if he'd witnessed something miraculous.

She didn't know about miracles, but what they'd just done could be measured on the Richter scale.

"That's one way to put it."

"That is the only way to put it." Randy lifted her with one arm to lay atop him. Impressive. "I like you up there."

Will placed a kiss in the middle of his chest. "It isn't the softest surface, but I kind of like it, too." Heat from his body radiated against her skin. With a deep breath, she closed her eyes and relaxed, enjoying the feel of Randy's fingers rubbing the small of her back.

That's when she noticed the sound.

"This isn't a water bed, is it?" she asked.

"If this is your way of saying you felt the Earth move, you're welcome."

Will rolled her eyes. "Don't you hear that running water? Where's that coming from?" Pushing off his chest, she looked around, but the light was fully gone now and Randy's bedroom didn't seem to have many windows.

In fact, she wasn't sure what the room looked like at all.

"That's the boys," Randy said, as if this statement explained everything.

"I'm going to need you to expand on that," she said.

Without another word, Randy scooted out from under her and headed for the wall to their right. Well, his right, her left.

So he didn't sunbathe naked. Good to know.

A click echoed in the silent room, then Will was blinded by a glowing light.

"Willow Parsons, meet the boys."

Blinking through the spots dancing in her vision, she finally made out three small fish swimming around a large tank filled with beautiful bright coral and wide-leafed ferns.

"You have fish?"

"Sure," he said, his usual chipper self. "Come over and meet them."

Will had never shaken hands with a fish before, but saw no reason not to humor the man who'd given her the best sex of her life. "Okay." She looked around for something to cover up with, toying with wrapping the comforter around her.

"The fish aren't really offended by nudity, and I've already seen all of you," Randy said, flashing her a wicked grin. "If you're cold, get over here and I'll keep you warm."

Pushing through her insecurities, Will joined Randy at the fish tank, but she couldn't help but cross her arms. In the throes of passion was one thing. In the blaring light of the tropical tank was another. Her breasts bordered on flat, something she'd always disliked about her body.

Her discomfort must have shown on her face.

"You're beautiful, Will. Every last inch of you." He loosened her arms and pulled her against him. "And I mean to get to all those inches eventually, if not tonight."

She couldn't have stopped the shiver any more than she could stop the sun from coming up in the morning. "Good thing we still have that chocolate torte to replenish our energy levels. Now introduce me to your boys."

Randy dropped a hard kiss on her lips, then turned to the tank. "This one is Harley. She's a Harlequin, and before you ask, no, she doesn't mind being called one of the boys. I think she likes it."

The man had seemed so sane only minutes before.

"This is Dizzy," he said, pointing to a flat round one with big eyes and zebra-print markings, only in a beautiful rusty-red color. "He tends to go in circles a lot. Swims along, then spins in place and shoots off in the other direction." In a whisper, Randy added, "He's not exactly the sharpest tool in the tank, if you know what I mean."

Mixed metaphors now. Was it possible for a person to be screwed stupid?

"And this is Shogun. The alpha of the group."

An alpha fish. Seemed legit.

Shogun was the prettiest of the bunch. "What kind of fish is he?" she asked, trying to be supportive.

"Koi. Swordtail to be exact. They're great company for meditation."

Will had tried meditation once. She'd ended up mentally writing her grocery list, inventorying her sock drawer, and projecting her taxes for the coming year. Her meditation skills needed work.

"How did I miss these guys the other day?"

"We didn't make it into the bedroom, remember?" Lifting back the lid on top of the tank, Randy poured tiny flakes across the top of the water. The boys pounced. "Though," he said, closing the lid again, "if I'd known how good the sex would be, I might have worked harder to get you to stay."

Will wanted to believe she'd have left anyway but had never been much good at lying. At least not to herself.

"Well," she said, sliding her hands down to his quite perfect derriere. "I'm here now. What do you think we should do next?"

His reaction was instant and evident in the nudge she felt against her stomach.

"I did promise to explore the rest of you," he said, his voice deepened by arousal.

"Tell you what," Will said, pulling him with her toward the bed. "If you promise to be a good boy and lie still, I'll explore you first."

"Whatever the lady wants," he said.

CHAPTER 18

Will had slipped on her dress, located her shoes, and shoved the strip of red lace that passed for a bra into her purse before waking Randy. It was past one in the morning, and he'd been asleep for about an hour. She'd dozed off with him, but years of living on alert had made her a light sleeper.

She'd never intended to spend the night. A little sex was one thing. Waking up together was another. As much as she'd like to stay curled against him until dawn, Will knew she had to go.

"Randy," she whispered, nudging the sleeping giant gently on the shoulder.

He didn't move. She nudged a little harder. Still nothing. Running a hand through her hair, she considered letting him sleep and slipping out, but that seemed rude after how they'd spent the evening. The man had given her more orgasms in one night than other men had given her in their entire relationships.

Not that it was all about the orgasms. He'd also held her for at least an hour doing nothing more than talking. Not many men were willing to do that.

Crawling onto the bed, she leaned over his face and poked with more conviction. Before she could say his name again, she found herself pinned beneath him, the light of the fish tank illuminating a wicked smile. Until he realized she was dressed.

"Why are you wearing clothes? If you need something to sleep in, I'll give you a shirt." He nuzzled against her neck. "But I'd rather you wear me instead."

Pushing his forehead up with her index finger, she raised one brow. "That might be the cheesiest line I've ever heard."

Randy nodded once. "It sounded better in my head. So what's with the clothing? Seriously."

"I'm going home," Will said, her voice not nearly as firm as she'd hoped. Sticking to her convictions wasn't easy with him all gloriously naked and pressing a knee between her thighs.

He didn't even have bad breath. How was that possible?

"Now why would you want to do that?" he asked, propping his head on one hand as if they were having a conversation over lunch. "I'm a very early riser. I'll make sure you're up in the morning."

And she knew exactly how he'd wake her. So tempting.

"Spending the night is too much," she said, pushing against him. He rolled to the side so she could get up. "We're helping each other out. A little sex to cure the drought. Waking up together is too much like playing house, and that's not what we're doing."

"I didn't think we were playing at anything." Randy rolled the rest of the way off the bed, opened a drawer of the dresser holding the fish tank, and slipped on a pair of shorts. "Sharing breakfast doesn't lock you into a marriage, Will. It's a meal, not a contract."

"No," she said, slipping on her shoes. "It's breakfast after a night of sleeping together. Besides, this is supposed to be a secret. Someone might see me leaving in the morning."

"Because being on the streets of Anchor at nearly two in the morning isn't suspicious at all."

This might be the first time she'd seen Randy show any hint of a temper. Though he'd been similarly pissed that night at the bar when he'd confronted her about not liking him.

Which made her realize, he wasn't mad. He was hurt.

Pulling the last strap into place, she walked around the bed, approaching him with a smile on her face. Sliding her arms around his rib cage, she looked him in the eye. "I don't regret one thing we did here tonight. And I'm all for repeating them again as soon as possible. But it's important to me that we stick with the program here. The clearer the boundaries, the less chance of anyone getting hurt."

The last thing she wanted to do was hurt this gentle soul. And if she wasn't careful, Will would be dealing with a broken heart of her own when this was over. Plus, there was Sid to worry about. Partly that she'd feel betrayed when she found out what was going on, but also because Will wouldn't put it past Sid to cut her into little pieces and scatter her at sea.

She'd cry while doing it, but Will would still be fish food before she knew what hit her.

Randy pulled her tight. "You're no fun when you're being all pragmatic like this."

With a wink, she answered, "It's always been my fatal flaw."

"Explains why you're so good with numbers."

That and the accounting degree, but no need to argue the details.

"Now that you're up, are you going to walk me to the door?" Not that he had to, but the gesture would be nice.

"Of course I am," he said, pulling her out of the room by one hand. "I'm not passing up the chance to coax a hot goodnight kiss out of you."

Randy was a good coaxer. The clock chimed two before Will finally reached her van, feeling more content than she'd been in a long time. And ignoring the demand from every pore in her body that she return to the house and let her new lover fulfill every promise he'd made in that kiss.

Instead, she drove home as fast as she could.

~

Randy was literally *up* bright and early, thanks to a dream that put Will back in his bed. They'd been enjoying a particular position they hadn't tried last night. He'd have to see if she was up for making that dream a reality. But first things first. This morning, he had an appointment with Sam Edwards.

Whistling as he strolled through the front door of the Anchor Inn, he rang the bell when he reached the front desk. Yvonne popped out from a back room almost immediately.

"Good morning, Mr. Navarro."

"We've been over this, Yvonne. First names." Randy leaned both elbows on the counter, saying with a smile, "You make me feel old when you call me mister."

"Sorry," she said. "Force of habit. Mr. Edwards said to send you in."

Stepping back, he asked, "Does he insist you call him Mr. Edwards?"

Yvonne graced him with a bright smile. "*I* insist on it. Some habits are harder to break than others. Referring to my boss by his first name is downright impossible."

Randy had to admit, he couldn't imagine Sam Edwards being on a first-name basis with his employees either. The man was amicable enough, but he had a formal air about him. As if he were all business all the time. In fact, Randy had never seen him in a real social situation that wasn't a Merchants Society function.

Reaching Sam's office, Randy knocked on the half-open door.

"Come on in," Sam said from inside. As Randy made his way in, the hotelier looked up from an open laptop. "Right on time, as always," he said, standing and extending a hand.

"Lucky for me," Randy said, "there was no traffic."

Sam let out a chuckle. "Another perk of living on this tiny little island."

There had been wild speculation across Anchor regarding Sam's reasons for setting up shop instead of selling off his inherited property. Whatever his reasons, the small size seemed to be a pro instead of a con.

"Yes, indeed," Randy took the chair offered. "Have you heard from *Prime Destinations* since Rebecca King left?"

"I have." The man across the desk unbuttoned his suit coat. "She's already turned in the article so we're good for the June issue. Last I heard, they were still deciding on what images to use, but my understanding is that Jude gave them more than enough shots to work with."

"Jude wasn't the most serious person I've ever met, but he seemed to know what he was doing behind the camera."

"That's good," Sam said. "We need this article to make Anchor look like *the* tourist destination."

"And that leads into why I'm here." Randy crossed an ankle over his knee. "As I'm guessing you know, Joe Dempsey and Beth Chandler are getting married on the deck of Anchor Adventures in a couple weeks."

"That's all anyone seems to be talking about lately," Sam said. "I'm not one to listen to gossip, but this wedding is inescapable."

The Dempseys were an important part of the island, so the talk made sense.

"A few of the out-of-town guests are staying here, aren't they?" Randy asked.

Sam reached for a green folder from the stack to his left. "Dempsey wedding. Five rooms reserved from Wednesday through Monday. Looks like all the details are set."

Randy didn't know if Will would need to confirm the rooms, but he'd fill her in that everything was a go the next time he saw her. Which if he had his way, would be tonight.

"What do you know about destination weddings?" Randy asked, dropping his foot and leaning forward. "Ever managed a hotel that specialized in them?"

"Can't say that I have." Sam dropped the folder back on the pile. "Are we talking Vegas and drive-thru chapels here?"

That was definitely *not* what he was talking about. "I'm not talking about rushed elopements or glitzy, booze-induced nuptials." Sitting forward in his chair, Randy continued. "I'm talking about making Anchor a desired wedding destination. Small, on the water, compact, with all the amenities right here. Almost like a cottage industry for the off-season."

"With all the amenities? As in the cake, food, and flowers?" Sam leaned his elbows on his desk, revealing Randy had piqued his interest. "Maybe have the wedding and honeymoon all in one place?"

"Now you're catching on. My venue would be one option, or maybe a spot on the beach. There's the park, with the draping trees to make it more intimate." Randy rose from the chair to pace the small space. "Nearly every business on the island would benefit. If we got a couple of nice-sized ones, we might even get a bridal magazine to give us some coverage."

Sam remained quiet for several seconds, one finger tapping his chin. "This idea has merit. Though we don't seem like the wedding coordinator types, we could create an office that would handle the details. Put someone with solid organizational skills and knowledge of the island in charge."

Randy hadn't thought of a special office to run the weddings, but he liked it. In fact, it would be the perfect business for Will. The person would be a kind of ambassador for the island, representing all the businesses and making sure the potential couples knew their options.

"It's not something we could implement before the season starts," Randy said. "But we could work out the details over the summer and hit it hard at the end of the season. Get the Merchants Society to pay for ads in a couple magazines."

Sam pulled a notepad from the top drawer on his desk. "The next Merchants meeting is supposed to be the day before the wedding, but I've had some requests to push it back a week. If we do that, then we'll have this wedding fresh in everyone's mind when we pitch the idea."

Something had told Randy that Sam would be the person to see the potential in his idea. Will's belief in Randy's vision for Joe and Beth's wedding had given him enough confidence to set up this meeting. The fact that if this came to fruition Will could have a good reason to stay on Anchor long term was an added bonus.

Not that they were working toward anything permanent. Will was very clear on that point. But that didn't mean he couldn't change her mind. Eventually.

"How about the week after the wedding we meet again, work out exactly how we'll pitch it, and then hit them at the meeting?"

Sam replaced the cap on his pen. "Sounds like a plan to me. And this is giving me ideas for my smaller property. I'm getting close to having the Anchor Inn where I want it, so I'll be changing focus soon. Now I have an idea of what could set the Sunset Harbor Inn apart from every other hotel around."

"Like I said, this could benefit all of us if we do it right." Of that, Randy had no doubt. Coming for a wedding would require more than a weekend stay. The longer the tourists stayed, the more money they pumped into the local economy.

Now he had to convince Will to consider the idea. She was a pro with numbers, had Beth and Joe's wedding planned down to the napkin folds, and knew nearly every business on the island intimately. She was the perfect person for the job.

~

"I'm not staying here forever!" Will yelled, her own voice echoing back from the rafters.

For some insane reason, she'd agreed to be Sid's boat for the day. On Sunday, the little wench wouldn't accept her help. Today she ordered Will to stand in the middle of the garage, arms extended for what felt like an eternity.

"Don't blow a gasket, woman. I'm almost done." Sid extended her measuring tape, only to let it snap shut as she took notes once again. She repeated the process over and over, moving Will forward and back. "A couple from the ends and we're done."

"Explain this to me again," Will said. "How am I a boat?"

"Your height and arm span work perfectly as a stand-in for the smaller boats in the harbor." The tape snapped again. "I want to make sure all the tools that require a cord or that will be attached to the walls will extend far enough for me to work the smaller crafts."

Great. First Rebecca the reporter had pointed out the expanse of Will's hips, and now she was considered comparable to a small water vessel. Nothing like a boost to the old self-esteem.

"My arms are about to fall off," Will said, dropping them to her sides. "When do all these phantom tools arrive?" The garage looked a thousand times better than it had when Sid bought the place, but was still mostly empty.

"Middle of May," Sid answered, without looking up from her clipboard. Biting her bottom lip, she measured between beams on the far wall, then quickly scribbled something down. "I want the layout set and ready to go when the shipment comes in."

Sid was talking faster than normal, fidgeting with the ink pen, and staring at the wall as if it might talk to her. From the looks of things, these tools must be the last step to getting the shop open for business.

"Sid."

"Huh?" she said, measuring the same two beams again.

"Sid!" Will said louder, finally gaining her attention. "The place is going to be great. Stop worrying."

"You really think so?" she asked, dropping the clipboard on the counter and plopping onto the stool beside it. Her gaze took in the garage from top to bottom. "If this doesn't work, I don't know what I'll do." Meeting Will's eyes, she said, "This is the only dream I've ever had besides Lucas. Maybe getting both is asking too much."

Will was always taken off guard by Sid's cute moments. The woman was 99 percent confidence, so when that 1 percent of vulnerability peeked through, it was like watching a baby panda waddle for the first time.

Taking the stool beside Sid's, Will perused the room much as Sid had. "You have a solid reputation in this area, and you have an incredible support group behind you. The business will be great. There are no limits on how many dreams we get to have. Not as long as we're willing to work for them when they come." With a smile, she added, "And you're the hardest working woman I know, second only to myself."

Sid gave Will an elbow that nearly shoved her off the stool. So much for cute.

After a moment of silence, Sid asked, "So what's your dream?"

The question took her by surprise. What *was* her dream? Once upon a time she'd wanted to get married and have a family. Settle into her own home, where she would live for years. No more moving around. She would spend her weekends at the ball field cheering on her kids in soccer or baseball or whatever they chose to pursue.

And she'd come so close to realizing it. Or thought she had. In truth, she'd dodged a bullet, if not the fist. And now she was further from her dream than ever.

"Gee," Sid said, pulling Will from her far-off thoughts. "I didn't mean to make you cry."

She hadn't even realized the tears were falling until Sid pointed them out. "I'm sorry. I have no idea where these came from."

"There's some serious shit in your past, isn't there?" This was as close to a personal question as Sid had ever asked.

"Yeah," she said, letting some honesty creep in. "Serious shit. But that's depressing and I'd rather talk about how awesome this place is going to be. Or the wedding. Anything more cheerful."

"Right. The wedding." Sid sounded disappointed.

"What's that about? You aren't happy about the wedding?"

Sid shrugged. "It's not that I'm not happy; it's that I'm not really a part of it."

"What do you mean?" Will asked. "You're the maid of honor. Outside of being the bride, that's as involved as you can get."

"So I get to hold her flowers and make a toast, which I'm dreading since Lucas says I have to keep it clean, but I'm not helping at all. Shouldn't I be doing more? Patty said that the maid of honor has all these duties and responsibilities, but I'm not doing squat."

It hadn't occurred to Will that Sid would want to do more. She was like the anti-girl. But there was that bit about her reading romance novels. And she did go all goopy when Lucas was around. Maybe there was estrogen in there somewhere. Under the motor oil and f-bombs.

"We still have the wedding shower to work out. I was going to talk to Beth about it, but if you want to take charge, then go for it."

"Really?" Sid said, perking up as if she'd been given free rein over a parts store.

"Why not?" Will tried not to answer that question in her mind. "We were shooting for next Saturday afternoon, with the bachelorette party to follow."

Sid hopped off the stool. "I can handle that. Leave it all to me."

Will was happy to see Sid so enthusiastic, but not looking forward to telling Beth what she'd just done.

CHAPTER 19

Randy spent the entire day smiling. Between the activities of the previous night and his meeting with Sam, everything seemed to be falling into place. He must have looked goofier than usual since no fewer than three people had asked what he was so happy about.

He'd answered each with a wink and a grin, then went about his business. Not that he could keep his focus on anything other than memories of Will's little red panties. Or the way her hair danced across his chest as she rode him. Then there was the way she'd clung to him as they said good-bye at his door.

If she hadn't been so determined to leave, he'd have coaxed her back to bed. But there would be no leaving tonight. He had a plan.

Randy spotted Will the second he stepped through the front door of Dempsey's. It was a stroke of luck that Joe had asked him if he wanted to grab a beer. Otherwise, he'd have had to come up with some other excuse to come see her.

"Hey there," he said, taking up residence on the stool a tourist had vacated. "Good crowd."

"It is," Will said, keeping her eyes on the drink she was making. "Especially for a month before Memorial Day." She finished off the drink with a cherry and disappeared down the bar without another word. Or even making eye contact.

We're keeping things a secret, remember?

Randy really didn't like that part. He knew the reason wasn't because they were doing anything to be ashamed of, but there was only so long she could use Sid as her excuse. There was no doubt Will wouldn't want to hurt Sid in any way, but there was more to this secrecy stuff. If no one knew what they were doing, then it was all in fun. No pressure. No commitment.

Then Randy remembered he'd spent more than ten years avoiding commitment like the clap. So why was he suddenly all gung ho about diving into one?

"You want a tea?" Will asked, snagging his attention.

"Sure."

After removing the cap and flinging it into the garbage, she lowered her voice as she passed over the bottle. "What are you doing here?"

He considered saying *to see you* in order to get a reaction. Instead he said, "I'm here to have a drink with Joe. Is he in here somewhere?"

If she could play their relationship off, then so could he. In fact, he *should* be as adamant about the no commitment thing. Commitment meant more than fun in bed. More than enjoying the other person's company and wanting to see her all the time, if only to catch a smile.

Wait, what?

"He's back in the poolroom, where else would he be?" Will moved on to the next customer before Randy could respond. Maybe that was for the best.

Carrying his bottle high to squeeze through the crowd, Randy found Joe at a cocktail table near the front corner. "This place is crazy," he said, taking a seat. "I guess this is what we've been hoping for, but I hate that they all seem to show up overnight."

Joe stopped with his beer bottle halfway to his lips, then set it back on the table. "What's up with you?"

"Nothing," Randy muttered, watching Phil Mohler, his least favorite Anchorite, sink a seven ball on the other side of the room.

"Bullshit. You don't bitch often, so it's easy to spot." Joe crossed his arms on the table. "Spill."

So much for keeping secrets. Maybe that's what had him all tense. Having to act like he had something to hide. Joe wouldn't tell anyone, not if Randy asked him not to.

"It's Will," he said, ignoring the guilt that came with the admission. He'd promised, but damn it, this crap was messing with his head.

"You two finally stop dancing around each other?" Joe asked, looking less than surprised.

"Dancing around each other?"

"I didn't see it," he said. "Beth had to point it out to me. But once she did, I couldn't believe I'd missed it."

Randy sat up straighter. "Missed what?"

Joe sipped his beer, then said, "The way you two look at each other. Like someone told you to eat your vegetables and you can't help eyeing the fried chicken." Randy raised a brow and Joe added, "Okay, that's not the right way to put it when you're involved, but you know what I mean. I get wanting something you don't think you can have. Not the greatest experience, is it?"

"It's not as if Will is engaged to someone else. I mean, there's no reason we couldn't do something. If we wanted."

That wasn't really telling Joe anything. He hadn't admitted they'd had sex.

"Your innocent face needs work, bro." Joe laughed. "So why are you two still acting like you barely like each other?"

Randy caved. "That's the way Will wants it. Says Sid's got it in her head I need a wife, and if she knows what we're doing, she'll cast Will in the role. That is apparently out of the question, though I'm still not sure why, so we have to keep everyone in the dark to keep Sid in the dark."

"Whoa." Joe sat back. "Did you hear what you just said?"

"I know it's convoluted, but I don't know how else to explain it."

"Man, you said you'd be fine with Will becoming your wife."

"What? I did not." Randy replayed his explanation, catching what Joe referred to. "I only meant that there's no reason we can't make this more permanent . . ." Well, hell.

"How did we get from making googly eyes at each other to till death do us part?" For some reason, Joe was finding this conversation hysterical.

Randy felt nauseated.

"Nobody is taking any vows here. We've only spent one night together."

Joe exhaled and patted Randy on the back. "I fell for Beth long before we had sex. As Patty would say, you're smitten, dude. Good luck with that. Will seems like a tough nut to pin down."

An hour ago, Randy hadn't even wanted to pin her down. Well, maybe in a different context.

"If she even suspects what I'm thinking, this will all be over before it goes anywhere."

Joe snorted. "If you've spent one night together, then it's already gone somewhere."

Randy ignored his friend. "I'll bide my time. Wait until she thinks it's all her idea." That might work. He had time. It wasn't as if either of them were going anywhere. "When she's ready, I'll be there."

"You do that." Joe finished off his beer. "Now I'm going to grab another beer and we can talk about what I wanted to talk about."

"What's that?" Randy asked.

"The bachelor party."

Randy felt the sudden urge to tell Will something. "Let me get the beer. I need to see Will for a second."

Joe shook his head. "You've got it bad, man."

Fighting the crowd once more, Randy reached the end of the bar and waited for Will to notice him. She held up a finger to say she'd be with him in a minute, so he took the opportunity to watch her move. The jeans hugged her slim legs, disappearing into the black boots. Her trademark bangle bracelets slid up and down her arm as gracefully as Will moved behind the bar.

The loose-fitting Dempsey's T-shirt was tucked into a waistband that hovered far below her naval. Randy imagined the ways he could get her out of the outfit.

"You drink the tea already?" she asked, leaning over the bar.

"Joe wants another beer," he said, holding eye contact. "And I want to see you tonight."

"I'm really tired—"

"I'll come to you this time." Randy would never force himself on a woman, and if she gave him a flat-out no, that would be it. But Will didn't look like a woman about to say no.

"I won't be home until after midnight."

He slid the empty bottle her way. "Then I'll see you after midnight."

Will finally flashed him the smile he'd been craving all day. Now he had to make it to midnight without losing his mind.

Randy's truck was nowhere to be seen when Will arrived home around twelve-thirty. She tried not to be disappointed that he hadn't been willing to wait. If he was ever there at all. It wasn't as if they couldn't see each other the next day. Or that she couldn't use a full night of sleep.

But he'd seemed so determined at the bar. Will never doubted for a second she had the final say. Still, the he-man thing was kind of cute. And she'd looked forward to not having to crawl out of his bed and drive home in the middle of the night. Now he wouldn't be crawling out of her bed either. Damn it, she'd been looking forward to seeing him for the last four hours.

First he made her want to see him, which she didn't want to do, then left her hanging.

Men sucked.

"Hello, gorgeous," said a voice from the darkness. Will froze in the driveway, about ten feet from the edge of her small corner porch. "My truck's under the house. Sorry if I scared you."

And her gentle giant was back. But why had he parked under the house?

Stepping onto the worn boards, Will started to ask the question, but before she could speak, Randy pulled her into a long, intoxicating kiss that had her clinging to his shoulders and sucking on his bottom lip. The question drowned in the wave of lust.

"That was worth the wait," Randy mumbled against her neck.

"I'm sorry," Will panted, struggling to steady her breathing. "Have you been here long?"

"I pulled up at midnight in case you got off early."

That was the sweetest thing she'd heard all night. Maybe all year.

Searching for her house key, she said, "We should probably go inside." Where she could reward him properly for being so sweet. "I always forget to leave the light on."

"Here," he said, laying his hand over her trembling ones. "Show me which one it is."

With as much focus as she could manage, Will flipped to the proper key and handed it over. "Thanks."

They'd been together less than thirty seconds and he already had her a quivering mess. Good thing they were keeping this light or she might worry about his effect on her. Her heart was already more engaged than she liked.

Randy unlocked the door, then pushed it open for Will to step through first. Which made sense, since she knew where the light switches were. But it still felt like a chivalrous gesture.

In the seconds before turning on the light, Will tried to remember in what condition she'd left the place. In all the time she'd lived in this little surfer shack, she'd only ever entertained Sid, and that didn't happen by choice. The first time Sid had shown up was an unexpected visit. Since then, she'd dropped by on occasion, always without warning.

Will had gotten used to it, and Sid didn't seem to care about the presence or lack of a mess.

Will flipped the switch and let Randy follow her into the house. Since every surface, including the ceiling, was covered with wood paneling, the place never got all that bright. But it was cozy and came fully furnished and she'd come to think of it as home.

Albeit a temporary one.

Hanging her purse and keys on hooks by the door, Will stepped into the kitchen and opened the fridge. "I have water and juice, but no green tea." Moving a bowl of cold spaghetti, she searched the top shelf. "There's a V8, but I have no idea how old it is."

Will didn't even remember buying a V8. Could that have been there when she moved in? Way to make yourself look like that gross person who never cleans out her fridge.

And why was she nervous and running this internal monologue like a woman who'd never had a man in her house before?

Because you haven't had a man in your house in more than three years.

"Water is fine," Randy said, appearing behind her, making Will jump and slam her head on the freezer door.

"Mother . . ." She cut the word off, grabbing the back of her head with both hands. Now she looked like the idiot who never cleaned out her fridge *and* smacked her head on things. Perfect.

Wrapping an arm around her middle, Randy pulled her clear of the refrigerator and closed the door. "This night isn't going to be nearly as much fun if you knock yourself out before I get you out of that T-shirt."

The wicked grin combined with the concern in his eyes were her undoing. Will pressed her forehead into his shoulder. "Can I ask a really big favor?" she murmured into his shirt.

Randy tensed, but said, "Anything."

She knew he assumed she would ask him to leave. And he would. For her.

Lifting her head, she met his eyes. "Would you give me ten minutes to take a shower? I'd be better at this if I could feel human again."

His shoulders relaxed as he dropped a kiss on the end of her nose. "Take all the time you need. I'm not going anywhere."

～

Thank God she hadn't asked him to leave. Not that he wouldn't have gone if that's what she wanted. But that definitely wasn't what *he* wanted. Waiting for Will to return, Randy leaned back on the tan couch with one foot propped on the large ottoman. He took in the small interior of the cottage.

Wood covered every surface, including the ceiling. He was surprised they hadn't used it for the countertop as well. Not that the place wasn't nice—it was. Dark, but nice. There was one large window along the back wall, which likely offered a killer view of the water. The cottage sat close enough to the sand that he imagined you could wade into the surf in about four steps.

A surfer's dream location.

No personal touches graced the walls or furniture. No hint of the woman who lived among the worn couches and outdated lamps. He'd expected a picture or two. A piece of sentimental bric-a-brac. Based on appearances alone, the place could have been occupied by a weekend vacationer.

How had she lived here for more than a year and not made it her own? Being a renter didn't mean you couldn't put a picture frame on the end table.

"Thanks for letting me do that," Will said, rubbing the bottom of her hair in a towel as she stepped into the room. "I feel so much better." Tossing the towel over the back of a small kitchen chair, she asked, "Did you get yourself something to drink?"

"I'm good," he said, smothering the urge to ask why there was no sign of her anywhere in sight. "I like the outfit." Will wore a thin gray shirt over black yoga pants. "I can get you pants like that with the fitness club logo on them."

"That's nice," she said, dropping down beside him, "but I'm anti-exercise."

Randy sat up. "You're wearing yoga pants. Yoga is exercise."

"Wearing the pants and doing the yoga are two very different things, my friend." Will crossed her ankles on the ottoman. "Ah, that feels good."

As dark lashes rested against pale cheeks and wet black hair scattered about narrow shoulders, all Randy could think about was how beautiful she looked. Not a stitch of makeup, and a tiny hole gaping from the side seam of the shirt. Nails free of paint, both fingers and toes. Not the slightest affectation to enhance the good or camouflage the bad.

On Will, the good needed no enhancement, and the bad didn't exist. She was perfect in his eyes.

"I can feel you staring at me," she said, eyes closed. "I hope you didn't expect me to put on makeup. At this time of night, what you see is what you get."

"I like what I see." Randy kissed her shoulder. "A lot."

She turned his way, granting him a blushing smile. "I'm happy to hear that," she whispered. Topaz eyes turned stormy. "What I'm looking at is pretty nice, too."

Lifting her hand to his mouth, he trailed kisses along her knuckles. "Want to see more?"

Her laughter danced around them. "There's a big bed in that room over there." Will kissed his jawline. "Want to go see it?"

"Lead the way."

She didn't need to take his hand. Randy would have followed her anywhere. But she did, and he did, and they reached the bed without another word being spoken. A lamp on the bedside table cast a dim glow across the ancient-looking quilt. Turning to face him, Will slid her hands up his abs, over his chest, then draped them around his neck. He brushed his knuckles over her cheek and she leaned into the touch.

"Thank you for letting me come over," he said, his voice soft, reverent.

"Thank you for making me feel special." Will stared into his eyes as if willing him to read her thoughts. To understand the silent message in her words.

"You *are* special, gypsy. Don't ever forget that."

A heartbeat later she was pulling him down, rising on tiptoe and kissing him as if their lives depended upon the connection. His hands slid under the shirt, wrapping around her back, soaking in the heat of her skin. Her lips and tongue were setting him on fire, demanding more with every breath.

Hands fisted in his hair, she edged them onto the bed, then grabbed the back of his shirt and struggled to pull it off. Randy broke the kiss long enough to give her what she wanted, then took a bit for himself, tossing her shirt away before taking her mouth again. There was no bra to remove, only tiny, pert breasts pressed against his chest.

When he dropped his hands to her bottom, she arched against him, revealing she was as ready as he was.

"Will," he said against her lips, using all his strength to rein himself in. "We need to slow down."

"No, we don't," she said, reaching for the button on his jeans. "We need to go faster."

Randy rocked back on his heels. "We're not teenagers having to hurry before your parents get home." He took her hands. "Let me do this right."

Planting her hands on his cheeks, she said, "You're doing this right. Last night was better than right. Three years, remember? You're killing me here."

He kissed each palm, then wrapped his arms around her. Spotting a silk sleeping mask hanging on the bedpost above the lamp, Randy got an idea.

"Trust me?" he asked, caressing her back and hips.

Impatient blue eyes narrowed. "I'm half naked with you on my bed. Odd time to ask that, don't you think?"

Leaning in for a kiss, Randy reached past Will, snagging the mask in his right hand. When he pulled back again, Will huffed.

"Are you *trying* to drive me crazy?"

"Not yet," he said. "But I'm about to. Lie down, Willow."

"I—" she started, but he stopped her with a look. Randy kept his hands crossed behind his back. "Fine. I'll lie down. But you're killing the mood here."

Once she was on her back, her body tense with irritation, Randy dangled the mask above her nose. "Put this on."

"What?" Will said, lifting off the pillow.

"Please," he said, the word laced with patience. "Trust me."

"You're not going to try feeding me weird things, are you?"

Randy chuckled. "You've seen too many movies. No food. Nothing but you and me and this mask."

She still hesitated.

"I will never hurt you, Will." Rubbing his thumb across her bottom lip, he held her gaze. "Ever."

Will reached for the mask and slid the band over her head.

CHAPTER 20

As everything went dark, Will's other senses heightened. She could feel the cool air drift across her bare chest. Hear the crickets chirping outside the window. She could even smell the shaving cream Randy must have used before he'd come over. That was nice of him, to spare her the beard burn.

The bed sagged to her right, followed by a weight pressed against her side.

"What are you doing?" she asked, already impatient and anxious. He'd gotten her to put the mask on, which she planned to rip off if this got too weird. The least he could do was move things along.

Randy kissed her shoulder. A chaste kiss, as if she weren't lying here half naked and blindfolded. "I'm looking at you."

She pulled her arms in to cover herself, but Randy stopped her with a gentle touch on her elbow. "You're beautiful, gypsy. Don't cover that up."

She didn't feel beautiful. She felt exposed and vulnerable. But she also felt anticipation and arousal. The fact that he saw her body as beautiful was enough to earn her cooperation.

Will decided to focus on Randy's breathing. To gain a sense of where he was, and what he might do next. Surely he planned to touch her eventually. His breathing was steady, unrushed. When was he going to do something?

And then he did something.

One finger trailed along her collarbone, leaving a trail of fire in its wake. With total certainty, Will knew she was not going to survive this. At least not for long. Then that finger trailed down her side, over the sensitized flesh of her right breast, and along her ribs. She didn't need her sight to know goose bumps were rising along her skin. It was as if she'd become one giant nerve ending.

One finger became two, trailing across her belly and up the other side. The moment his palm brushed her left nipple Will nearly latched onto his neck, but she remained as still as possible. Which was taking a herculean effort. The weight by her side shifted again, lifting away until she felt the bed sag along her other hip. She focused again on Randy's breathing.

Slightly quicker now, and from above instead of by her side. At least she wasn't the only one being affected by this slow torture.

And then the bed moved again and his weight disappeared completely.

"Where are you going?" she asked, using all her willpower not to remove the mask.

"I'm taking off my pants."

Will wasn't sure how to respond to that. "Oh," she said, possibly the lamest response ever. "That's good."

"I thought it was only fair considering what I intend to do next."

Was that a clue? He was taking off his pants because . . .

And she had her answer. A firm hand slid beneath the waistband of Will's yoga pants. He moved with slow deliberation, trailing across her hairline, then sliding toward her hip. Instead of pulling down from both sides, the hand retreated.

Had she called this torture? Was there a word *worse* than torture? Because this was worse. Much worse.

"I don't know how much more of this I can take," she whispered, her voice sounding distant in her own ears thanks to the blood pounding through her head.

"You need to be patient. We've barely started."

Easy for him to say. He wasn't lying here at the mercy of someone else.

He joined her on the bed again, most of his weight low on the mattress. As if—

"Oh, God," she said as he kissed her. There. Over the thin material that suddenly felt like thick wool against her burning skin. Will had never been one to call on any deity during sex, but this was an extreme circumstance.

The next kiss was above the waistband, but not by much. Moist breath teased her skin as his tongue licked the fire threatening to burn her from the inside. Determined to see this through, and certain the patience for which he asked would be justly rewarded, Will grabbed two handfuls of quilt and bit her bottom lip.

Both of his hands were on her now, easing the black pants down. Dropping kisses on every inch of newly revealed skin. He blew on her clit and she clenched the blanket tighter.

Once the pants were gone, Randy kissed the bottom of her foot, then her ankle. Next was the inside of her knee. The inside of her thigh. And again below her naval. Powerful legs straddled one of hers, pressing a knee firmly between her thighs. She couldn't help but press down, fighting the need to take charge and make demands.

Big hands slid up her torso and finally touched her breasts. He gave them gentle attention, then pinched each one just enough to send a bolt of heat to her core. Will whimpered. She could do this, but his time would come. He would see she could give as good as she got.

His mouth took one nipple, suckling and biting in turns, while he kept the other busy with his talented fingers. Will dropped the quilt to touch the man who was driving her crazy. A sheen of perspiration covered his skin, and his movements were quicker, more demanding, as if he were fighting his own struggle to keep things slow.

"I need you, Randy. Please." She would not make demands, but she *was* willing to beg.

In response, he nudged her legs open wider, sliding a hand between her body and his knee. One finger drove in hard and Will half screamed, half growled Randy's name. Wet and ready, she pulled his head up until their lips met in a rush of longing and need. Her hands slid over his slick back, pressing him closer.

He withdrew his hand to rub circles over her clit. Will's hips lifted off the bed as the orgasm scorched her body. Sensations toppled one over the next, her limbs tense, then limp. And as the wave began to crest, Randy entered her in one deep plunge, sending her back into the storm.

He was as lost as she was now. Setting a driving pace that took Will's breath, her ability to think or speak. Raw animal instinct took over, and she held on with all she had, knowing the next wave would take them both. When it did, a guttural moan echoed around the room. Will clung to the man buried inside her, one thought filling her mind.

She never wanted to let go.

~

Randy remained as still as possible as air pumped in and out of his lungs. That was a good sign. At least he was still breathing. There was no bright light coming toward him. Another good sign that he hadn't died. Though he *had* just gone to heaven.

A cheesy thought, but he was too sated to care at the moment.

He opened his eyes to find Will peeking at him from under the mask, a goofy smile on her face. "You alright there, stud?"

Laughter shook his body. "I'm better than alright. How about you?" he asked, giving into the temptation and taking her mouth in a leisurely kiss. He was still inside her and growing hard already. Not a bad recovery time for a guy his age, though he'd never last as long a second time.

Will pulled the mask off and held it above their heads. "I could learn to love this little thing. Is that a frequent party trick of yours?"

She gave him way too much credit. "First time."

Her arms dropped to the bed as her mouth fell open. "You lie."

"Scout's honor. I'd do the salute thing, but I can't move my arms yet."

This time it was her laughter that made him shake. "I'm feeling a bit numb myself. Though I see something else isn't having any trouble lifting." Long nails traced his rib cage, sending him squirming to the side. Will leaned up on one elbow. "Oh my gosh. Tell me you are not ticklish."

"Okay, I won't tell you." Randy hurried off the other side of the bed before she could attack his weakness. "Is the bathroom around here somewhere?" He needed to dispose of the condom he'd managed to slip on after taking off his pants.

"Five feet to your left," Will said, sitting up on the bed. "That's another perk of wearing a mask. Once you take it off, it's as if you have night vision."

Randy did his business with little fuss, then joined Will back in the bedroom. She'd pulled the covers down and crawled beneath the sheet. "Got room in there for one more?"

"I'm not used to sharing, but I'll make an exception for you." She threw the covers back and patted the pillow next to hers. "Come on in."

As he lowered onto the bed, Will laid her head on his chest, drawing invisible circles around one of his nipples. The blanket would look like a pup tent if she kept that up.

He considered asking her about the lack of personal items in the place, but the timing didn't feel right. Truth be told, he didn't feel like talking at all. Randy would be content to hold Will in silence for the rest of the night. Or longer.

"I'm tempted to ask what you're thinking, but I hate when people do that." Will abandoned his nipple to twirl a finger in his chest hair. "But you're so rarely quiet, I can't help but be curious."

Should he tell her he was having long-term thoughts that involved the two of them spending lots of time in this exact position? Something told him the timing wasn't right for that either.

"I'm thinking about how hot it was to realize you didn't bother with panties after your shower."

She threw a leg over his, pressing against his hip. "No sense in wasting a clean pair of underwear when they were going to come right back off."

Sometimes her honesty took his breath away. "Have I told you lately how much I like you?" he asked, before pressing a kiss into her hair.

"No," she said, lifting her head to look into his eyes. "But you've shown me, and that's even better."

"I'll happily show you anytime."

Will leaned up high enough to kiss his chest. "I think it's time for me to do a little showing in return." As she spoke, Will scooted down his body, disappearing under the blanket. When she glanced up from the vicinity of his naval, the smile on her face set his temperature soaring.

"If you really want to," he said, his mouth too dry to say anything more. When she gripped him at the base, his eyes nearly rolled back in his head. When she kissed the tip, he grabbed the cast-iron headboard.

When she took him to the hilt, he saw God.

~

Will expected Randy to leave in the middle of the night, as she had the night before. But when she brought it up, the man had been ready with an answer on every front. He'd parked under the house, so no one passing by would know he was there. And no one would miss him at home, since he'd fed the boys before coming to her house.

Then there'd been the promise of morning sex. A promise he'd diligently kept. Twice.

If the man hadn't possessed an innate ability to make her feel cherished and safe simply by smiling at her, or holding her hand, she might have caved. If she'd been in her right mind, she'd have shoved him out the door. Sleeping together, meaning actually sleeping, and then waking to his charming face only made matters worse.

She could place the blame on that damn mask. Still shocked that she'd even agreed to wear it, Will knew that if it had been any other man, there would have been no deal. Not even a moment's consideration. Putting on that mask required total trust. Will didn't trust anyone. Couldn't afford to. It was as if Randy had slipped beneath all of her defenses when she wasn't looking. Taken her by surprise and done more than offer her some long-overdue sex.

He had her thinking long term. Mentally searching for ideas of how she could stay on Anchor forever. Make the past a nonissue. Defuse the threat that had hounded her for three years.

But there was no use, and she knew it. Jeffrey wasn't going away. He'd get close, and she'd have to run again. It had happened too many times for her to think anything would change. And she had no more power against him now than she ever had. The remote anonymity of Anchor provided better protection, but her luck was bound to run out eventually.

Besides, she was damaged goods. Randy would want a family. That's something she could never give him. He deserved more than Will could ever be, and that meant reinforcing the boundaries on their relationship. Which she would do, as soon as Randy finished his shower.

"I've got it all figured out," Sid yelled as she stormed through Will's front door.

Oh, shit.

Will stood frozen in the kitchen, coffee mug halfway to her lips. "What are you doing here?" she asked, hoping her voice didn't reveal the panic screaming through her brain.

"The shower and bachelorette party thing. I've got it all planned."

"But it hasn't even been twenty-four hours since you agreed to handle it."

And why the hell hadn't she locked that front door last night, Will thought. *Because you were too busy having crazy hot blindfold sex with your best friend's brother, dipshit.*

Sid waved her words away. "I work fast. Or rather, Opal does."

"Opal?" Will asked, trying to determine if the shower was still running.

By all that is holy, please do not let him walk out here.

If Will's concern showed on her face, Sid didn't notice. "We're having the shower up at Lola's place. Everyone gets to make some wedding-related piece of jewelry to take home, and Opal is going to provide the food. Lots of cake and pie, so Beth should have plenty to eat."

Will stepped around the edge of the counter, moving closer to the bedroom door. She was only half listening to Sid. "Sounds good." Nothing but silence came from the bedroom. Maybe Randy would hear his sister's voice and remain in hiding until she left.

"Hey!" Sid said, gaining Will's full attention. "Did you get that shirt from Randy?"

Crap on a cracker. Will had forgotten she was wearing Randy's T-shirt.

"I—" she started, unsure how to answer.

"The least he could do is give you one in the right size. Geez. That thing is floating on you."

Thank the stars Sid could be dense as a day-old doughnut.

"You're right," Will said, setting her mug on the counter and ushering Sid toward the door. "I'll make him give me another one in a smaller size."

"Why are you pushing me?" Sid asked, standing her ground. How could such a tiny woman be so strong? "I haven't even told you about the bachelorette party yet."

"How about you come by Dempsey's tonight? I need to get in the shower." Fishing for some imaginary appointment, Will said, "I'm helping out at the real estate office today. Season's almost here." She threw her hands around her head like a lunatic. "Phones are ringing off the hook."

"Your water pressure is better than I expected," Randy said, walking out of the bedroom with a white towel hanging low on his hips, using another to dry his hair. He had yet to look up and see that they had company.

Will looked from her lover to his sister. From surprised brown eyes to an identical pair reflecting shock and hurt. This wasn't supposed to happen.

"Sid, I can explain," she said, unable to stop the most clichéd and overused phrase in the English language. How was she going to explain why Randy was naked in her house first thing in the morning after she'd adamantly argued that they were no more than friends and never would be anything but friends?

How could she explain that she had lied?

"I'm not an idiot," Sid murmured. "At least not anymore. Sorry I interrupted." Without another glance, she practically ran to the door.

Randy yelled, "Sid!" but she didn't stop.

Ripping the towel out of Randy's hand, Will wrapped it around her waist and ran after her friend, reaching the door as Sid slammed it behind her. Yanking it open, she charged onto the small porch.

"Sid, please wait. You can't leave like this."

"I can do whatever the fuck I want. You sure as hell have." The dark-haired pixie climbed into the jacked-up truck and tried to slam the door, but Will threw her body between it and the cab.

"Damn it, would you listen to me?" Will smacked Sid's hand away when she reached for the handle. "You are so stubborn sometimes."

"*I'm* stubborn?" Sid yelled. "You preached at me that you were not going to get involved with my brother. That you would only ever be friends and nothing more could ever happen. And then you turn around and start fucking him and I'm the one being called stubborn? At least I'm not fucking bipolar."

She deserved that, and Will knew it. She'd turned this entire thing into a giant cluster and hurt the first person who ever made her feel like she belonged on this island. A person she really cared about.

Taking a deep breath, Will met Sid's angry glare. "You're right. And you have every right to be mad and hurt. I'm sorry."

Sid didn't answer, only stared out the windshield. "Get away from my truck, Will. Now."

Honoring the request, Will stepped away from the door, feeling for the first time the jagged rocks that were cutting into her bare feet.

Holding the towel around her waist with one hand, she stepped slowly to the front of the pickup, giving Sid room to leave.

Will didn't move for a full minute after Sid's truck had disappeared into the distance. Staring at the cloud of dust, she wondered how she ever was going to fix this.

CHAPTER 21

By the time Will stepped back into the house, Randy had slipped on his jeans. He couldn't put his shirt on since Will was wearing it. He'd considered going out to settle Sid down, but her truck had been long gone before he'd been decent enough to walk outside.

"You okay?" he asked Will as she dropped onto the ottoman, eyes unfocused.

She shook her head from side to side.

"You want to tell me what I'm missing here?" he asked, squatting down in front of her. "Why is my sister acting as if she caught us burying a body?"

"More like burying our friendship." Meeting his eyes, she added, "Hers and mine. I'd told her in no uncertain terms that you and I would never be anything more than friends. She's so lovesick with Lucas that now she's determined to see you in the same condition. I didn't want her thinking that would happen between us."

Randy took several seconds to process the explanation. If Sid had been pushing her about getting involved with her brother, then it was no wonder Will had been so determined to establish the boundaries going in. But he could also see his sister balking at what she would consider being lied to by her friend.

Taking Will's hand, Randy moved to the couch and maneuvered

her onto his lap. "We have a bit of a mess here, but nothing that can't be straightened out."

Will shook her head again. "She won't forgive me. Not when I was so hateful about the idea of you and me dating or becoming a couple. Think about what we're doing," she said, turning toward him. "How do I say, 'Your brother is having sex with me because I haven't gotten any in three years?' I might as well say, 'I'm using your brother for sex and standing in the way of him finding the woman he deserves.'"

"Let's clear one thing up right away. I'm not having sex with you because you need it. I'm having sex with you because I want to, and that would be true whether you went without it for three years or three weeks."

"But we—"

"Still my turn," Randy said, cutting her off. "I wasn't looking for a wife before we started this, and I'm not going to revert to some wife hunt if you get out of the way. Right now, right this minute, I want to be with you. Clothes on or clothes off. I wasn't gung ho about this secrecy thing, but you made a good argument so I went along. But regardless, what we do is no one else's business, including my sister's. You said you told her we were becoming friends, right?"

"Yes," Will said.

"And we are friends, aren't we?"

"To say the least."

He planted a quick kiss on Will's lips. "Then give me my shirt so I can go talk some sense into my pain-in-the-ass little sister." Before she could get up, Randy took her chin, forcing her to look him in the eye. "One more thing. I never again want to hear that you're not the woman I deserve. Any man would be lucky to have you in his life. Right now, I'm that man, and that makes me the luckiest bastard around. Are we clear on that?"

"If you knew—"

He laid one finger against her lips. "There's nothing that could change my mind, gypsy. Are we clear?"

In her charmingly honest way, Will said, "You scare me when you talk like that. I can't help but want to believe you."

"Good," he said, rising off the couch and taking her with him. "Then we've made more progress than I thought."

$\approx$

Randy tried Lucas's law office first. Since she'd popped into Will's around nine in the morning, he knew Sid hadn't been on a charter with Joe. If she were mad or hurt, she'd go to Lucas first. And he'd been right, except she'd cut out before he got there.

Lucas was a bit confused as to what was going on, and Randy couldn't blame him. This snafu was clearly a product of how the female brain worked, which would make untangling the mess that much more complicated, but Randy was determined to do it. Though she hadn't told Lucas where she was going when she left, both men agreed that Sid would be found sitting on the pier behind her house.

And that's where Randy found her, pouting and telling her side of the story to the seagulls flapping around, waiting for the chance at a quick snack.

"Mind if I sit down?" he asked, stopping beside the woman he'd do anything for.

"Go away," Sid muttered, refusing to look his way.

Randy sat down. "So you're mad at me, too?"

"No," she said. "But I know you're here to defend her, and I don't want to talk about it."

"Good, then listen. Remember that day when I told you I'd seen Lucas's car in your driveway early in the morning? Do you remember what you said to me?"

Sid remained silent.

"I'll take that as a yes. What you and Lucas did that night was none of my business, and other than wanting to make sure you knew what you were doing, I didn't interfere."

"You threatened to kick his ass."

"And I still will if he ever hurts you. That's my prerogative as your big brother."

She finally turned to face him. "Do you know what you're doing, Randy? Do you know that Will has said over and over again that she wants nothing to do with you?"

He kept his voice level. "She told you the two of us were becoming friends, didn't she?"

"*Friends*," Sid emphasized. "Not fuck buddies."

"So that's only okay for you?"

Red crept up Sid's neck and he could almost see the steam coming out of her ears. "That was different and you know it. I'd known Lucas for half my life."

"And you'd loved him for half your life," Randy added. "Which means you had a lot more to lose than I do."

"I didn't lose." Sid crossed her arms, staring out over the water. "She doesn't plan on staying here, Randy. She told me that last year." Slapping her palms on the pier, she threw her head his way. "What do you think of that?"

With a sigh, he gave one concession. "I think that would suck, but she's told me as much herself. Look, there are things that happened to her before she got here. Things that scare her and make her think she needs to keep moving." Watching a gull dive into the water, he said, "I want to convince her she's safe here, but it's going to take time. I'm willing to put in the effort, and I need you to give Will the benefit of the doubt."

Sid pulled her legs up to cross them beneath her. "What happened to her?"

"I don't know exactly, but whatever it was, she's pretty scared. I'm hoping the fact that she's been here so long means she trusts us." If she'd trust him enough to let him help, maybe this *for now* stuff could stretch a little longer. "I know you feel like she lied to you, but that was for your own benefit. Your happiness with Lucas has you love crazy, and you're pushing it on everyone else."

Scratching at the plank beside her foot, Sid said, "I don't see what's wrong with wanting you to be happy. Don't you want a wife and kids? A family? We had so much family back in Miami."

"Is that what this is about?" he asked. "You miss having lots of family around?"

Sid lifted one shoulder. "It's stupid. Forget I said anything."

Lifting her chin, he smiled into familiar brown eyes. "I miss them, too. But you have the Dempseys now. They're going to be your family. And Beth will pop that baby out in the fall. Once you and Lucas throw your hat in the baby ring, we'll have munchkins all over this island."

In a rare moment of softness, Sid said, "I can't imagine myself as a mom. Do you think I could do it?"

"I think you're going to be the greatest mom ever. But right now, I need you to be a less nosy sister. Deal?"

With a roll of her eyes, Sid said, "Deal."

"Good." Randy climbed to his feet. "Will is still at home. Go tell her you're sorry."

"What?" Sid asked, jumping up with him. "Why do I have to apologize?"

"Were you nice when she ran after you this morning?"

Her eyes dropped away. "Maybe not. But I was pissed."

"Now you're not pissed. So go apologize. Will feels like hell." He threw his arm around Sid's shoulder as they walked toward the house. "Let her off the hook."

"Fine." Sid kicked a shell out of her way. "I didn't want to stay mad at her anyway."

"That's my girl," Randy said, adding a quick squeeze for good measure. "I like this softer version of you."

His payback for that comment was a stiff elbow to the ribs.

~

Will put the last of the breakfast dishes away before putting her boots on for work. She hadn't heard from brother or sister since Randy had left that morning. Not that she expected to hear from Sid. Not after she'd been such a bitch about not pairing up with Randy and then getting caught practically in the act of pairing up.

As she tied the last knot in her black boot, a knock sounded at the door. Most likely Randy come back to say Sid hated her and would never talk to her again.

To Will's surprise, Sid stood on the other side of the door. "Can I come in?" she said as Will hovered speechless in the doorway.

Stepping back, she pulled the door open wider and motioned Sid in.

"I know you're heading out, but I need a minute." Sid stopped at the counter and turned. "You shouldn't have lied to me about you and Randy."

"No, I shouldn't have," Will said, finally finding her voice. "But so you know, Randy and I didn't have sex until two nights ago. I didn't lie to you on Tuesday. We hadn't taken that step yet as of that night."

Sid nodded. "Fair enough. And I shouldn't have pushed you so hard about him."

"You want him to be happy." Will closed the door. "There's nothing wrong with that."

"I want you both to be happy. He's my brother and you're my best friend aside from Curly." Sid toyed with a fingernail, then shrugged and crossed her arms. "Would have been cool to have you as a sister, that's all."

Will blinked back the moisture in her eyes. "I don't have any brothers or sisters. That would be kind of nice." Swiping at her cheek, she caught her breath. No sense in dreaming of what could never be. "Whoever Randy ends up with will be lucky to have you as a sister-in-law."

Pinching her lips, Sid stared at the floor for a brief moment before meeting Will's eyes again. "And that absolutely can't be you, huh?"

Wishing it weren't so, Will shook her head no.

"Right." Jerking up the sleeves of her hoodie, Sid closed the distance between them. "Friends, then," she said, offering a conciliatory handshake.

Taking a risk, Will reached out and swept Sid into a hug. "I really am sorry," she said, holding on tight. When Sid squeezed back, Will knew they would be okay.

As the hug ended, Sid stepped back. "You probably need to get to work."

"Yeah," Will said. "But I want to hear about the bachelorette party stuff. Will you stop in and see me later?"

"I can do that."

They walked to the door together, and Will asked, "You're not bringing in a stripper, are you?"

"I thought about it." Sid reached the door first and pulled it open. "But Lucas refused to do it."

Their joined laughter filled the air as they left the house.

~

The weekend had been crazy at Dempsey's. Many tourists seemed to be taking advantage of the unusual spike in temperature to kick the season off early. Though the crowds were more than welcome, and encouraging considering the magazine article had yet to hit newsstands, by Monday night Will was exhausted and ready to sleep for a week.

She'd spent every night of the weekend at Randy's house. He'd stopped in to see her at work Friday night, letting her know he'd be happy to rub her feet (or any other body parts she wanted) when the night was over. Will clearly remembered turning him down, but found herself holding an overnight bag on his front porch at one-thirty that morning.

What happened next was the real shocker. After taking a much-needed shower, she'd curled up with Randy on the couch and promptly fell asleep. When she awoke the next morning, still clothed and feeling like a new woman, Will thought maybe she'd dreamed the part about going to Randy's house. Until she opened her eyes to the sight of three colorful fish swimming in a tank six feet away.

Coffee and breakfast were waiting for her, and after slipping on some yoga pants under her T-shirt, she'd joined Randy on the back porch with mug in hand. Against her own better judgment, Will started the next three mornings the same way, only she'd made sure to save up enough energy to let Randy rub whatever he'd wanted during the nights.

"Are you sure you don't want someone to ride up with you?" Will asked Randy as he dished up her scrambled eggs Tuesday morning. He was due at the tuxedo shop by one for his final fitting.

"You're the only person I'd want to spend the day with, and since you have to work, that means I go alone." He set the empty frying pan in the sink, then moved to grab the whole wheat toast from the toaster. "I'll be up and back in no time."

Will had to admit, she was dying to see the finished product. Actually see Randy in the tux, not busting out of the thing. But she did have to work. And tonight she was meeting Sid and Beth at Opal's for their regular girls' night and to put the final touches on the shower and bachelorette party, both of which would be held on Saturday.

"If you really liked me," she said, "you'd bring me some of those dumplings I had the last time."

Randy slid her plate onto the island. "That can be arranged. What time do you think you ladies will wrap up tonight? I can heat up the dumplings and have them ready when you get here."

Will buttered her toast. "You're going to make someone a fine wife someday, Mr. Navarro."

"Is that a proposal, Ms. Parsons?" Randy asked, keeping his eyes on his toast.

She knew he was joking. He had to be. But a tiny part of her wished they could have this conversation for real. Which is when Will knew she was in deep, deep trouble. It was also the moment she considered saying yes.

"What if it is?" she asked, moving to her second piece of toast. The words caught Randy's attention.

Setting his butter knife down gently on his plate, Randy dropped the toast on top of his scrambled egg substitute and sat up straighter. "I'd say yes. Are we still playing here or are you serious?"

Will wasn't sure. She knew she wanted to be serious. And she believed Randy would say yes. But if they were going to do this, it was time to share her secrets. All of them. He had to know what he was saying yes *to*.

"We need to have another conversation before I answer that. I'd better start at the beginning."

CHAPTER 22

Randy lost interest in his breakfast as his entire body became focused on the woman across from him. Having her with him these past few days had confirmed his feelings. He wanted Will to be the last person he saw at night, and the woman he woke up with every morning. He'd been reasonably sure she was beginning to feel the same way but hadn't figured out how to bring her around to it.

Now she seemed to be coming around all by herself.

"I grew up with my mom, who was what you might call a free spirit. Not in the hippie way, more in the 'girls just want to have fun' kind of way." Will pushed the eggs around her plate as she spoke. "By the time I was seventeen, we'd moved about twenty times. Mom would move somewhere for a man, get tired of him, or he'd disappear, and we'd move again. It took another year before I learned why she didn't like to stay in one place."

"Why was that?" he asked, unable to suppress his curiosity.

"She didn't want to be found. You see, my mom grew up in a very wealthy family. As an impetuous and rebellious eighteen-year-old, she fell in love with the gardener. Or one of them, anyway. That's when she got pregnant with me." Setting the fork next to her plate, Will sat back. "Her parents demanded she get rid of the child and forbade her from ever seeing my father again. That's when they ran off together."

"Mom might have wanted to make her own choices, but she wasn't prepared for poverty. She'd gone from having servants to living in a hovel overnight, but she was stubborn enough to refuse to go home. Before I was born, she left my father and our nomadic life began."

Surely Will didn't think there was something wrong with her because her parents had never married. It took everything Randy had to remain silent as she sipped her coffee.

"Anyway, Mom didn't really have any job skills," Will continued. "So when I was old enough, I started working to support us both. She had what people would call sugar daddies, but they were never dependable. That's why I went to college in the evenings for accounting. I'd been working finance and numbers since I'd learned to count."

Randy blinked. "You're an accountant?"

With a sheepish grin, Will said, "Yeah. That's why I knew what to do with your books. Which were in pretty good shape before I got hold of them. Nice job with that."

"Um . . . Thanks." As much as he was interested in learning about Will's past, nothing she'd said so far explained her fear or her refusal to consider a real future with him. "But why pretend to be a bartender?"

"I'm not pretending. I am a bartender," she said, as if he'd insulted her in some way. "I was tending bar long before I went to college. One of the perks to being tall and not sticking to one place long enough for people to know much about you is that no one knows your real age and most assume you're older than you are. Tips were cash in hand and I didn't want to wait tables, so I learned how to mix drinks."

She must have been an adult from age ten. What teenager took it upon herself to learn how to mix drinks? And what was her mother doing allowing her underage daughter to work in bars?

"After I finished college, things got better. I was making enough money to get us a nicer place, and I'd convinced Mom to stay put for a while." Will was fully into the story, as if it wouldn't have mattered if he were present or not. "At that point, I didn't know her history. I had no idea that she'd kept us moving so her parents wouldn't find us. I guess once I was an adult, she figured there was no more reason to run. Until she got sick."

"Sick?" Randy said.

Will nodded in the affirmative as she stared into her coffee mug. "When I was twenty-five, Mom got diagnosed with liver cancer. It was pretty advanced by the time they caught it, leaving her with little chance of beating the disease." Meeting his eyes for the first time since she'd begun the tale, Will said, "That's when she asked me to take her home. Back to the family she'd left behind when she was pregnant with me."

He took her hand across the island. "Did they welcome her back?"

"They took her in. Paid her medical bills. But they weren't the most affectionate people. Mom was their only daughter, and she'd tainted the bloodline by having a child with my father."

Tainted? Who the hell even thought like that anymore?

"Were they mean to you?"

"What?" Will jerked her head up, as if surprised by the question. "Oh, no. I mean, they didn't lavish me with gifts and show me off to their friends, but we found some common ground over Mom. At the end, shortly before she died, is when I made one nearly fatal mistake."

Randy remembered what she'd said to him once. "When you said hello to the wrong person. You leaned on someone to get through your mother's death."

"Unfortunately." Will's movements became jerky, and she hopped off the stool to pace the kitchen as she spoke, all the while staring at the floor. "His parents were friends with my grandparents, though much younger. They all ran in the same rich-people circles. But I thought he was different. Turned out he wasn't. In fact, he was much worse."

Randy clasped the edge of counter, his knuckles white. "What did he do to you?"

Stopping near the back door, she stared out across the surf. "A couple months after Mom died," she said, her voice cracking with emotion, "he asked me to marry him. I said it was too soon, but he wouldn't take no for an answer. When I told him we needed to take a break, that I needed time to grieve, he put me in the hospital."

Randy's teeth nearly cracked under the pressure in his jaw. He had never wanted to commit a violent act the way he did in that moment. If the man who'd laid his hands on Will were in the room, he would have died an ugly and painful death.

Breathing through his nose to control the rage, Randy kept his voice as level as possible as he asked, "Where is he now?"

Will turned to him, narrowing her eyes as if trying to read his thoughts. "Probably where I left him. As soon as I was able, I left the hospital without telling anyone, and I've been running ever since."

"Why didn't you tell the police? Have him arrested?"

"When I say these people are wealthy, I mean old money, lots of influence kind of wealthy." Looking as if she'd set down something heavy, Will moved back to her stool. "He warned me that if I told anyone, he'd make sure I never talked again. To anyone. Yet he was sick enough to still want me. Even though he'd taken away my ability to have children."

Randy froze. "He did what?"

"I didn't know it until the doctor told me, but I'd been six weeks pregnant when he beat me. The blows and kicks to the stomach were likely the cause of the hemorrhaging. They had to take it all."

The words were spoken as if she were discussing a car totaled in an accident. As if a man had not kicked and beaten her until she'd nearly died, killing her unborn baby in the process.

"He's still looking for you, isn't he?"

Will's brows went up with her shoulders. "I can't know for sure, but I don't doubt it. That's why I couldn't have my face in the magazine. Why I was afraid someone had recognized me in Nags Head that day."

"And why Rebecca King was sure she'd seen your face before."

With a nod, she replied, "I was a missing person on the news back when I first left. She could have seen me there, or she could know someone who looks like me. There's no way to be sure."

Charging around the counter, Randy cupped Will's face in his hands. "He's never going to hurt you again. Do you hear me? Never."

She placed her hands over his, a sad smile settling across her lips. "There's no way to know that for sure. This man has enough money and power to do anything he wants. I've been safe here, on Anchor, but that could change in an instant. Do you see why I can't give you anything more than today?"

"He might have been able to get to you when you were alone," Randy said, dropping his hands to her shoulders. "You're not alone anymore. You don't have to run ever again."

Will gazed into his eyes, tilting her head to the side. "You're such a good man. You deserve a woman who isn't dragging around baggage like this. A woman who can give you a family, trust, and love whole-heartedly." Kissing the back of his hand, she sighed. "I wish that woman could be me."

What was she talking about? Didn't she understand she was that woman? Maybe she couldn't have babies, but they could still be a family.

"There are other ways we could create a family, Will. But why did you decide to tell me this now?" he asked, certain her true feelings for him had been the reason.

"It's all this playing-house stuff, I guess," she said, pushing the plate of cold eggs to the center of the island. "Wanting things to be different. Wanting the past to disappear so there might be a future for us." Leaning her chin on her hand, she said, "Wishful thinking."

"Nothing you've told me changes how I feel about you." Randy watched her bottom lip quiver and realized she'd told her whole gruesome story without shedding a tear. His gypsy was stronger than she realized. "I'm thirty-five years old. I could be dead in five years or I could live to be a hundred," he said. "Does that change how you feel about me?"

"Of course not," she argued. "And you are not going to be dead in five years. Don't talk like that."

"Don't you see? Life doesn't come with guarantees. All we have for sure is today. Why don't we spend whatever todays we have left together?"

Was that a proposal? After what she'd just told him? The man was out of his mind, and heaven help her, she was feeling a bit insane herself.

"Is this one of those living in the moment things?" she asked, dabbing at what were quickly becoming happy tears. "You know I'm not good at those."

"No ring," he said. "We live each day as it comes and if someday we want to do the ring thing, then we'll do it. Whether that's in two years or twenty years doesn't matter."

Will thought of all the reasons to say no. The biggest being that if Jeffrey learned of her whereabouts, and that she'd become involved with another man, more than her life would be on the line. But maybe he would never know. He hadn't found her yet. And the reporter had disappeared without another peep.

"I can't believe I'm saying this, but yes. I'd like to spend my todays with you." Will let the laughter bubble over, feeling real, true happiness for what might have been the first time in her life. "I think we've both lost our minds."

"We're crazy in love, that's all." As if the words were as much a surprise to him as to her, Randy stopped and stared wide eyed into hers. "Whoa. I said the L word, didn't I?"

Will nodded, the smile on her lips making her cheeks hurt. "You sure did."

"Too soon?" he asked, brown eyes twinkling.

"Perfect timing." She laid a hand along his cheek. Glancing to the clock over the stove, Will did some quick math. "We each have to leave in less than an hour, and neither of us has taken a shower. I think this means we should take one together."

Sweeping her off the stool, Randy carried Will toward the bathroom. "Today is getting better already!"

～

Randy wouldn't have been surprised to learn that the tires of his truck never touched the pavement all the way to Nags Head and back. His determination to win Will over had paid off, and sooner than he'd expected. The move felt sudden, but at the same time as if he'd been waiting a lifetime for this day to come.

For a guy who made a hobby out of taking risks with his life, Randy had never been as daring with his heart. Until Willow Parsons came along. He hadn't imagined wanting to protect her would lead to the life he never thought he'd have, but then again, miracles happened all the time.

Kind of nice to have one happen to him.

With his perfectly fitting tux hanging safely in his closet, Randy strode through the door of Lucas Dempsey's law firm whistling a classic Bob Marley tune. "Hey there, Gladys," Randy said, smiling at the brunette behind the reception desk.

The older woman returned the smile with bright blue eyes. "Howdy, Randy. Are you here to see Mr. Dempsey? I was about to call it a day, but I'm sure the counselor will be here for a while."

"Don't let me hold you up." Randy stepped toward Lucas's office door. "I'm sure Frank is waiting to see you."

Gladys tossed a lock of mousy-brown hair over her shoulder. "That old coot won't be seeing much more of me if he doesn't fix that fence between our houses like I told him to."

Gladys and Frank had been together for as long as Randy could remember, even though they'd divorced years ago. They lived in neighboring houses and during the peaceful times, Frank's truck was usually in Gladys's driveway. When the war resumed, as it always did, the truck stayed in the mister's driveway while the mister did anything and everything to make Gladys talk to him.

They were a cute couple, in an insane, masochistic kind of way.

"You have a good night then," Randy said, avoiding eye contact so as not to encourage a rant about all the ways Frank was no good. As Gladys headed for the exit, Randy knocked on the office door.

"Come in," replied a voice from the other side. Upon seeing Randy enter, Lucas leapt from his chair. "Is Sid okay? Where is she?"

Was popping in to see his future brother-in-law so unusual that it would take a tragedy to make it happen?

"Sit your ass down. Sid is fine." Closing the door behind him,

Randy faced the man behind the desk with arms crossed, wearing his sternest personal trainer expression. "Can't I come to see you without the dramatics?"

In all honesty, Randy liked Lucas well enough. The lawyer doted on Sid, which made him a smart man, as well as indicated he had excellent taste and an abundance of patience. But keeping him a little afraid of her big brother seemed like an extra layer of protection for Sid's heart.

Lucas remained standing. "Randy, you've only come to see me once, and that was to tell me you'd twist me into a pretzel, tie chum around my neck, and drop me as far off the coast as possible if I ever hurt your sister." Motioning for Randy to take a seat, Lucas returned to his chair. "A threat your sister swears is empty, but we both know better, don't we?"

"Sounds like we do." Randy accepted the offer to sit and got right to the point. "I need to talk to you about a legal issue."

With raised brows, Lucas stared hard across the desk. "Are you asking for legal advice?"

That was one way to put it. "Yes."

"Do you want this conversation to stay in this office?"

"Definitely."

"Then you need to hire me." Lucas pulled a large leather-clad book from his desk drawer.

Randy bit his cheek and reminded himself his sister loved this man. "Extorting money from your future brother-in-law? That's pretty shitty, don't you think?"

To Randy's surprise, Lucas rolled his eyes. "Now who's being dramatic? Give me ten dollars as a retainer. I'll buy you some of those nasty teas you drink this weekend."

Once he'd pulled the money from his wallet and tossed it over the desk, Randy said, "This has to do with Will, but you can't let her know I talked to you. At least not yet."

"I'm intrigued," Lucas said, pocketing the ten. "But whether I can keep it from her will depend on what you're about to tell me."

Sharing Will's secrets without a guarantee the deed wouldn't get back to her was a risk, but Randy was used to those. "There's a man in Will's past. A man who hurt her. Bad." His jaw flexed as he pictured Will's face as she'd told him the story. "She believes he's looking for her and, if he finds her, will hurt her again."

Lucas grew serious, sitting forward in his chair, "This sounds like a case for the police, not a lawyer. Did she press charges?"

"She says he's rich and powerful, and no one would believe her if she told. The bastard put her in the hospital, then had the balls to threaten her not to rat him out." Randy didn't see the need to share the part about Will no longer being able to have children. "She took off from the hospital and has been running ever since."

A silence fell over the room, broken only by Lucas tapping a pen on the desktop. "Then who is she?"

"What?"

"If she's on the run," Lucas said, "then she's not using her real name. Unless she's an idiot, and Will is in no way an idiot."

Randy hadn't even thought of that. It wasn't as if he dealt with people trying to stay invisible on a regular basis. Now it was all starting to seem like something out of a movie.

"I have no idea. She didn't say anything about her name." So he'd agreed to spend the rest of his todays with a woman whose name he didn't even know? "I was so stunned by what she'd told me, I didn't think to ask."

The pen stopped tapping. "Then you don't know who the asshole is either, do you?"

Shaking his head, Randy answered, "I did ask where he is, but she evaded the question. I think she knew I'd go find him."

"You'll have backup if that ever happens." Lucas turned to a clean page in the yellow legal pad on his desk. "What else do we know?"

Randy replayed the conversation in his mind. "That's it. He hurt her. He's looking for her. And she's afraid of him."

Lucas set the pen down slowly, then rubbed his temples. "What exactly did you want me to tell you here? We don't know where he is. We don't know who he is. Hell, we don't even know who Willow is. Was this supposed to be a 'What if?' conversation?"

"We need to protect her," Randy said, bolting from the chair. "There has to be some legal way to get him out of her life. To make sure he can't hurt her again."

"I can't eliminate a threat if I don't know what it is." Lucas kept his voice calm, almost soothing. "Are you sure there isn't anything else? Something we could use against him, if we ever get his identity? Something besides threats that only she can verify?"

The baby.

"There might be something."

Randy debated what to do. If he told, it would be breaking the ultimate confidence. But Lucas could help them. As much as Randy would rather break the son of a bitch in half, getting his ass thrown in jail wouldn't help anything.

"Give me something I can use, or we're wasting our time."

Dropping back into the chair, Randy tapped a nervous rhythm on his knee. She'd said there was a doctor. Surely he or she could back her up. Deciding he had no other choice, Randy told Lucas the rest of the story.

CHAPTER 23

"Spill," Beth said, popping up beside Will's chair and scaring the bejeezus out of her.

"What the heck is wrong with you?" Will held a hand over her heart. "I nearly peed myself."

Beth set her pie on the table and slid into the chair across from Will. "I'm going to be a barge soon. I'm taking advantage of still being able to sneak up on people." She buried her fork deep in the cherry filling. "From what I hear, you've been aflutter all day. Patty said every time she saw you, you were humming a happy tune. I'm sure this has to do with Randy, so I'm giving you the chance to fess up before Sid gets here."

Trying unsuccessfully to wipe the smirk off her face, Will cut her rhubarb pie into pieces. "You know she called me bipolar last week? I think she might have been right."

Freezing with the fork in midair, Beth looked skeptical. "Are you saying a mental disorder and not regular sex with Randy Navarro is what has you looking so happy?"

"I didn't say that." She pondered a car passing outside. "Maybe the regular sex is making me bipolar? Regardless, it's making me more limber."

"You finally putting those yoga pants to work?" Sid asked, taking the chair next to Beth with a cupcake in her hand. "It should be illegal to stay so damn thin without doing a lick of exercise."

"She's exercising," Beth said. "But it's not yoga." Shoving a large bite in her mouth, the mom-to-be tried looking innocent but failed miserably.

Sid stopped removing the paper from around her dessert. "You're talking about sex with Randy, aren't you? Please spare me the details. I'm happy y'all are both getting some, but there are things I don't want or need to know about my brother."

"After all the PDA we've had to endure from you and Lucas, it's only fair we get to torture you back. But it's not the sex that has me happy. At least not today."

She'd made the conscious decision that morning to leave the past where it belonged. It had been well over a year since Will arrived on Anchor, and Jeffrey had yet to find her. He'd most likely given up or, God forbid, found another woman to obsess over. That was the awful part, knowing he could do to another what he'd done to her. But then maybe another woman wouldn't be the easy target that Will had been.

Both women stopped eating and stared expectantly. "Come on," Beth urged. "Tell us."

"I'm not sure how to explain it." It wasn't as if they'd decided to get married. That would be crazy after such a short romance. But they'd sort of agreed that someday they might consider getting married. Of course, she'd have to tell him her real name by then.

"You're killing me, woman," Sid said. "Did you win the lottery or something? What?"

On a steadying breath, Will said quickly, "Randy and I have agreed to be a couple."

No excitement came from the other side of the table. Instead, the women looked at each other, perplexed. Finally, Beth said, "I thought you already *were* a couple."

"No. We were having sex."

Beth snorted, then covered her mouth. Sid was less successful at holding in the laughter.

Will didn't understand what was so funny. Then she thought about what she'd said and started laughing with them. As they each caught their breath, she said, "Let me try this again. Randy and I were kind of having a fling. Sex only. I was serious about not committing to anything."

"So what changed your mind?" Beth asked, wiping her eyes. "I'm assuming you're committed now."

"She should be," Sid said. "Wasn't it last week we had this serious talk about why you couldn't settle down and be in a real relationship? How there were *complications* none of us knew about? What happened to those?"

That was the tougher question. Technically, those complications still existed, only now Will refused to let them rule her life.

"Let's say I'm working around them."

Licking cherry filling off her finger, Beth said, "So this is real? You and Randy are the real thing?"

Will smiled, feeling a pleasant heat travel up her cheeks. "Yeah. We're the real thing."

After several seconds of silence, Sid raised a large chunk of chocolate cupcake into the air as if making a toast. "It's about fucking time."

∼

Rebecca King had done her homework. She'd even triple-checked her sources. Maybe right now no one knew where Maria Van Clement might be. But everyone would know Sunday morning when her whereabouts would be headline news, with Rebecca's name in the byline.

Rebecca gave herself a mental pat on the back. No more shitty travel jobs. No more twenty-four-hour flights in coach. No more being ignored and invisible in the world of journalism.

But this story would do more than get her credit as a true reporter. No, this story would get Rebecca's face on television. That's where she belonged. In the spotlight. On camera. Not buried on some remote island making dorky pirate crap sound like fun for the whole family.

Will Parsons would likely be on TV as well. Quaint that she'd been using her father's last name. The Van Clements wouldn't like that part. It was obvious from the research that their golden child sinking to reproduce with the gardener had been a blow to family pride.

Their old money wouldn't be able to protect them when this story hit the stands. Though Rebecca was curious if Maria knew she was the last remaining heir. The bartender was a very wealthy woman. Seemed a waste to hide out on that dinky island when she could likely buy the whole damn thing.

"What are you up to, Rebecca?" asked Jude as he stormed up to her cubicle.

She spun in her chair, smile firmly in place. "Since when do you wander freely around the *Globe* offices, Jude? And shouldn't you be on some assignment in Timbuktu or something?"

"Don't piss with me. You swiped the disk of pictures from that Anchor assignment," Jude said. "What do you want with those images?"

The man was such an idiot, he didn't even know what he had on that tiny disk. Flicking the edge of her nail, she went for ignorance. "I don't know what you're talking about. I have no use for pictures of water, sand, and useless souvenir shops." Which was technically true. "You'll have to look elsewhere for your disk thief."

With a huff, the annoying Brit crossed his arms. "What do they have you doing here anyway? Writing up the obits? Checking for spelling errors in the articles written by real reporters?"

The man was such a shit. "This conversation is over," she said, smacking the spacebar on her keyboard to bring the screen to life. "I have work to do."

"I bet you do." Jude leaned his elbows on the edge of the cube. "If I see a single one of those pictures show up anywhere they're not supposed to be, I'm coming for you. Remember that, my darling Becks."

He stared at her for several seconds, as if he might intimidate her into tears, before walking away. Rebecca didn't realize she'd been holding her breath until the wind rushed out of her. Let him come after her. By the time Jude saw that picture, she'd have done what she set out to do.

~

Lola's Island Arts & Crafts looked as if a party store had been thoroughly raided. Dark blue and white crepe paper were braided together and draped along every shelf. Some had even been stuffed inside vases, making it look as if the ceramics had eaten it, then thrown it back up.

Not exactly gaudy, but close.

A large sign wishing Beth and Joe the best of luck hung across the wall behind the front counter, with a large chunk missing from the corner.

"What happened to the sign?" Will asked Lola, who had greeted her at the door with a punch-filled paper cup.

"The only one Sid could find was for a graduate, so she cut the picture of the cap off." Pointing to the other corner, she added, "The diploma is supposed to be the marriage certificate. No one has had the heart or guts to tell Sid it's not fooling anyone."

"Speaking of the little party planner." Will searched the room for the dark-haired pixie. "Where is she?"

"Helping Opal load up the dessert trays in the back room. From what I've seen, there's enough food to feed the entire island." Lola held up her own cup of punch. "Not that I'm complaining." The older woman led the way farther into the store. "Beth is back by the jewelry section. Come on."

Will was surprised to see tourists milling about in other areas. "You're still open to the public?"

Lola motioned for Will to pass through a walkway too narrow for the both of them. "I didn't want to lose the Saturday business, but Sid was so excited about this party, I couldn't turn her away either. Beth said the more the merrier, so we're open for business *and* a party."

"Alrighty then."

The party wasn't due to start for another fifteen minutes, but Beth was already surrounded. Opal's granddaughter Kinzie, Lola's soon-to-be stepdaughter Yvonne, Patty, Daisy, and Georgette sat in a circle around the bride, each holding a white paper cup full of punch.

The presence of Georgette and Daisy meant Annie was holding down the fort at Dempsey's for the afternoon. When she'd made the schedule, Will told the women to decide who would cover and who would enjoy the shower. Looked like Annie had drawn the short straw.

"Where's the table for presents?" Will asked, joining the group.

Beth jumped up and gave her a hug as Kinzie took the silver bag Will was carrying. "I told you not to buy me anything. Taking care of all the wedding details has been present enough."

Will leaned back from the hug. "Let's say this present is more for Joe and leave it at that." Randy had helped her pick out the gift online, and they'd ordered a little something for their own fun as well. Though they had to pay a hefty price for the overnight shipping.

Rubbing her stomach, Beth grinned. "If it's lingerie, that's how I got into this condition in the first place. Though the wine is probably more to blame."

"Alcohol has a reputation for that sort of thing." Taking in their surroundings, Will said, "Is there a scrap of crepe paper left on the Eastern Seaboard?"

"It is overkill, isn't it? I think this is Sid's idea of girly. It's a foreign concept to her, you know, but I appreciate her willingness to try." Beth glowed as she sipped her punch. Though she wasn't the type to crave the spotlight, Will knew the bride was enjoying the attention more than she'd admit. "How did you get her to do all this, anyway?" Beth asked. "I'm guessing you had to pay her."

"Nope," Will said. "Sid was feeling left out, so I suggested she handle the shower and bachelorette party. Aren't those traditionally the responsibility of the maid of honor?"

"I suppose, but I didn't think she'd want anything to do with this stuff."

"Maybe being with Lucas is raising her estrogen levels."

Beth laughed. "Maybe so."

"The sugar is served," Sid declared, setting a tower of cupcakes on a long table at the end of the bead display. Opal appeared next, carrying a platter covered with slices of pie and cake. "Dig in, everyone."

Sid edged Will's way, then pulled her away from the crowd. "What do you think?"

Will could see the worry and doubt in Sid's eyes. "It's perfect," she said. "Better than anything I would have come up with."

"You're full of shit," Sid said, "but I'm going to pretend you mean it." Her eyes followed Beth as she sized up the desserts. "I wanted to make it nice. Curly deserves something special."

"There's a lot of special going on around here." Will waited until Sid turned her way. "It's great, and I mean it."

Shuffling her feet, Sid crossed her arms. "Then maybe you could return the favor some time."

Will wasn't sure what that meant. "You want me to throw you a party?"

"You said this stuff was what the maid of honor was supposed to do. So what do you say?" she asked. "Want to be my maid of honor when my turn comes around?"

Pride swelled in Will's chest. "Try and stop me."

Nodding as if they'd agreed to have coffee together, Sid said, "Cool. But do me a favor."

"I thought being your maid of honor and throwing you parties was the favor."

"Alright then, one more favor."

"What's that?"

"Don't let Opal talk you into playing these stupid shower games we'll be doing today." Sid turned away from the crowd and dropped her voice. "I tried to tell her no, but the woman is a master at getting her way. I think she puts something in that chocolate buttercream that makes people loopy."

With a straight face, Will said, "No games. Got it."

A week ago she'd been convinced staying on Anchor, or anywhere, would be impossible. But this island had become her home, and these people her family. After a lifetime of feeling like an outcast, it felt good to finally belong somewhere.

Watching Sid wander over to Beth, and then seeing Beth throw her arms around the mechanic, who looked as comfortable as a frog in a tutu, Will felt something heal inside her chest. This is what she'd always dreamed of having. Sid had been right.

It *was* about damn time.

CHAPTER 24

Randy wasn't sure he could take any more male bonding. After spending the day on Joe's boat fishing with the three Dempsey men, they were now building a bonfire on the beach, waiting for the women to join them.

The fishing trip had been to keep the men occupied while the women had the wedding shower. As the sun faded in the horizon, they'd rolled into what was supposed to be the bachelor party. Sitting on Tom and Patty's porch, Lucas and Joe had enjoyed a couple of beers and some brotherly trash talking, while Tom and Randy had stuck with the non-alcoholic beverages and discussed the symptoms and signs of heart disease.

Not exactly the most exciting bachelor party he'd ever attended. Truth be told, they were all killing time until the women joined them, though none of them would admit to it. At the beach, Manny, who worked for Randy at Anchor Adventures, Marcus, Lola's newly found former sweetheart, and Chuck Brighteyes, a friend of Joe's, had joined them.

The reinforcements proved fruitful once the bachelorette contingent arrived, most of them having imbibed enough alcohol to increase their volume to a substantial level.

"You call that a fire?" Sid yelled, charging over a dune with her arm around Opal's granddaughter Kinzie. "I can barely see it from back here!"

Lucas leaned toward Randy. "Is she drunk?"

"Yes, she is," he said. "And she's all yours."

With heavy steps, Lucas crossed the sand to reach Sid.

"Heya, hot stuff," Sid said in greeting, throwing her arms around Lucas's neck, smacking him in the back of the head with the beer bottle in her hand. "Where've you been all my life?"

Randy doubted Sid would remember any of this in the morning. Good thing he was sober and could remind her of it in full detail.

"We tried to slow her down," Will said, sliding up beside him. "But she informed us she was drinking for two."

He looked Will's way. "What does that mean?"

Will pointed to Beth. "Said she had to drink Beth's share for it to be a real bachelorette party, but I think she drank enough for all of us."

As Lucas helped Sid wobble over to the fire, Kinzie was left staggering on her own. Her arms were out to her sides as if she were balancing on a high wire when Manny stepped in where Sid had been seconds before. A crooked smile covered Kinzie's face as she stared up into Manny's dark features.

"You're so pretty," she said, looking very happy to see him.

"So are you, *querida*." Manny caught Kinzie as she stumbled. "Maybe we should go sit by the fire."

Kinzie nodded, holding on tight to his arm. "Yes, I'd like to sit down."

Kinzie wasn't usually the party girl type. "Is that Sid's influence?" Randy asked Will.

"I think Kinzie was having a good time and lost track of how many she had." Will wrapped an arm around his waist and cuddled into his side. "How was your day? Any good blackmailing stories us womenfolk shouldn't know about?"

Randy pulled her tight. "I spent the entire day waiting for this. It was the longest day of my life." Smiling into her blue eyes, he brushed a lock of hair out of her face. "You're so pretty."

Chuckling, she replied. "Where have you been all my life?"

"Like I said, waiting for this."

He took her mouth and it wasn't long before they were both out of breath.

"Get a room!" came from the other side of the bonfire. Randy looked over to see Lucas cover Sid's mouth, waving an apology. The man really did have the patience of a saint to put up with Sid in all her glory.

"That's not a bad suggestion," he whispered in Will's ear.

She laid her head on his shoulder. "We just got here. I've been looking forward to roasted marshmallows all day."

Randy took a deep breath. If his girl wanted roasted marshmallows, she would have them. "We can do that. Let's hope Sid doesn't breathe too close to the fire and send us all up in smoke."

≈

Will had barely unlocked the front door of Dempsey's on Sunday morning when Sid showed up holding her head as if trying to keep it from falling off. She sat down gingerly at the bar. "Water," she said, her voice sounding as if she'd gargled a handful of sand.

"What's the matter, Sid? Not feeling so well this morning?"

With eyes closed, Sid warned, "I may not be able to kick your ass right this second, but once this marching band quits stomping through my brain, I will come back for you."

Will tsked. "We tried to stop you, but you were determined to drink your weight in liquor. You did it to yourself, woman."

Georgette picked that moment to slap her tray on the bar next to Sid. "Heard you had a good time last night," she said, standing too close to be poking the angry bear, in Will's estimation. "The head a little sensitive?"

With lightning speed, Sid turned and gathered a fistful of Georgette's shirt. "I will pee on everything that you love. Don't think that I won't."

Leaning across the bar, Will disengaged Sid from the waitress's shirt. "Why don't we all take a little break," she suggested, keeping her voice as low and soothing as possible. "Georgette, you might want to check on the customers who just took a booth in the corner." With more force, she added, "And avoid this area of the bar for the foreseeable future."

"I was only joking around." Georgette straightened her shirt as she stepped out of Sid's reach. "I won't do that again."

"Smart woman." Will watched the waitress cross the dining room. "Have you taken any pain pills?" she asked Sid.

"Not yet. I couldn't find them and Lucas kept laughing at me, so I got pissed and came over here."

"Good," Will said. "Those things can screw you up when they hit the alcohol still soaking your system. I'll be right back." She stepped to the kitchen door and almost yelled her instructions to Chip, the sous-chef, then remembered Sid's headache. Crossing to his station, she gave instructions for a fruit smoothie with OJ and a hit of carrot juice.

Returning to the bar, Will filled a glass with water. "Drink this until Chip brings out the smoothie."

Sid raised her head for the first time since Georgette had walked off. "Smoothie? You've been around my brother too much."

"You need the vitamins to replenish your system. Trust me," Will said with a smile. "I'm a bartender."

Two minutes later, Chip delivered the drink and let Will know she had a call waiting in the office. After pouring the concoction into a tall glass, she made her way through the kitchen to the back.

"Will here," she said into the receiver. "What can I do for you?"

"Do you have any idea how fecking hard you are to track down?" asked a man with a strong British accent.

"Jude?" A thorn of apprehension straightened Will's spine.

"Are you really this Maria Van Clement person Rebecca says you are?"

Dear mother of . . . "What are you talking about? When did Rebecca say that?"

"Today," he said. "On the front page of the *Boston Globe*."

Holding the phone between her ear and shoulder, Will forced her lungs to continue working as she keyed the newspaper URL into the computer. She knew the website from having checked its financial news daily when she'd been living and working in Boston. There, looking back from the screen, was Will standing behind the bar looking as if she were about to face a firing squad.

And very shortly, she would be.

"I need to go," she said, hanging up the phone before Jude could say anything else.

~

Randy finished dealing with the business finances in record time thanks to Will's professional input from the week before. She was sorely wasting her talents behind the bar. In fact, he planned to talk to her about starting her own accounting service on Anchor. Not that he wanted to leave Tom and Patty without their manager, but Will should be doing what she really loved, which oddly enough was working with numbers, not shot glasses.

He'd putzed around the house, did some maintenance on the weight machines at the fitness center, and tried to focus on the reopening plans for Adventures until caving and doing what he really wanted to do—which was go see Will.

What he hadn't expected to find was Sid behind the bar.

"What are you doing here? I expected you'd still be sleeping off the effects of last night."

"Lying in bed made the headache worse, and Lucas was too amused to be helpful." Sid didn't look amused at all. "So I came in here looking for solace and a quick bite to eat."

"And ended up behind the bar?" Randy surveyed the room. "Where's Will?"

Sid paused in the task of pouring beer into a glass. "You haven't seen her?"

"I came here to see her," he said. "She's working today."

"She was. Then she got a call and said she needed to take care of something." Sid set the glass down. "This is normally Lucas's thing, but she didn't leave me much choice. Will lit out of here as if her ass was on fire."

"Did she say who was on the phone?" Randy tried to ignore the feeling of foreboding that landed like a weight on his shoulders. "Or where she was going?"

"Nope. Got the call and headed out."

There was only one reason Will would bolt out of Dempsey's without a word, without telling Sid what was wrong. But if the asshole from her past had appeared out of nowhere, why hadn't she called him? Why hadn't she gone to Randy right away?

"How long ago did she leave?"

Tossing the empty longneck into the recycle bin, Sid glanced to the clock behind the bar. "A couple hours. I thought she'd be back by now. I need to get out to the garage."

Randy's heart raced. That was long enough for her to get off the island already. If she took off, he'd never find her. Hell, he wasn't even sure who the hell to look for since he'd never gotten around to finding out her real name.

Maybe she wasn't gone. Maybe he was overreacting and she'd been looking for him. "I need to use the phone," he said, charging around the bar.

"It's in the office," Sid said. "Probably sitting on the desk. But who are you calling?"

Ignoring the question, Randy jogged through the kitchen and stepped into the office. The phone was on the desk as Sid had assumed, but when he pressed the button, the line was dead. Locating the base near the door, he followed the cord to the wall, where it had been unplugged.

The moment he clipped the end into the base, the phone rang in his hand. Caller ID showed a 617 area code. "Dempsey's Bar and Grill, how can I help you?" he answered.

"I'm looking for Maria Van Clement. I understand she works there?" said a nasally voice with a strong northeastern accent.

"There's no Maria Van Clement here. You must have the wrong number."

"You might know her as Will?" the caller said.

Randy gripped the receiver tighter. "What did you say?"

The sound of papers rustling sounded down the line. "Says here she's going by the name Will Parsons. If she's around, I'd really like to talk to her. Do you know her?"

"Who are you and where are you calling from?" Randy asked through a clenched jaw.

"I'm a reporter—"

Randy hung up the phone and headed for his truck. By the time he was halfway through the kitchen, the phone started ringing again, but he kept going.

~

Will rolled into Myrtle Beach as the sun faded in the west, exhausted, hungry, and battling the sinus headache from hell thanks to crying her way down the East Coast. She'd let herself believe the running was over. That she could be happy on Anchor, safe from the past and the constant fear of being discovered.

The truth was, she wanted to believe it because she'd fallen ass over elbow in love with Randy Navarro. He'd made her feel invincible and special, as if she deserved some good in this life. But it was all an illusion, and now reality was back with a vengeance.

Randy was the best man Will had ever met, and she'd let him believe they could have a future together. As much as it broke her own heart to do so, leaving Randy angry and hurt was preferable to having Jeffrey do something far worse.

"Welcome to Mammy's. What can I get for you?" asked a pretty young waitress as Will slid onto a retro-looking stool at the counter. Before she could answer, the waitress dropped a peach and green laminated menu on the counter in front of her.

Will had pulled her hair back in a slick ponytail in case she crossed paths with anyone who'd seen the article. The odds of that happening were slim the farther south she drove, which was why she'd headed this way.

"A glass of water, please," she said, skimming the menu. "And I'll have the grilled chicken."

"Comes with two sides," the brunette said, pen poised above her notepad.

"Oh." Will's eyes slid down the menu until she'd located her options. "How about the sliced tomatoes and coleslaw?"

"That'll work." Tucking a stray wisp of hair behind her ear, the woman stepped a few feet down to a computer behind the counter. Will exhaled, just as she had after every encounter throughout the day.

She'd only stopped a few times, for gas, bottles of water, and bathroom breaks. No one had looked twice at the unremarkable woman with her head down, using body language to make it clear idle chitchat was not welcome.

Will had been nervous that her time on Anchor had tarnished her skills at looking unapproachable, but she'd fallen into the old routine with little effort. Sitting there, waiting her turn to pull onto the ferry, Will had almost changed her mind. It wasn't too late to go back, she'd thought. Randy would never have to know she'd almost left.

But the panic pushed her forward. He'd likely found the note by now, she thought. Maybe he'd crumpled it up and thrown it away. No, that wasn't something he would do. Randy was more likely to read it several times, trying to figure out where she might have gone.

He couldn't know, of course. Even if he'd found the note right away, once Will was off the ferry and out of sight, her whereabouts would be almost untraceable. Or so she hoped.

The waitress set a glass of water on a small napkin. "Your food will be up shortly. Anything else I can get you?"

"No, thank you," Will said, peeling the wrapper from a straw.

"Well hey there, Miss Johnny," said the waitress as a large woman ambled onto the stool two down from Will. The width of her hips was enough that she overlapped onto the stool between them.

Hanging a metal cane from the edge of the counter, the woman huffed as she settled her weight, a grunt of pain escaping her lips as she reached for her left knee.

"Evening, Livie," her new neighbor said, pushing the wire-rimmed glasses up on her button nose. "Get me a cup of hot tea, would'ya?"

"Of course." The waitress disappeared into the kitchen, leaving Will and the woman alone at the counter.

"Pretty night, isn't it?" the older woman asked.

Will nodded as she sipped her water. If only she had something to read. That usually kept the talkers at bay.

"You get in today?" she asked, shaking three sugar packets as if she were going to pour them onto the counter. "Long trip?"

Great. A nosy local. Not what Will needed.

"Passing through," Will said, opting to stare at the muted television hung over the open window between the front counter and the kitchen. A newscaster with Ken-doll hair was speaking into the camera. What he was reporting was anyone's guess.

"Gerald made fresh apple pie this morning," the waitress said, setting a small coffee cup and slice of pie on the counter. "Let me get the milk and some whipped cream for you."

Livie was gone again and the smell of warm apple pie filled Will's senses. What she wouldn't give to be back at Opal's right now, cutting into a slice of rhubarb pie and laughing with her friends.

"That girl is hell on my diet," Miss Johnny muttered. Will assumed the statement was meant to be funny, since the woman was nearly as wide as she was tall. To be fair, Miss Johnny was likely only five feet tall, but still.

Returning her gaze to the flashing screen, Will saw the last thing she expected.

Hovering above the reporter's right shoulder was the photo of herself, taken at Dempsey's a few weeks before. This was seriously not her day.

CHAPTER 25

Will snatched a menu from between the ketchup and salt and pepper shakers. "You look like a regular. What would you recommend?" she asked, holding the menu out toward the other diner.

"Since you look like you could use something substantial, I'd suggest one of the seafood meals." Miss Johnny stirred her tea and lifted her eyes to the TV.

"But which one?" Will asked, practically slapping the woman in the nose with the menu.

"It's all good," she said, ignoring the flapping menu. "Hold on a second, hon. I want to see this."

Will followed the woman's gaze to find the weather forecast covering the screen. The breath she'd been holding whooshed out of her lungs. That was entirely too freaking close.

And why the hell was her story being carried all the way down here? A missing woman from Boston shouldn't be news in South Carolina. It wasn't as if she were famous, though at this rate she would be.

"More sun," Miss Johnny said. "Thank the heavens. I've had all the rain I can take for a while." Looking over to Will, she said, "I don't know where you've been lately, but we've had belly washers galore here for a couple weeks now."

Livie reappeared with a can of whipped cream and, without asking permission, squeezed out a giant dollop on top of Miss Johnny's pie. "Have you heard about that heiress lady?" she asked. Will held her silence.

"Makes you wonder," Miss Johnny said, spreading the whipped cream to cover the corners of her pie. "Why would a girl set to inherit all that money disappear into thin air? Though I suppose she's being flooded with reporters asking that same question by now."

Livie crossed her arms. "No one's found her yet, far as the news says. She was supposed to be up on Anchor, though why anyone would want to hide out there I do not know. Anyhow, they say if she was there, she isn't anymore."

Will resisted the urge to defend her little island home. Not that it would ever be her home again. Eyes down, she sipped her water and pretended to mind her own business. Then Livie's question finally registered.

"Did you say heiress?" Will asked.

"You don't know?" Livie replied. "It's been all over the TV today."

Will shook her head. "I've been driving since this morning."

"Some young woman who disappeared from a Boston hospital a few years ago turned up on Anchor Island. It's a remote little place up in the Outer Banks," Miss Johnny said. "Turns out while she's been missing, her grandmother died and left her everything. The girl is rich as that idiot with the crazy hair who likes to fire people on television, but no one knew where she was to tell her."

"I'm sure she knows," Livie said. "How could you *not* know? I think she's running for love."

"That's because you're a hopeless romantic," Miss Johnny said, looking much more skeptical than the young waitress. "A grown woman wouldn't give up all that money for a man. At least not for long."

But she would give it up for a child. Will's mother had. And her grandmother had left her everything? Maria, the gardener's daughter? That had to be a mistake.

"Maybe Livie is on to something," Will said, letting herself pretend the subject of this bizarre conversation was someone else. "You say she was supposed to be on some island but no one can find her?"

"That's the latest. And even the people on the island are claiming they don't know her. What's the woman's name?" Livie asked Miss Johnny.

"Maria Van something," the older woman said. "But that's not the name she was supposedly using on the island. Maybe they're all protecting her."

"Oh," Livie exclaimed. "Maybe the guy she loves is on that island. Think he left with her?"

"No," Will said, her voice nearly a whisper. "I mean, have they mentioned anyone else disappearing from that island? They'd have mentioned that on the news, right?"

The two locals looked at each other. "Not that I've heard," Livie said. "How about you, Miss Johnny? Maybe I've missed something since my shift started."

"I haven't heard any mention of a man, at least not one being with her. I can tell you right now," Miss Johnny said, tapping a finger on the counter. "A woman disappears because of a man, it's not because he was good to her. I'd bet my knitting needles she's running *away* from a man, not *with* one."

The words were so frighteningly accurate, a chill ran down Will's spine.

Livie pouted. "You're no fun, Miss Johnny," then abandoned them to wait on two bearded bikers who'd taken a seat at the far end of the counter.

An heiress. She'd never imagined. Will took a second to mourn the grandmother she never really knew. Nancy Van Clement had been aloof, but she'd also taken her daughter back without a breath of hesitation. In her own way, Nancy loved Will's mom, and maybe she'd loved her granddaughter as well.

Sadness mixed with the weight of exhaustion. Three years of running. Three years of fear and heightened senses. Of worry and anxiety and now she had one more thing Jeffrey had taken away from her—the chance to have known her grandmother. Something new and powerful took root in Will's brain.

Maybe she had done enough running. Maybe Jeffrey had taken enough.

Maybe it was time to get her life back.

"I bet if she knew about the money, she'd go home," Miss Johnny said before slipping a bite of pie between her lips. "If she doesn't, she's an idiot."

"I think you're right," Will said, knowing exactly what the missing heiress would do next. "Could you tell Livie to cancel my order? There's someplace I need to be."

Will headed for the exit when Miss Johnny yelled, "Maria?"

Without thinking, Will stopped and turned, realizing too late what she'd done.

Miss Johnny smiled, eyes twinkling behind thick lenses. "Airport is down Highway 15. If you hurry, you can get a flight out tonight."

I never meant to hurt you.

Those were the words Randy read over and over again while sitting on his back porch drinking a beer for the first time in nearly ten years. He didn't feel like making the healthy choice tonight. His health didn't mean much at the moment.

According to Sid, the phone had blown up at Dempsey's the second he'd left. In fact, most of the businesses on the island had fielded calls from newspapers, magazines, and even major network news departments, all looking for the lost heiress, Maria Van Clement.

The name didn't match up with the dark-haired gypsy Randy knew. The serious woman who could stop his heart with a smile. Who wore combat boots with dresses, slept in holey T-shirts, and drove a dented VW Bus.

No. Nothing about Willow Parsons read old-money heiress. At least the name thing explained why Lucas couldn't find so much as a birth record on her. Their efforts to locate the doctor who'd treated Will when she'd lost the baby were clearly no longer necessary.

"Hello?" came a voice out of the darkness, somewhere to his left. "Are you back here?"

Randy glanced over. "I'm not in the mood for company," he said.

"Joe told me you'd say that." Without an invitation and ignoring his less-than-friendly brush-off, Beth climbed onto the porch and sat beside him on the glider. "Sid said Will left a note."

He nodded. "Yep."

"Any mention of where she might have gone?"

A different shake of his head. "Nope."

Beth sighed. They sat in silence for what felt like an hour but was probably less than a minute. Then she took his hand. "Will had to have a good reason for all this," she said.

"Maria," Randy said, his voice clipped. "Her name is Maria."

"Doesn't suit her, does it?" Beth said, staring into the darkness. "No, she'll always be Willow to me."

The pain in his chest swelled. "Yeah," he said, hating the crack in his voice. "Me, too."

Wrapping herself around his arm, Beth cuddled in tight against his side. "You can't give up."

It was Beth's way to cling to the good. To believe the person they cared about hadn't really left them with nothing more than a note.

Hadn't driven off without a good-bye or explanation. Not that the reason she left was a mystery, but Randy would never understand why she didn't give them a chance to stand with her. To face her demons with the support of her Anchor family instead of running away again.

And they were a family. Something even he hadn't realized until today. Not one person on the island was willing to talk to the press about Will. Instead, they'd all pulled together, feigning ignorance of the whole thing.

"She's not coming back, Beth. I don't think she ever intended to stay in the first place."

That's what hurt the most. He'd believed her when she said they could be together. Spend their todays making each other happy, facing whatever came side by side. She hadn't meant a word of it, and he'd lapped it up like a starving dog.

Leaning her head on the back of the bench, Beth asked, "What is she running from? What's so horrible about who she is? I can't imagine anyone giving up the fortune they say is rightfully hers."

Randy figured it didn't matter now what he told anyone. Any debt of confidence became null and void when Will drove off the island.

"She's running from a man. He beat her, then threatened to do worse if she told."

Beth sat up. "Someone beat her? Oh my God, that's horrible. That's never mentioned in any of the news stories."

After finishing the last of the beer, he said, "She never told anyone." Randy looked down, picking at the label on the bottle. "Except me, I guess. I thought that meant something, but I was wrong."

A small hand gripped his chin, forcing him to turn Beth's way. "You listen to me, Randy Navarro. That woman loves you. She may not be making the best choices right now, but that doesn't change anything. Don't you dare give up on her."

Removing the hand from his face, Randy placed a kiss on Beth's knuckles, then tucked his best friend's girl beneath his arm. "What was it we agreed to?" he said. "Never say never?"

Beth patted him on the chest. "That's right. Never say never."

But Randy knew. Will was never coming back to Anchor Island.

~

Sun glared off the giant wall of windows of the *Boston Globe* headquarters. Standing beside her luxury rental car, Will took a deep breath, steadying herself for the meeting to come. It was possible that Rebecca wouldn't even be in, but doing this over the phone didn't feel right. What Will had to say needed to be done face-to-face. Which made taking this chance necessary.

With shoulders back and head held high, Will marched up the dark, marble steps and through the main entrance of the building. At the front desk, she asked to see Rebecca King.

"Is she expecting you?" the security guard asked.

"No, but she'll want to see me,"

He picked up the phone receiver. "Who should I say is here?"

Hoping the guard wouldn't recognize the name, she said, "Will Parsons."

The guard pressed four buttons on the phone, then relayed the message. He listened, nodded, then said, "I'll tell her."

Will held her breath.

"Ms. King will be right down. You can have a seat over there to wait." After indicating a seating area to the left of his desk, the man returned his attention to the papers on his desk.

She breathed a sigh of relief that he hadn't recognized her. Though to be fair, Will was no longer sporting long dark hair, nor did she look like the dazed and confused bartender included with the article in the Sunday paper.

As she waited, Will concentrated on the particles of dust floating in the beams of sunlight streaking through the windows surrounding the entrance. Everything hinged on this meeting. There was a Plan B, but it involved lawyers and going public with what Jeffrey had done to her. That was the messy plan.

Plan A was the cleaner, simpler option, at least for Will. But she needed Rebecca's cooperation to make it work.

The elevator opened moments later, spewing the blonde reporter into the lobby as if she'd been catapulted out. Rebecca looked left and right, skipping over Will several times. The straight, shoulder-length red hair along with the large sunglasses were clearly working.

"Ms. King," Will said, rising to her feet and gripping her purse strap like a lifeline. "I appreciate you taking the time to see me."

Green eyes went round, then the reporter looked right and left again, as if expecting someone else to be in attendance. "I didn't expect to see you so soon," she said, visibly nervous.

Good. Rebecca being nervous boded well for Plan A.

"Is there someplace we can talk?" Will asked. "In private?"

"Yeah. Right." Rebecca tapped the up button for the elevator, and the women held a mutual if tense silence until they'd closed the door and taken a seat in a small conference room on the third floor. "So," the blonde began. "What can I do for you?"

Will looked the reporter in the eye. "You're going to undo the damage you did with your article."

An empty, unsure laugh escaped Rebecca's perfectly lined lips. "What I did was reveal your true identity, Maria. I don't think forcing an heiress to step forward and admit her identity is all that damaging."

Will remained calm. "Did you ever stop to think there might be a reason I was hiding? Some threat that would make a woman pretend to be someone else? Especially considering that claiming her true identity would make her a very wealthy woman?"

Though she hadn't known about the inheritance before the story broke, Rebecca didn't need to know that.

"A threat?" Glossy lips pinched into a straight line. "No, I hadn't thought of that. Are you telling me that my revealing your identity puts you in danger?"

Instead of answering, Will held the woman's gaze, letting the revelation sink in.

"I had no idea." Rebecca shifted in her chair, openly uncomfortable now.

"I'm sure you didn't." Will opened her purse. "That's why I'm going to give you the opportunity to fix the situation." Withdrawing the documents she'd created the night before, Will laid the papers on the table and pushed them Rebecca's way.

"What is this?" the reporter asked, refusing to take the offering. "Are you serving me with papers?"

As if a woman of Will's means would serve her own papers.

"No. I'm giving you the opportunity to write another story. One that will advance your career much more than anything you could write about me."

"What?" the woman asked, laying a finger on the edge of the papers. "Did you witness a crime or something?"

"Something like that." Will zipped her purse shut. "What I have here will give you everything you need to expose Jeffrey Hillcrest as an embezzler with ties to organized crime. The catch is, you can't ever reveal this information came from me."

"Did you say Jeffrey Hillcrest? The up-and-coming politician from Back Bay? He's the epitome of old money in this town." Rebecca opened the papers now, scanning their contents. "Is this for real?"

Jeffrey had hinted at political aspirations while they were dating. Another reason Will hadn't believed their marriage would work. She could never be a politician's wife.

"This is very real. But that information leaves with me unless you agree to one small request." If Rebecca didn't agree, plan A was dead in the water. Thankfully, the reporter was practically salivating over the papers in her hand.

"You can't tease me with this and then take it away," she said. "Is this guy what you were running from?"

"The request is simple," Will said. "Write another article about me, stating that I came forward to claim my inheritance, then left the country immediately for parts unknown to avoid the media spotlight. Hint that I might be somewhere in South America or Asia. Wherever you want, so long as people believe I'm out of the country."

Smiling now, Rebecca sat back in her chair. "Why didn't you give this story to someone else? I can't be your favorite person right now."

"You're hungry. You're smart enough to do the homework required." Will raised one brow. "And you owe me."

With a nod, the reporter stood and offered her hand. "It was nice to meet you, Maria Van Clement. I hear you have a plane to catch for Buenos Aires. You should probably get going so you don't miss it."

Will slid her hand into the one offered. "Don't be silly. A woman with my money never flies commercial."

"Touché," Rebecca said with a laugh. When they reached the door, she sobered. "I'll make sure this guy never gets to you again. Can I ask where you really intend to go?"

Feeling true relief for the first time in longer than she cared to think about, Will said one word.

"Home."

CHAPTER 26

The small wedding party hovered inside the front door of Anchor Adventures, waiting for what would hopefully be a brief shower to pass. With Will's departure, Randy was now escorting Kinzie down the aisle, which put Manny on edge. Watching the young man squirm made Randy smile, and he'd had little reason to do so this week.

"Did the radar look like this was moving out?" Beth asked, holding on to Joe and chewing on her bottom lip. "Please tell me this will all be gone by tomorrow."

"Last I checked, we looked due for a clearing." Randy didn't have the heart to answer the second question. According to the forecast, Beth and Joe were going to have a soggy wedding day.

"Relax," Joe said, even-keeled as always. "Rain or shine, we're getting married. And that's all that matters."

"But—" she began.

Joe set a finger over her lips. "That's all that matters."

Beth calmed, smiling into her fiancé's eyes. "You're right. That's all that matters."

The pair beamed, looking as if everyone else in the room had disappeared. Randy felt as if he were intruding on something personal and wandered off without the couple noticing.

"How you holding up, big guy?" asked Sid, shoving a red, plastic cup into his hand. "Hear anything yet?"

Sid had asked him this question every day. As if it were a given that Will would call or send an e-mail or a smoke signal maybe. Randy wasn't sure when his sister became such an optimist, but he indulged her mostly because it was the easiest thing to do.

"Not yet. You?" he asked, knowing the answer would be the same.

"Nah." His sister stared into her cup as he raised his to his lips.

Catching a whiff of the contents, Randy stopped and said, "What the hell is in here?"

"Jack," she said, as if handing him a cup of straight whiskey at three in the afternoon were normal. "Call it fortification."

"Call it something I'm not going to drink." Randy set the cup behind the counter to throw away later. "Tell me you have something less alcoholic in that cup." He gestured toward the Solo cup in her hand.

"I'll tell you anything you want to hear as long as you leave me and my cup alone."

As Sid tilted the plastic for another drink, Lucas appeared, swiping it out of her hand. Ignoring his protesting girlfriend, he said, "Great weather for a wedding, don't you think?" and placed the cup next to Randy's. "Any chance we'll get out there soon? The natives are getting restless, and the preacher has a book club meeting in an hour."

"Book club?" Randy and Sid said in unison.

"The answer involves hobbits so I didn't press." Lucas leaned toward the front window, squinting up at the sky. "Looks like we have a window of opportunity here. Better grab it."

Within minutes, the small gathering had taken their places on the lower portion of the deck. Joe stood at the front with the preacher, while Sid, Lucas, Randy, Kinzie, and Beth lingered at the back. Tom escorted Patty to their seats in the front row. Instead of a bride's side and a groom's side, there would be a sign telling guests to sit wherever they liked, as there were no sides in this union, only one large island family.

That had been Will's touch, Randy learned. One of many reminders about how much she'd done to make this day special for Beth and Joe. It was a shame she wouldn't be there to see her efforts come to fruition.

Right. That's why he wanted her to come back. To see the wedding.

Not because he missed her so bad it felt as if someone had ripped his heart out and mounted it on a pike.

Dragging his brain back to the task at hand, Randy offered an arm to Kinzie and escorted the pretty little baker down the aisle. Manny looked tense until the bridesmaid went her way and Randy joined Joe on the other side. Lucas and Sid were next, and then Beth took the walk by herself.

There had been much discussion about who would give the bride away, but in the end, she'd opted to go it alone, saying she could give herself away and didn't need any man to do it for her. No one argued after that.

Beth had reached the front row when Sid said, "Ho. Ly. Shit."

The entire rehearsal looked her way, then followed Sid's gaze to the upper deck. A tall redhead lingered there, wearing an expensive-looking blue dress and large sunglasses. Sunlight broke through a cloud, glistening off the shiny tan heels.

As they all stared, wondering who would have the nerve to crash Beth and Joe's rehearsal, the woman removed her sunglasses, revealing familiar blue eyes Randy would know anywhere.

Holy shit was right.

~

Will wasn't sure what to do next. In all honesty, she hadn't thought far beyond this moment. She'd hoped to arrive earlier, to catch Sid and Beth alone first, but she had hit the Friday traffic through the Outer Banks, which added significant time to the drive. Maybe this way was for the best.

This way, she would know if there was a chance for her here. If this family of her heart would let her back into the fold. Not that she wouldn't have to earn their trust again, but she was willing to do whatever it took to make that happen.

As hard as she tried, she couldn't keep her eyes from straying to Randy. Wearing khakis and a dark blue polo shirt, his eyes bore through her, as if determining if she were real or some twisted product of his imagination. The anger was there, but not the hatred she'd feared. Will took that as an encouraging sign.

Beth said something close to Joe's ear. He nodded and she walked down the aisle in Will's direction. Randy moved at the same time, but Joe's hand on his arm held him in place. Will had no doubt Joe's actions were in direct response to whatever Beth had whispered.

"Hi," Beth said, joining Will on the higher deck.

"Hi," Will said, feeling vulnerable and on the edge of breaking apart. She took a deep breath. "I'm sorry about the timing."

"Of when you left or this unexpected return?" Beth asked.

The wind blew a wisp of hair across Will's face. She brushed it away as a cloud drifted in front of the sun. "Both," she replied, her eyes once again going to Randy. He watched her intently, a muscle ticking in his jaw. "I panicked. That's no excuse, but it's the truth."

A second passed before Beth asked, "Do I have to call you Maria now?"

A flicker of hope ignited in Will's chest. "No. I'm still Willow."

Beth smiled softly. "You don't look like Willow."

She looked down at herself, tucking another wind-blown lock behind her ear. "A temporary necessity," she said. "This is my best effort at going incognito."

Turning to the wedding party again, Beth said, "I think there are some people down there who want to talk to you. Joe will hold Randy as long as he can, but my guess is that power will run out very soon,"

"Does he hate me?" Will asked.

On a sigh, her friend said, "You hurt him. A lot. But Randy isn't the kind of man who could hate anyone, especially not the woman he loves."

Will slid her sunglasses back into place. "I hope you're right," she said, stepping toward the parking lot. "I'll wait for him."

Will reached her car, then leaned on the front fender to wait. The VW Bus had been replaced by a silver Chevy Malibu. As she now had enough money to buy yachts and ride around in limousines, one new car hadn't seemed like much of a splurge.

From over her shoulder, she heard Beth yell, "Let him go," and knew the next few moments would determine the rest of her life.

~

Randy found Will leaning against the front fender of a shiny new Chevy Malibu, staring at the stone beneath her expensive-looking shoes. She was an heiress now. He needed to remember that. The down-to-earth bartender was long gone. In fact, had never existed.

The woman he'd loved had never existed.

"Why did you come back?" he asked, foregoing a friendly greeting. He wasn't feeling very friendly at the moment. Even if every nerve ending in his body was screaming out to hold her.

Without looking up, Will said, "Because this is my home." She removed the sunglasses and met his eye. "And because of you."

Hands fisted by his sides, Randy ignored her second statement. "Your home is a mansion in Boston," he said. "That's what the news says, anyway. The long-lost heiress returned to claim her fortune. Right, Maria?"

"Parsons was my father's last name," she said, her voice calm. "My mother started calling me Willow when I was nine years old. It's been my name ever since." Pulling away from the car, she added, "Willow Parsons is who I am. Much more than Maria Van Clement will ever be."

He hadn't expected there to be a string of truth in the Willow he'd known. Regardless, the woman standing before him might as well have been a stranger. "So you didn't lie by virtue of a technicality." Randy nodded. "Convenient."

"I don't blame you for being angry," she said, crossing her arms and clutching the sunglasses against her side. "I'm sorry that I hurt you. What I put in the note was true. That's something I never wanted to do. If I could go back a week, I'd do things differently. But I can't."

She stepped to the car door and reached for the handle. "I'd like to stay for the wedding, but after tomorrow, I'll leave Anchor for good if that's what you want." She stood behind the open door, the light dimmed in her eyes. "My best todays will always be the ones I spent with you."

The words nearly brought him to his knees. Letting her climb into that car and drive away was the hardest thing Randy had ever done. And quite possibly the stupidest.

~

Sitting on the balcony of her Anchor Inn hotel room, Will contemplated where she would go next. Boston wasn't an option, especially since Maria was supposed to be out of the country. Through the family lawyer, she'd learned of a distant cousin with a wife and four kids. Will had always thought the sweeping Victorian where her mother had grown up needed a real family to bring it to life.

She respected the Van Clements enough not to sell the ancestral home, but that didn't mean she had to live in it herself. Roger Van Clement and his brood had agreed to take up residence, which had solved the dilemma of what to do with a vacant mansion.

Now, what to do with a heartbroken heiress? That was a tougher problem to solve. Will wanted to live on Anchor. Maybe start an accounting business, though the thought of doing everyone's taxes didn't sound all that fun anymore. And it seemed after her landlord had learned of her hasty departure from the island, he'd had her cottage emptied and the locks changed.

A bit extreme considering she'd only been gone for five days, but she was currently homeless nonetheless.

There were other islands along the coast. Perhaps she could go find Miss Johnny in Myrtle Beach and learn how to knit.

But the other islands didn't have Randy. And knitting didn't sound any more attractive than endless tax forms.

As she let the sadness take over, Will stopped thinking about the future. Stopped trying to be optimistic about some newly invented future. Instead, she closed her eyes and saw Randy. His eyes dark and drawn. The shadows beneath revealing he'd lost sleep since she'd left. The hurt that made his words tight and bitter. He'd ignored the part about her coming back for him. Which she deserved. If she'd cared, if she'd really meant the things she'd said, why had she left him in the first place?

Will had been asking herself that question for days and wasn't any closer to an answer now than she'd been on that plane flying into Boston on Sunday night. A lifetime alone ingrained certain habits.

Certain reactions. Maybe she wouldn't change any of it. The events of the last week had given Will something back. Not only her life, but herself.

It wasn't the money that had given her the power. It was her bond with this place. Her love for Randy that made her willing to find a way. Determined even. Whether he ever spoke to her again or not, Randy gave her the gift of strength she'd needed to face her demons. She'd always love him for that.

Tears blurred the moon in the distance. The stars looked like disco lights, spinning as she blinked the moisture away. At least the stars were a good sign. That meant the clouds had cleared, and Beth and Joe might have sunshine for their big day.

Will stepped inside to grab a tissue when a knock sounded at the door and a voice from the other side yelled, "Room service!"

She hadn't ordered anything from room service, which meant the waiter had the wrong room. Will opened the door to clear up the mistake, but instead of a waiter and cart, she found Randy holding a small white box.

Will froze, unable to speak or even breathe. All she could do was stare at the gorgeous man filling the doorway to her room.

"Can I come in?" he asked. No anger accompanied the request. No tense jaw or heated glare.

"Um . . . Sure." Will stepped back, allowing Randy to enter and move past her. The fresh scent of his aftershave was like a punch in the gut. She tucked her hands beneath her armpits to keep from touching him.

Randy set the white box on the counter between the tiny kitchenette and a seating area. Will had splurged and reserved a suite.

"Rooms are nice," he said, taking in the decor as if this weren't a moment of great consequence. "Sam did a good job with the place."

"Yes," she said, feeling as if she'd been sucked into a weird movie in which nothing made sense. "He seems to know what he's doing." Not the best line in the script, but Will was too off balance to make intelligent conversation. "How did you find me?" she asked, her best effort at not asking why he was there.

"Small island," Randy said. "I was surprised to see you today." He crossed the room to the open balcony doors. "Nice view."

If he was trying to confuse her, the man was doing a bang-up job.

"I should have called first," she said, moving closer, but keeping a good distance between them. "The week was a little crazy, and I didn't have much chance to stop and think through how to handle this."

"I thought about it a lot," he said, leaning against the doorjamb, his eyes focused on something in the distance. "Nothing about today played out the way I imagined."

Will could only guess at what he'd imagined. "Should I ask if it was better or worse?"

He finally looked her way. "A little of both. I stopped breathing when I realized it was you. That part I'd expected."

Still not a clear answer. Will felt as if she were swimming through quicksand, unable to get a grip on anything solid. "Seeing you was wonderful for me," she said. "Bittersweet, but still wonderful."

"I wanted to protect you," he said, stepping onto the balcony. "You were this wounded thing that I could nurture back to health." Leaning on the railing, he glanced over his shoulder. "I didn't realize until today that you didn't need protecting. You were wounded, but when the time came, you took care of yourself."

"Thanks to you." Will joined him at the railing. "I took care of myself because I had a reason to fight. You were that reason. You gave me the strength I needed to get my life back, and you deserved more from me than a note."

Randy turned until his body was facing hers. "It was a pretty good note, though. As far as 'I'm leaving you' notes go."

"You think?" she said, feeling a knot untangling in her chest. "It was a hard note to write. Took me a couple tries."

Instead of answering, Randy smiled and Will thought he might reach for her. But then he strolled back into the room. "Sid told me once that a woman expected gifts as part of being wooed. Ignoring the fact that Sid is a complete cynic, or possibly because of it, I've since decided to take her advice."

Before Will could wrap her head around the possibility that Randy was talking about wooing her, the man lifted the small white box he'd carried in and held it before her. "This is for you."

What Will hadn't noticed before was the logo for Opal's Sweet Shoppe on the top of the box. "For me?"

Randy nodded as she took the box. Sliding it open, Will found one large slice of rhubarb pie.

On a choked sob, she said, "This is my favorite."

"I know. Sid told me."

Will had yet to talk to Sid. "She must really hate me."

"Not quite," he said. "She threatened to kick my ass if I didn't stop you from leaving again." Holding up a hand, he added, "Not that I didn't plan to come over here. I'd already bought the pie before she stormed into my house."

Sid on a rampage could be a sight to behold. Will was almost sad she missed it. Almost.

"That must have been a treat," she said, returning the white box to the counter. "So is this a peace offering to let me know I'm welcome to live here, or is there something more?"

"You did catch my mention of the whole wooing thing, right?"

"I did," Will said with a nod. "But I'm afraid to believe you mean it in the traditional sense of the term."

Stepping closer, Randy brushed a finger over her cheek. "I mean it in every sense of the term. The whole shebang. Today and tomorrow and all the tomorrows after that. Just please tell me you're home to stay."

Unable to resist any longer, Will wrapped her arms around him. "You're my home, Randy Navarro, and I'm with you for as long as you'll have me."

"That's what I wanted to hear," he said, leaning in to seal the words with a kiss.

CHAPTER 27

After a long night of making love, Will woke at dawn curled against the man she would never leave again. They started the day much as they had ended the night, then proceeded to coffee and catching up over a breakfast of granola bars and sugar-laden cereal. Needless to say, the granola was Randy's idea.

Will learned Beth had spent the night at Sid's place, with Lucas camping out with his parents and Joe home alone. The idea of embracing the tradition of not sleeping together the night before the wedding seemed odd when the couple had lived together for nearly a year and the bride was already pregnant.

But then traditions existed for a reason, and if the sleeping arrangements were important to Beth, Will was happy to hear everyone else was willing to go along. Especially Lucas, considering he and Sid hadn't spent a night apart since the fall before when they'd become a permanent item.

Though Sid had been on Will's side the night before, pushing Randy to find her, Will wasn't so sure all would be forgiven this morning. She'd still hurt the woman's brother, something for which she would readily apologize, but that didn't mean her friend wouldn't want to inflict her own punishment. Taking a deep breath and thinking nonviolent thoughts, Will knocked on Sid's front door.

It opened in a rush, with the screen door being flung at her so quickly Will nearly lost her nose.

"It's about damn time you got here," Sid said, dragging Will into the house and slamming the door behind her. "She's freaking the hell out."

Sid disappeared down the hall, with Will following behind. The greeting had been unexpected, and a bit confusing, but at least it wasn't painful.

"What are you talking about!" she asked, stepping into a room that looked as if it had been ransacked by criminals. "Holy shit. Did you get robbed?"

"What burglars would go out in the rain?" Beth whined, dropping onto Sid's bed in a sobbing puddle of terrycloth.

The question required some pondering. Would burglars go out in the rain? If they didn't want to leave evidence behind, then they probably wouldn't. Shaking her head, Will realized what she was doing. Perhaps bridal insanity was contagious.

"See?" Sid said, standing near the end of the bed, hands on her hips and one foot tapping a staccato beat. "She's been like this for an hour. It isn't even raining."

"But it's cloudy," Beth said, bolting up like a woman possessed. "Don't you see those thunderheads in the distance? It's a bad sign. It's bad luck!"

The crying continued in earnest as Sid stared at Will, pointing silently at the crazy woman who had invaded her bedroom.

Holding her hands up as if to say *let me see what I can do*, Will eased toward the bed.

"Beth? Hon? I'm sure that your day is going to be beautiful no matter what. Why don't you take a hot shower while Sid and I clean up this room and get it ready for putting you into that gorgeous dress of yours? What do you say?"

"It won't be gorgeous once it gets wet," she replied, the words muffled against the twisted sheets.

Sid rolled her eyes as Will patted Beth on the shoulder. "I promise you it will not rain during your ceremony. I checked the radar before I came over here, and it's all moving out." As the lie rolled off her tongue, Will sent a woman-to-woman prayer out to Mother Nature. "You have my word on it."

"What are you doing?" mouthed Sid, but Will waved her off.

"Now come on, sweetie," she said, tugging on Beth's shoulders. "Your eyes are going to be all puffy, and we don't want that. Hop in the shower and don't give the weather another thought."

Beth shoved damp curls away from her face. "Are you sure? The clouds are really going away?"

Holding up three fingers, Will said, "Scout's honor."

Waterlogged green eyes brightened as a smile tugged at the bride's lips. Then her face fell again. "I must look horrible," she said, smacking her hands against her cheeks.

Will shook her head quickly. "A little ice on the eyes after the shower and you'll be good as new. Even better." Scooting Beth toward the bathroom, she added, "Now get in that shower so Sid and I can get moving in here."

"You're right." Beth nodded as she followed Will's directions. "If Sid had told me about the radar, none of this would have happened."

Sacrificing herself, Will lunged to cut off Sid's attack. Beth didn't seem to notice the imminent danger as she closed the bathroom door.

"That woman is freaking nuts. And you weren't a Girl Scout any more than I was, were you?"

"No, but Beth doesn't need to know that. She's hormonal and nervous. I expect nothing less on *your* wedding day." Will turned to face her friend. "Though I hope you don't plan on being pregnant, too. If this is what incubation does to Beth, I expect you to turn completely homicidal."

"I have no intention of producing a spawn any time soon." Straightening her oversized T-shirt, Sid glanced around the room. "She looked out the window, then started throwing shit. I couldn't get her to stop. Drillbit is lucky I put her out of the room before Beth could throw her, too."

As if on cue, the gray tabby stuck her head inside the room, meowing as if to ask if the coast was clear.

"What is all this stuff?" Will asked, picking up two bras and reaching for three pair of panties. She froze with her hand a full foot above the underwear. "Please tell me it's all clean."

"It's the stuff from my underwear drawer. Beth ripped it open and started using what was inside as giant bits of confetti."

Straightening, Will asked, "Why do you have so much fancy stuff? I figured you for the simple white, tan, or black. Not lace, bows, and . . ." She lifted a bit of white fluff off the chair. "Are these garters?"

Sid jerked the delicate items out of Will's hands. "I like pretty stuff. Don't act so surprised."

Unable to keep the smile from her face, Will continued straightening the room. "You know what I like most about you, Sid?"

"My endless charm?" the younger woman asked.

"Besides that dry sense of humor of yours," Will said. "I like that you're the most down-to-earth person I know, yet you never fail to surprise me. You're funnier, smarter, and deeper than you let people see." Sitting down on the edge of the bed, Will stared at her toes. "And you're forgiving. Or so it seems."

Sid stuffed a handful of bras into a drawer, then scooted onto the bed next to Will. "I was really pissed when I found out you were gone. Especially since I was the last person to talk to you."

"I'm sorry."

"Then I saw Randy when he realized you were gone." The hurt in Sid's voice was tough to take, but the unwavering concern for her brother is what tightened the knot in Will's chest. "It was like the color drained right out of him. Like he'd been deflated and the only thing holding him up was his pride."

"I don't deserve him," Will said, feeling like the evil villain who'd ruined everything.

"And then you came back, and he was alive again." Sid turned to face Will. "I'm not saying he couldn't live without you, because he could. But he wouldn't be happy. At least not for a long time. So promise me all this crazy secret identity shit is over, and you're not going to hurt him again."

"It's over." Though Will couldn't be sure what Jeffrey might do in the future, she knew she had a family on this island that would face whatever came right along with her. "No more running. No more lies. No more looking over my shoulder for the boogeyman."

"So what was that all about anyway?" Sid commenced the cleaning, and Will rose to make the bed. "Who was this boogeyman hunting you down?"

With a fluff of the pillow, Will turned to her friend. "Tell you what. Let's get through today, get Beth and Joe off on their honeymoon, and then I'll tell you all the gory details of my past."

Folding the last towel from the floor, Sid said, "Gory, huh? That sounds sucky."

Will shrugged. "There's some good stories, too." She glanced around the now neat bedroom. "That was easier than it looked. When will Kinzie be here? Isn't she coming to play out her bridesmaid role?"

"Kinzie was only standing in until you came back," Beth said, exiting the bathroom wrapped in a short pink robe and toweling off her hair. "But she is coming over to do my hair and makeup." The bride turned the clock on Sid's nightstand. "Three hours until the ceremony and I already feel like I want to puke. And I'm not talking morning sickness."

Unable to avoid being the bearer of one more disappointment, Will said, "But I don't know where my dress is. I didn't take it with me, and I don't know where the stuff I left behind is now."

Sid dragged a suitcase from her closet. "All the clothes we could find are in here. The dress is hanging up."

Staring at the two women before her, Will could do little more than open and close her mouth, with nothing coming out.

"Curly was sure you'd come back," Sid said. "As you can tell, it's not worth arguing with her these days. So we stashed your stuff until you did."

The best thing to ever happen to Willow Parsons had been landing on Anchor. And in that moment, she sent up a prayer of thanks for all the good and bad that had led her there.

Blinking back tears of joy, she said, "I love you guys. Now let's get ready for a wedding."

There would be many more happy tears shed that day. Will nearly lost it when she spotted Randy in his tuxedo waiting to escort her down the aisle. Making a mental note to send Mr. Lee a thank you card, she tucked her hand in the crook of Randy's arm, feeling as if she might be dreaming.

Mother Nature had clearly heard Will's prayer. The clouds had parted thirty minutes before the ceremony and held off until nearly an hour after. By then, all the revelry was safely under the tent, the dance floor covered in swaying bodies, and the happy couple staring into each other's eyes as if they were the only people on the planet.

Will understood the feeling wholeheartedly.

"You did a great job with this wedding," Randy said as they danced to an old Bob Marley song. "That touch with everyone sitting wherever they wanted instead of having sides was pretty good, considering Beth's side would have been empty otherwise."

Enjoying his arms around her, Will twirled a finger in Randy's hair and leaned closer. "I think the layout on the deck was pretty good, too. And that was all you. It seems we make a good team."

"That we do," he said, dropping in for a kiss. The song ended before the kiss did.

Upon leaving the dance floor, Will and Randy found Sam Edwards hovering in a far corner, looking more like an unwitting observer than a wedding guest.

"You look like you're afraid of being contaminated," Randy said, stopping beside the hotelier and tucking Will against his side. She didn't know much about the man, but Mr. Edwards certainly knew how to wear a suit.

Will briefly wondered how such a small island could harbor so many attractive men.

"There does seem to be something going around," Sam answered in a deep voice that carried the slightest hint of a southern accent. As if he'd made a concerted effort to purge the telling lilt from his dialect. "This must be the Ms. Parsons I've heard so much about."

Randy made the formal introductions, and the tall man in the perfectly tailored suit extended a hand. "I hear you had a hand in putting this event together," Sam said.

"I did," Will said, feeling proud of her efforts. "I'd never planned anything like this, but I find with organization and a solid checklist, any project runs smoother."

Sam's eyes lit up. Turning to Randy, he said, "I like her. Is she still available?"

Will nearly fell off her strappy heels as Randy said, "I don't know. You'll have to ask her."

What the hell? "Am I missing something here?" Will asked, miffed that the man who'd practically proposed was now acting as if they were playing some game. "Maybe you want to answer that question again."

Randy smiled. "Maybe Sam should have phrased the question better. He wants to know if you're available to run a wedding planning business for the island. Since you're an accountant by trade and now a woman of means, would you want to run a small business bringing weddings to Anchor?"

Now the conversation was starting to make sense. Which was good, since she'd been considering shoving Randy off the deck seconds before. "I don't know," she said. "I haven't thought that far ahead." To Sam she said, "You think we could bring weddings to Anchor on a regular basis?"

Sam nodded. "We're thinking of focusing on the off-season months first. See what other businesses might want to come on board."

Since Will wasn't even sure if there would be a life for her back on Anchor, she really hadn't thought of much beyond begging forgiveness from Randy and her friends. And considering her inheritance, she didn't need to work at all. But Will would go nuts with nothing to do, and centering her life around spreadsheets and bank statements was far less appealing than it had once been.

"Are you starting this business and looking to hire?" she asked, wanting to know exactly what she was being offered. The idea of making it her own business, being her own boss, would be more attractive. "Because if I were going to do it, I'd want to take it on myself."

The smile on Sam's face widened. "I'm already running two hotels, with one about to undergo renovations in the fall. Though I definitely want to be involved, having a capable person doing the heavy lifting would be my first choice."

Heavy lifting *and* being the boss. That sounded like a challenge. "Then I am definitely interested. How about we discuss the details next week?"

"Give me a call on Monday and we can set up a meeting."

It had been years since Will had taken a meeting. To know she'd be more than just a person being dictated to felt good. Better than expected. She and Sam shook hands, as did Sam and Randy, then the hotelier made his excuses and left the reception.

As she watched the broad shoulders cut a path through the crowd, Will asked, "Has Sid met Mr. Edwards?"

"Maybe in passing," Randy said. "I don't think they have much reason to cross paths. Why?"

"You know she's in a matchmaking mood these days." Will's eyes were still watching Sam's departure, noticing the way several women in the room watched as well. "And that is one eligible bachelor."

"I hope you're not looking to be matched." Randy pulled her tighter against him. "I like Sam. I'd hate to have to kill him."

Will laughed, patting Randy's chest. "You have no worries there. I'm good and matched. I was simply making an observation."

"How about you make an observation over this way." Randy pulled his tuxedo jacket out far enough to reveal a small black box tucked into an inside pocket.

A hand fell over her lips. "Is that?"

"It is," he said, watching the crowd instead of Will. "I was saving it until later, so we wouldn't take anything away from Joe and Beth. But it's killing me not to give it to you."

The blood drained from Will's brain. "Think they would mind if we left early?" she said, aware that she was either going to whoop for joy or break into sobs at any moment.

"My guess would be no," he said, nudging Will to follow his gaze. Beth and Joe were sneaking out the side of the tent. No one else seemed to notice.

Shoving aside the corner of the tent closest to them, Randy motioned for Will to take the lead. She pulled him across the deck and down to the pier. The rain had died down to a drizzle, but she barely noticed the mist landing on her lashes.

There, on the pier where she'd fallen into lust, Will finished falling into love.

"Will you?" he asked, swiping a damp curl off his forehead while holding the little box in her direction.

Her cheeks strained from the force of her smile. "I will. I most definitely will."